A CANDLELIGHT INTRIGUE

CANDLELIGHT ROMANCES

214 Pandora's Box, BETTY HALE HYATT
215 Safe Harbor, JENNIFER BLAIR
216 A Gift of Violets, JANETTE RADCLIFFE
217 Stranger on the Beach, ARLENE HALE
218 To Last a Lifetime, JENNIFER BLAIR
219 The Way to the Heart, GAIL EVERETT
220 Nurse in Residence, ARLENE HALE
221 The Raven Sisters, DOROTHY MACK
222 When Dreams Come True, ARLENE HALE
223 When Summer Ends, GAIL EVERETT
224 Love's Surprise, GAIL EVERETT
225 The Substitute Bride, DOROTHY MACK
226 The Hungry Heart, ARLENE HALE
227 A Heart Too Proud, LAURA LONDON
228 Love Is the Answer, LOUISE BERGSTROM
229 Love's Untold Secret, BETTY HALE HYATT
230 Tender Longings, BARBARA LYNN
231 Hold Me Forever, MELISSA BLAKELY
232 The Captive Bride, LUCY PHILLIPS STEWART
233 Unexpected Holiday, LIBBY MANSFIELD
234 One Love Forever, MEREDITH BABEAUX BRUCKER
235 Forbidden Yearnings, CANDICE ARKHAM
236 Precious Moments, SUZANNE ROBERTS
237 Surrender to Love, HELEN NUELLE
238 The Heart Has Reasons, STEPHANIE KINCAID
239 The Dancing Doll, JANET LOUISE ROBERTS
240 My Lady Mischief, JANET LOUISE ROBERTS
241 The Heart's Horizons, ANNE SHORE
242 A Lifetime to Love, ANN DABNEY
243 Whispers of the Heart, ANNE SHORE
244 Love's Own Dream, JACQUELINE HACSI
245 La Casa Dorada, JANET LOUISE ROBERTS
246 The Golden Thistle, JANET LOUISE ROBERTS
247 The First Waltz, JANET LOUISE ROBERTS
248 The Cardross Luck, JANET LOUISE ROBERTS
249 The Searching Heart, SUZANNE ROBERTS
250 The Lady Rothschild, SAMANTHA LESTER
251 Bride of Chance, LUCY PHILLIPS STEWART
252 A Tropical Affair, ELISABETH BERESFORD
253 The Impossible Ward, DOROTHY MACK
254 Victim of Love, LEE CANADAY
255 The Bad Baron's Daughter, LAURA LONDON
256 Winter Kisses, Summer Love, ANNE SHORE

PEREGRINE HOUSE

JANIS FLORES

A CANDLELIGHT INTRIGUE

Published by
Dell Publishing Co., Inc.
1 Dag Hammarskjold Plaza
New York, New York 10017

*To George and Laura Dickens
for orange-striped kittens,
chocolate milk shakes on Sundays,
and a rabbit called Munch-Munch...*

All of the characters in the book are fictitious, and any resemblance to actual persons, living or dead, is purely coincidental.

Copyright © 1977 by Janis Flores

All rights reserved. For information address Doubleday & Company, Inc., New York, New York.

Dell ® TM 681510, Dell Publishing Co., Inc.

ISBN: 0-440-17073-7

Printed in the United States of America

Reprinted by arrangement with Doubleday & Company, Inc.

First Dell printing—July 1979

CHAPTER ONE

It was on a dark, cloudy afternoon that I first saw Peregrine House. It stood high on a cliff, overlooking the rumbling sea below, made of stone that could have come from the sea itself, so closely did it harmonize with the landscape surrounding it. Perched on the cliff as it was, with the glittering sea as a backdrop, it should have appeared diminutive; instead, it seemed to dominate the sea and the sky, a towering, three-storied structure that bore down on me as I gazed upon it for the first time. The lead-paned windows across the face of the house glinted in the waning afternoon light like so many sightless eyes staring blankly out at me. A sudden feeling of unease came over me: it was as though someone—or something—was watching our arrival, and was not pleased.

Disturbed by this flight of fancy, I turned away and focused my attention on the grounds surrounding the house. A small expanse of carefully tended rolling green lawn ended abruptly in rock gardens which dotted the areas to the sides of the house. Here and there were clumps of evergreen trees whose full-skirted shapes rustled in the rising wind. It was a scene of desolation, I thought, totally unwelcoming to me, and I wondered briefly if it was possible for me to be happy here in the face of such bleakness. I forced my mind away from such thoughts.

The wind was bringing with it sheets of fog, which came stealing in from the sea, silently covering everything in its path. Soon the whole house would be shrouded in that gray blankness. I shivered and looked at Julian, wondering why we did not proceed into the house, but he was busily engaged in supervising the unloading of our baggage from the carriage and seemed to have forgotten me.

The muttering sound of the sea attracted my attention once again. I had never seen the sea before. I wanted to go to the stone fence flanking the edge of the cliff and look down on the immensity of steel-gray water below, but I was afraid Julian would frown on such a childish act. And I had enough to face in the next few minutes without incurring Julian's displeasure.

I felt Julian's hand on my arm, propelling me up the stone steps to the front door. My knees were shaking in anticipation, and I had to admonish myself to assume a semblance of calm and hopefully a dignity beyond my nineteen years. I would need all the poise I could muster when I met Julian's family. He had said little about them, impatiently brushing off my few questions, until I felt that there was something ominous in the omission. Well, I would soon know for myself, I thought, as we passed through the front door. The thought was not one to give me courage.

The front door opened onto a long gallery that was ablaze with light, though no one was there to greet us. Julian gave an exclamation of annoyance; I felt the conspicuous absence of any member of the family to greet us demonstrated clearly how displeased they were with Julian's hasty marriage. This was going to be more difficult than I thought.

I looked covertly at Julian; his face was drawn into a ferocious frown as he stood tapping his foot impatiently while waiting for someone to appear.

"Perhaps your message was not received," I ventured.

He looked down coldly at me. "What nonsense. Of course it was. Mother is just being difficult."

Further conversation was interrupted as an elderly man, closely followed by a plump little woman, came hurrying down the length of the gallery. "Master Julian!" the man, whom I judged to be the butler by the uniform he was wearing, exclaimed as he reached us. "I'm so sorry we were not here to greet you. We had no idea you were arriving this early."

Julian glared at him and the man dropped his eyes in the face of that fierce stare. "Where is my mother, and the rest of the family?" Julian asked in an ominous tone, completely ignoring the man's stumbling apology.

"I believe they have gathered in the drawing room, sir," the butler replied hesitantly.

"I see," Julian replied in the same forbidding tone. "Well, we will meet them later. I suppose the confrontation is inevitable." He turned to me, as if suddenly remembering my presence at his side, and said curtly to the plump little woman, "Mrs. Harmon, take Mrs. Synclair to her room—I trust a room has been prepared?"

"Oh yes, Master Julian," Mrs. Harmon replied, not in the least abashed by Julian's rudeness. "Your mother had the red room aired yesterday as soon as we heard you were coming home. She thought that since it was the largest—"

"Yes, yes," Julian interrupted impatiently. "We need not go into all that now. As you can see, my wife is nearly dropping with fatigue. Take her up immediately."

I was not dropping with fatigue, as Julian suggested; I was extremely curious about the lack of welcome, and more than a little piqued at such rudeness. However, I held my tongue; it was not for me to argue in the presence of servants.

I nodded to Mrs. Harmon and she smiled sunnily and said, "Come along, my dear. A nice hot cup of chocolate and a little rest before dinner will have you feeling as good as new."

She moved away briskly, and I was left with no choice but to follow, for Julian was already striding away in the opposite direction, his heels striking loudly on the stone floor.

I followed Mrs. Harmon to the end of the gallery and up a wide staircase hung with portraits that looked down darkly at us as we ascended. The second floor was lined with doors all facing a balcony that gave a view of the gallery below. We turned several corners and at last Mrs. Harmon stopped before a door and opened it with a flourish, gesturing me across the threshold.

The room was huge. A large fire blazing in the great stone fireplace at the end of the room cast an orangered glow over the walls, but as Mrs. Harmon bustled around, lighting the lamps that stood on various tables, I could see that the glow from the fire was not responsible for the overwhelming redness of the room. Crimson velvet draperies hung heavily at the windows, a red satin quilted coverlet was spread over the huge carved mahogany bedstead, and red and gold paper covered the walls. There was even a scarlet rug spread before the fireplace.

For a moment, I could only stare speechlessly at the overwhelming furnishings until my eye caught the only bit of relief in the oppressive room: a bowl of white roses on a table near the curtained window.

Mrs. Harmon, who had been watching me carefully, saw me looking at them and said, "I put those there for you, my dear. Sort of a welcome, they are."

"Thank you, Mrs. Harmon," I said gratefully. The white contrasted sharply with the rest of the room, and I tried to focus on the roses in an attempt to forget my revulsion at the heaviness and oppressiveness surrounding me.

Mrs. Harmon bustled around, leaning down to poke up the fire, stooping to pick off an imaginary speck of lint from the immaculate coverlet. I was certain she was trying to give me time to adjust to all this magnificence, but I was too tired to do much more than undo my bonnet and sink wearily into one of the crimson overstuffed chairs by the fire.

"Your trunk will be brought up directly, and I'll have Betsy bring you a nice cup of chocolate. Dinner won't be for an hour at least, so you will have time to rest awhile," she chattered. "My, you look pale as a sheet, poor dear. Can I do anything before I leave?"

I shook my head, wishing her only to be gone so I could have a few precious moments alone. She looked at me doubtfully, but I smiled reassuringly, and soon the door closed behind her.

Tears stung my eyelids. I brushed them away impatiently; it would do no good to cry, I told myself. The bargain was made; it was done, and I would just have to make the best of it.

A muted pounding sound from behind the draperies caught my attention. I went to the window and pushed back the heavy curtains, peering outside into the darkening light.

The sea was below me, pulsing with a life all its own, the waves rushing toward the rocks and breaking into frothy fragments before drawing away to begin their fruitless journey again. I stood mesmerized for a time until I realized that there was a small balcony just outside the window. Suddenly I longed to be away from the oppressive room behind me and out into the fresh air. I searched for a door in the expanse of glass and finally found one cleverly hidden in the pattern of the diamond-shaped panes. As I opened the door and the salt-tinged air brushed over me, the feeling of faintness that had threatened to overcome me vanished. I stepped close to the stone railing that ran the length of the small balcony and looked down. The sea rumbled and thrashed far below me and for an instant I felt giddy as I stared at the rocky expanse of the cliff that swept down and away from the house to the sea; the balcony seemed a precarious perch and I moved back from the rail.

The fog was rolling in in earnest now, great puffs that softly covered everything in their path. Soon even the waves below were obliterated, the only evidence of their presence the continual crashing against the rocks.

I was about to go back in when a low growl from the end of the balcony made me freeze where I stood. The sound sent a chill through my body and for a moment I did not dare move even my head to locate the source.

At last I forced myself to look in that direction, turning my head slowly. The growl came again. It was fairly dark by this time, and I could see nothing until a dark shape detached itself from the wall and moved closer to the light that shone weakly through the parted curtains.

Two eyes stared at me. One brown, one pale blue. The effect of the different colors was startling, and for an instant I was convinced they were looking through me, so steadily were they trained in my direction. I stared, too fascinated to be frightened. Even in the dark, I could see the black pupil of that pale blue eye expanding and contracting; when the whole iris was obliterated by the pupil, I had the feeling I was impaled by that penetrating stare, and that the owner of the eye could somehow read my thoughts. I could not move.

Suddenly the shape moved closer to me, and as its body came into the light, I could see it was a huge dog. My relief was so great I let out an exclamation, and the spell, if I could call it that, was broken. The slight sound from my lips caused the dog to bristle and growl again. I was not afraid of it; I had come to more harm at human hands for me to be frightened, even of such a huge specimen. I bent down and stretched out my hand in a gesture of friendship, thinking how absurd I had been to allow my imagination to run away with me. The dog looked at me suspiciously, its eyes narrowing in an almost human look of appraisal. One huge paw came forward, then another, until its nose almost touched my outstretched fingers. It sniffed me mistrustfully, but finally, when I made no move to touch it, a brief wag of the plumed tail gave me permission to stroke the massive head. I did so, feeling the thick fur and silky ears.

Suddenly the dog stiffened beneath my touch and looked toward the window. At the same instant, a harsh voice commanded, "Berus! Down!" The dog dropped instantly to the floor while I stared up into Julian's angry face.

"Julian—what is the matter?" I asked, confused.

"Have you lost all your senses? Can't you see that dog is dangerous? You could have been badly mauled!"

"But, Julian . . ."

"Leave him at once—carefully!"

The peremptory tone in his voice compelled me to obey, though I cast one look over my shoulder at the dog, lying as still as stone on the floor of the balcony. I risked one last plea: "Julian, it's so cold and wet out there—could he not at least come in by the fire?"

"The dog is not your concern," he replied coldly. "I can't understand how he came to be here on the balcony anyway—unless . . . If I find out who put him there, knowing how dangerous he is, I'll . . ."

The unspoken threat hung in the air between us, and I realized with shock that Julian thought someone had put the dog on my balcony with the intention that he would harm me.

But I had no time to wonder about the reason anyone would do such a dangerous thing, for Julian was continuing angrily, "Dinner will be in an hour. My mother will send her maid, Louisa, to attend you shortly, since you do not as yet have a maid of your own. Pray see to it that you do not disgrace yourself or me this evening. You can be certain Mother will be searching for flaws, and I do not intend to be made more a laughingstock than I already am."

With these curt remarks, he turned on his heel and disappeared through a side door I had not noticed before, which presumably led to his own room. I heard him call to the dog still on the balcony, and realized that the balcony joined both our rooms. The only access to it was through either Julian's room or mine, and someone had led the dog up here with the hope that I would go out onto the balcony and be attacked by the dog. But who would do such a thing? And why?

My thoughts were interrupted by a brisk knock on my door. Before I had time to answer, a brisk young woman in starched apron and mobcap entered carrying a tray. She set the tray on the table in front of the fire and turned to bob a curtsy.

"I'm Betsy, ma'am," she said, staring at me with bold black eyes.

Her scrutiny unnerved me; I wondered how much she knew. But with Julian's last words still ringing in my ears, I was determined not to betray my nervousness. Stiffly I said, "You may unpack the trunk and lay out the ivory satin for tonight, Betsy."

She nodded briefly and went to the trunk, which stood in the center of the room, but not before I noticed the shrewd glance of appraisal she flung at me before lowering her eyes.

I forced myself to walk calmly to the tray and pour a cup of steaming chocolate, hoping my unsteady nerves would not betray me by the rattle of the cup against the saucer. I sipped at the chocolate, and as the warmth penetrated me, I steadied somewhat and watched Betsy moving swiftly about the room, folding and putting away, hanging gowns in the wardrobe, until at last all traces of new arrival were gone. I wondered idly what she would say if she knew that all the gowns were new—chosen and ordered by Julian, fitted hastily by a seamstress before we left for our journey to Peregrine House.

As she was leaving, an older woman came in and introduced herself as Louisa. Louisa was too well trained to openly betray her curiosity about the new bride of Julian Synclair, but several times as she dressed my hair I caught her studying my reflection in the mirror. I was surprised at the skill with which she first twisted the heavy, unruly length of dark auburn hair into a cluster of curls and waves on top of my head, then took it all down and arranged it into a smooth coil at the nape of my neck, declaring critically that she thought a simpler style suited me best. I was not so certain, but her no-nonsense attitude would allow no protest, and in any event I was too tired to argue. When at last she helped me into the ivory gown and smoothed the skirts, standing me before the mirror, I had to admit her taste was unarguable. The heavy skirt of the gown flowed richly about me, making my waist seem smaller than usual, and the heels on the new ivory satin slippers made me appear taller. The low-cut bodice of the gown with its puffed sleeves just off the shoulder gave me an air of poise which normally I lacked, and which is so difficult to come by for persons of short stature. The smooth hairdo added just the right touch—I could only hope Julian would be pleased.

Louisa declared herself satisfied and took herself off just as Julian stepped into the room. Against my will, my heart gave a treacherous lurch when I saw him. He had changed to evening clothes, and the black of his coat accentuated his blue-black hair and deep blue eyes. He was wearing an embroidered satin vest in blue and yellow, and the linen of his shirt was immaculately white. Even his black shoes shimmered with a glossy polish. He looked tall and strong and distantly handsome as he stood and stared at me, noting every detail of my toilette. I stood quietly, knowing that he was not seeing me, but only the effect I would make on his family.

At last he nodded to himself, saying he was satisfied with my appearance—save for one thing. From his pocket he drew out a diamond necklace, from which hung a large ruby. Coming forward, he put the necklace around my neck, moving in back of me to fasten the clasp. As his fingers touched me, I was unable to repress a shiver and he stepped back, annoyed.

"We'll have to put a good face on it, my love"—he stressed the endearment sarcastically—"no matter how we dislike each other. It's going to be bad enough without our making it even more difficult."

He had misinterpreted my reaction at his touch, but the coldness of his words prevented me from declaring my true feelings. Helpless in the face of his antagonism, I was silent for a moment, then said, "The necklace is lovely. Is it an heirloom?"

"Yes," he said crushingly. "But what would you know about such things?"

Tears sprang into my eyes at his cruelty; I looked away so he wouldn't notice and saw myself in the mirror. The ruby glistened in the lamplight like a drop of blood, and I wondered if this was the way our life was going to be: constantly wounding each other because of things neither of us could change. I resolved that if it were in my power, I would not allow this to happen; somehow I would soften Julian's attitude toward me, and we would learn to make our marriage at least bearable.

I knew Julian was referring to my lack of background, and I felt the old familiar sense of loss. My mother had never mentioned anything about her family, save that she had been disowned by her parents after marrying my father. She had been bitter about the estrangement, and I couldn't blame her, for my father had been a gentleman of moderate means when she met him, gentle and kind, steady and respectable, or so she had thought. But soon, to her shocked and bitter dismay, my father had gambled away everything, and in his despair shot himself, leaving my mother to pay his debts and take care of a small daughter as best she could. I think my mother could have survived even this, but the knowledge that her family had been proved correct in their assessment of my father had turned her inward, making her severe and uncompromising, even in her humiliation and disillusionment.

It wasn't until I was older that I understood what sacrifices my mother had to make—first for my father, then later for me. We had gone to live with one of my father's relatives, my Aunt Flora, who was none too pleased to have the two of us foisted upon her—as she so often said. My mother had been a lady, and how she had endured the treatment she received at my aunt's hands I will never know. She was treated as a sort of unpaid companion, in return for which my aunt paid for my education—an arrangement I was not aware of until much later. But by then it was too late.

Julian's voice broke into my thoughts and I started violently, unaware that he had been addressing himself to me. "I said, are you ready to go down now? What is the matter with you? You stand wool-gathering while the family waits impatiently for the new bride?"

I winced at the undisguised tone of contempt in his voice. "I'm sorry, Julian. Yes, I am ready."

He opened the door and held out his arm. I took it, hoping that the sudden tremble of my fingers was not noticeable. We walked downstairs in silence, until at last Julian paused before the door of the drawing room. I looked up at him anxiously, and was surprised to find a reassuring smile on his lips. My hand was still on his arm; he brought up the other hand and brushed mine with his fingertips. This slight gesture gave me confidence and I was able to enter the room with my head held high.

CHAPTER TWO

The drawing room was large, as indeed all the rooms at Peregrine House seemed to be, and richly furnished, but I scarcely noticed at the time, being preoccupied with the small group who fell silent at our entrance. I could sense the current of animosity that seemed to crackle in the air and could only hope I would not make a fool of myself by stumbling, or something equally disastrous, as we advanced across the room.

Julian halted before a silver-haired, autocratic-looking woman who seemed to dominate the group and said, "Mother, may I present my wife, Larissa. Larissa, my mother, Dorothea St. John."

I was startled by the fact that her name was not Sinclair; Julian had not told me. I murmured a greeting before sweeping into a low curtsy, as befitted

Julian's mother, and could only hope my hesitation was not noticeable.

When I straightened, I could see that Dorothea St. John was a formidable woman. She sat in the high-backed chair with the air of a queen, her long-fingered hands curled around the arms of the chair. As I dared to look into her eyes, her thin-lipped mouth tightened into a grimace of distaste, and her fingers tightened into clenched fists. She acknowledged the introduction with a frigid nod of her well-coifed head, while her eyes remained an icy blue.

Julian shrugged slightly and turned toward the other occupants of the room, who had maintained their frozen stance. He said, "Larissa—my sister, Dorcas, and her husband, Mathew; my brother, Norman."

Mathew gave me a brief nod, his pale eyes flicking uneasily back and forth between Julian and me. Norman lounged away from his place by the fire and insolently lowered himself into a chair, his eyes taking in every detail of my appearance. I had no opportunity to observe him further because Dorcas moved swiftly forward until she was standing directly in front of me. I fought down an impulse to step back as her malignant gaze hit me with the force of a blow.

"So," she said contemptuously, "this is the bride. I wonder at your temerity at setting foot in this house—after you were so brazen as to trick Julian into marrying you."

"That's enough, Dorcas," the icy tones of Julian's mother interrupted before either Julian or I had an opportunity to reply to such an attack.

"But, Mother—"

"I said that will be all." Dorothea St. John rose majestically from her chair and walked toward me. When she reached the place where I was standing, still stunned at this reception, she put her hand up to my face, turning my head this way and that. Her cool blue gaze raked me in a manner that unnerved me, but I remained silent. At last, still cupping my chin in her cool fingers, she turned to Julian.

"I see you have already given her the ruby—a pity it clashes with that peculiar shade of hair. Really, Julian, you have surpassed yourself this time. All your other peccadillos pale to insignificance in the face of this preposterous marriage. I *had* counted on you to do better."

The contempt in her tone made me want to shrivel inside. I jerked my head away from her grasp, fighting back tears. She looked at me in feigned surprise and said coolly, "Well, what did you expect, my dear— open arms and a loving greeting? Surely you are not that naïve?"

Julian broke in, his voice deceptively calm. "Mother, I think you have all played your little charade to the hilt. Larissa is my wife, and she will be treated as such in this house." He paused, his eyes touching each of them in turn, before adding, "And I will thank you to remember that it *is* my house!"

Dorothea St. John laughed, a sound without mirth. "Of course, my son," she said contemptuously before turning to me with a look of hatred in those glacial blue eyes.

Suddenly I could remain no longer in this room. I looked at Julian and said, as calmly as I could, "Julian, if you will excuse me? I fear I shan't make a suitable dinner companion tonight, after all." I turned toward the predatory little group and added, "Traveling is so wearying; I'm sure you understand. I shall look forward to continuing this most interesting conversation tomorrow. I must say I enjoyed meeting you so much; it's so reassuring to receive such a welcome from my husband's family." I smiled sweetly, and curtsied again, looking at Julian's mother from under my lashes. Dorothea St. John tightened her lips and looked away, and Mathew shifted uncomfortably in his chair. Dorcas turned crimson with anger, while Julian's brother, Norman, merely seemed amused.

But when I turned to go, I heard someone let out a breath like a hiss, which I pretended not to hear. I held out my hand, indicating that I assumed Julian would accompany me to the door, as a husband should. I did not know what I would do if he refused, but fortunately he took the cue and I dared to glance at him, expecting him to be furious with me for my behavior toward his family. I was surprised to see a glint of admiration in his eyes, though he said nothing. I thought perhaps he would save his anger until a more private time; curiously, I was not upset at the thought. I was too angry at the rude reception I had been given by his family.

My anger sustained me until I reached my room. Julian had remained behind with his family, a fact for which I was grateful, as I would not have wanted him to witness the sudden trembling that overtook me. Reaction to that painful scene in the drawing room set my teeth to chattering and my legs refused to hold me. I collapsed into a chair, holding my arms about me, feeling thoroughly chilled.

The situation was worse than I had feared. And now I had made enemies of at least two of Julian's family. But I could not help it; I refused to remain silent in the face of what, I thought, was undeserved malice. And what did Dorcas mean when she said I had tricked Julian into marrying me? I had had no choice in the matter—it had been arranged between Julian and my aunt.

But now I wondered. My aunt had made it clear during the years that my mother and I had lived with her that she thought little of the responsibility she had assumed for us. Was it possible that she had somehow coerced Julian into marrying me? I knew she was capable of the act, for she was a selfish, greedy woman who would think nothing of deception to gain her ends. I remembered the first time I had met Julian. My aunt and I were attending the theater—a rare occasion for me, since my aunt did not seek my company in public—and during intermission, Julian had been introduced by a friend of Aunt Flora's. My aunt had lost no time in learning Julian's identity and thereafter had given several parties to which Julian was invited. She had insisted that I attend these parties, another fact that surprised me, since I was not often required to be present when my aunt entertained. Suddenly Julian became very attentive toward me, and the next thing I knew, my aunt informed me that Julian had asked for my hand in marriage. She also informed me that I had no choice; I must marry him. I owed a great deal to her, she said, and the marriage would be an excellent means to repay the debt. Cunningly, she told me that my mother would have wished it. I knew that to be true; one of my mother's fondest dreams had been that I would make a suitable marriage. After that, there was nothing more for me to say; Julian and I were married only two months after our first introduction at the theater.

And now Dorcas' cruel remark about my tricking Julian into marrying me set off the memory of an unpleasant scene that had taken place after our marriage ceremony. I remembered it now and wondered at the significance of it.

I remember Julian was handing me into the carriage that was waiting to take us to my aunt's house for a small reception. Aunt Flora was determined that none of her friends would be able to say she had not done things properly; none of them need know that it was also done grudgingly. At any rate, I was occupied with trying to keep my voluminous skirts free of dirt, and scarcely noticed the man who had come up to Julian and handed him some kind of note. When I was settled in the carriage, I turned to ask Julian something, and I remembered even now the fierce look on his face as he read the note and then crumpled it furiously before stuffing it into his pocket. The man who had given him the note disappeared as quickly as he had appeared, and Julian turned to the crowd that had gathered around the church, seeming to search for someone who was no longer there. Alarmed by his manner, I tried to ask him what was the matter, but he glared at me and would not answer. The ride to my aunt's home was silent and strained, Julian sitting like a statue beside me, and I afraid to ask him any more questions. Somehow I managed to get through the reception, accepting best wishes from friends of my aunt, pretending that Julian was not standing beside me with that thunderous expression on his face, ignoring or scarcely acknowledging the congratulations from people who came up to us. At one time he left my side, and in a moment I saw him in conversation with Aunt Flora. His dark head was bent close to hers as though he did not want their conversation to be overheard, and my aunt, her lips curved in a self-satisfied smile, was shaking her head and shrugging as though to deny whatever Julian was telling her.

Immediately after his conversation with Aunt Flora, Julian came over to me and told me to change; we would be leaving in ten minutes. Bewildered at the sudden change in plan—we had previously agreed to stay the night in London before leaving the next day for Julian's home—I saw by his taut expression that it would do no good to question him. I did as he asked, and before I knew it, the coachman was whipping up the horses and we were on our way.

We stopped about midnight at a small inn. The innkeeper's wife, given terse instructions about separate rooms, silently led me upstairs while I followed in an agony of embarrassment, having intercepted a knowing look between the innkeeper and his wife about the curious arrangements. But by the time I had struggled unassisted with seemingly endless buttons at the back of my gown and had slipped into my nightdress and climbed into bed, I was furiously determined to demand an explanation from Julian the moment he entered the room. Two hours passed, and my temper did not improve; the more I thought about it, the angrier I became that Julian would treat me this way. At last, when I heard the clatter of boots and muffled cursing on the stairs, I leaped out of bed, determined to meet him at the door and let him know that whatever else his problems were, I was not going to be treated in this manner.

The noise retreated down the hall and I opened the door a crack, wondering what had happened. I saw Julian being assisted by the burly innkeeper, who, even with all his bulk, was having a difficult time propping Julian up against the wall while he struggled with the key to open the door. I had never before seen any man inebriated, but I knew without question that Julian was drunk. He sagged against the wall in a most disgusting manner, his head thrown back against the paneling. When the innkeeper finally wrestled the door open and pulled at Julian's arm, Julian stumbled heavily against the man before the two of them disappeared into the room and closed the door.

After that, there was nothing to do but climb into my own bed and try to sleep. I would demand an explanation in the morning.

But the next day, when Julian appeared in my room after my solitary breakfast, he was so abrupt that I did not dare question him. At first I thought he was avoiding me because he was ashamed of his conduct, but when the next several days went by, and each evening Julian left me at the door of my own room while he went to his, I knew he was avoiding me for some other reason. As his attitude toward me became more and more aloof, I was relieved that he did not choose to spend the night with me as a husband should. I was not wholly ignorant of the ways of married couples, as Aunt Flora had given me terse instructions on the duty of a married woman, but I did not think I could give myself to Julian knowing that he felt contempt for me.

The situation was unchanged by the time we arrived at Peregrine House, and I, having allowed too much time to lapse without asking for an explanation of Julian's strange conduct, could not ask for it now.

But perhaps Dorcas' unfortunate remark offered me an opportunity I had lost; tonight, when Julian came to my room, I would ask him what she had meant. It was obvious that Julian had said something to his family; otherwise, why would they have greeted me with such coldness? And if Julian had said something to them, I felt I deserved an explanation also.

I felt better after coming to this decision and sat down to wait. But when several hours had passed, I knew Julian would not come that night. A feeling of depression settled over me, and I felt alone as I had never done before. The great house seemed to press down on me, smothering me, and the crimson furnishings of the room were more oppressive as the night wore on. At last I decided to retire; perhaps in the morning things would look better. When I had changed into my nightgown, I sat down at the dressing table and opened the little jewel box that had belonged to my mother. The only thing it contained was a brooch; it was all I had left of my mother's things. The brooch was unlike any I had ever seen. It was gold, shaped in the form of a ram's head with one small diamond for the eye. My mother had never worn it—but, for some reason of her own, had kept it; and I thought it must have reminded her of someone. Perhaps my father had given it to her. At any rate, it was mine now, and I treasured it for the memory of her. It comforted me tonight; holding something that had been my mother's, I did not feel so alone. I took one last look at it before putting it carefully away in its velvet nest. Then, turning out the lamp, I climbed into the big bed.

I was awakened by the sound of the sea. It was morning and I could see weak sunshine filtering in through the draperies. Suddenly eager to be up and out, I threw back the covers and dressed in the chilly room. As I struggled with the buttons on one of the new woolen dresses that Julian had bought for me, I hoped that today I would make a new start with Julian's family. I had been innocent of any wrongdoing, and perhaps, when they became aware of that fact, they would be able to set aside their animosity and we would be able to live peacefully together.

I went downstairs, hoping I would be able to find the dining room, and met Betsy on the stairs. She looked at me strangely, and when I asked for directions, she pointed the way, saying that breakfast was served on the sideboard for everyone to help themselves.

There was no one in the dining room, when I found it at last, and I helped myself to coffee and a muffin, going to the window and looking out to the sea as I sipped the strong beverage. A voice behind me startled me so violently I spilled some of the coffee into the saucer as I turned.

"Up and about early, I see. Surveying your domain?" he said, as he poured himself a cup. "In case you don't remember, after my brother's hasty introduction last night, I'm Norman St. John."

"Of course I remember," I said.

"I think you might be puzzled at the family relationship—or has that close-mouthed brother of mine bothered to explain?" Norman asked, sipping his coffee.

I did not want to admit that Julian had indeed not explained; that our marriage was not based on confidences. I said nothing.

"Yes, I can see he neglected his duty. Well, as you might have guessed, Julian and I are half brothers. My father was Bernard St. John. My mother married him after Julian's father died. Julian has always regarded that as the ultimate betrayal of his mother— hence his aversion to me. When Mother and I came back to Peregrine House after my father died, it was almost more than dear Julian could bear, but of course he had to swallow his pride and let us in. After all, Mother denied that shocking rumor he confronted her with in no uncertain terms, so there wasn't much else he could do, was there?"

Norman glanced at me and appeared surprised at my puzzled expression. "Oh, you haven't heard?" he asked, obviously pleased at the prospect of explaining this piece of news to me.

I shook my head, hating myself for listening to him, but unable to say anything to stop him.

"Well, of course, it's all hearsay, and of course Mother denies it to this day, but the rumor was that Julian . . . well, actually, that Julian is illegitimate."

I gasped, and Norman shook his head at me. "I wouldn't worry about it. After all, Julian senior made him his heir, and that's all that matters, isn't it?"

He smiled engagingly before he turned to fill his plate, and I did not respond. I could think of nothing to say in reply to his outrageous statement and decided that it would be best to forget such an insidious piece of gossip. It was some time later before I would recall Norman's words and wonder at their significance.

As Norman stood before the various dishes arranged on the sideboard, I had an opportunity to study him. He was almost as tall as Julian, but much younger, and did not have the same dark handsomeness. Instead, his eyes were pale blue, his hair light brown, and he did not carry himself with the same assurance that Julian did. His hands, I noted, were long-fingered and soft-looking. He was dressed with the utmost care, as though his appearance were most important, but instead of appearing casually elegant, as Julian did in anything he wore, Norman had the faint air of a dandy.

I was trying to think of something to say to him when Dorcas bustled into the room, closely followed by her husband, Mathew. Upon seeing me, she stopped and stared aggressively. "Well," she said sarcastically. "Have you recovered from the rigors of the journey? Perhaps you did not sleep well, so far from the more luxurious accommodations you are no doubt accustomed to in London!"

I winced; I deserved her sarcasm after the little scene last night, but I did not understand her remarks about being accustomed to luxury. Deciding it was best to ignore her statement, I said simply, "I hope you will forgive me; I'm afraid I was over-tired last night."

"Ha! Yes, I can imagine that you were tired—all that scheming to snare a rich husband. What a blow it must have been to fall into your own trap!"

"Dorcas," Norman interrupted, "there is no need to quarrel."

"Oh yes there is," she hissed, her anger at me turning toward Norman. "After what she's done—do you think it likely that I will say nothing?"

"No," Norman answered, "that really would be too much to expect, wouldn't it?"

I thought it was time to speak for myself; I did not care for her insinuations. "Dorcas," I said, "what exactly do you mean?"

"As if you didn't know, you—you adventuress!"

"Dorcas!" Mathew said, shocked.

"Well, it's true!" she shrieked. She turned to me again, her face crimson with anger. "Do you think we are not aware of how you tricked Julian into marrying you? Pretending you were an heiress to snare him, when all the time you had nothing—nothing!"

"Dorcas, I don't know what you are talking about," I answered, so shocked at her accusation that I hardly knew what I was saying. "But I refuse to listen to your recriminations any longer. Please excuse me."

I turned to go, so caught up in fury and outrage that I failed to see Julian standing in the doorway until I was almost upon him. I didn't know how long he had been standing there, and I was dismayed at the look on his face. He seemed to be staring at me with the same look of contempt as that of his sister. "Dorcas, I warned you once," he said tightly; "pray see to it that Larissa is not subjected to your malice again." He looked at me and I wanted to shrink back at the look on his face. "Larissa, I want you to join me in the library. We have a few things to discuss."

The library was warm, the fire blazing, throwing light onto the walls full of leather-bound books, but I felt as though I would never be warm again. Julian gestured me to a chair by the fire, and I sat down hesitantly.

"Dorcas has never learned to guard her tongue," he began.

25

"Nevertheless," I said with a calm I did not feel, "she accused me of tricking you into marrying me. What exactly did she mean?"

Julian stared down at me for a moment, his face an unreadable mask. I forced myself to look directly into his eyes, reassuring myself that whatever the reason for this horrible nightmare, I had had no part in it except to agree to marry him.

Finally, after what seemed an interminable wait, he said, "Do you really expect me to believe you didn't know your aunt assured me you were an heiress?"

I could feel my face tighten with shock. Was it possible that even Aunt Flora could have concocted such a monstrous lie? One look at Julian's face assured me that not only was it possible, she had actually convinced him that it was so.

I could feel an anger such as I had never known building in me. So, I thought bitterly; this was the reason for the hasty wedding plans. Julian, anxious to marry because he thought I could bring him a substantial dowry; my aunt, equally anxious to marry me off before Julian discovered the lie she had so carefully built up. And I, in the middle, naïvely believing that Julian wanted to marry me for myself, knowing nothing of the arrangements between the two of them. It was no use berating myself for being a fool; the deed was done. But how I wished I had been clever enough to know that such a man as Julian would never have given me a second look if he had not been convinced I had money behind my name.

I was angry and hurt; I said the first thing that came into my head, wanting to hurt him too, and hating myself for it: "When did you discover the truth, Julian? Was it in the note that was handed to you outside the church? And confirmed later at the reception by my aunt? I should think you would have taken pains to learn my financial status—since that seems to have been the uppermost consideration—before the marriage ceremony; not after, when it was too late."

Julian stiffened, his brows drawing into such a forbidding frown that I hesitated. But some sense of pride, long dormant under my aunt's domination, came to me. I stood and faced him. "It seems we were both deceived. You, because you were led to believe I was an heiress; I, because I foolishly believed in something that did not exist. I have only one consolation now; your behavior toward me since our marriage has been explained. For the sake of appearances, I will act the part of the dutiful wife, but you need not feel I expect more. I hope that is to your satisfaction?"

I did not wait for his answer; I was afraid I would burst into tears of humiliation if I was forced to continue this conversation any longer. I gathered my skirts in one hand and left the library, my head held high so that the tears stinging behind my eyelids would not spill over and humiliate me further.

I went back to my room, the only place in the whole house where I felt safe from prying, accusing eyes. The balcony beckoned me, and I went out into the fresh air. As I stood there, with the cool air blowing over my flushed face, I could see, far below me on the beach, a man on a horse, galloping rapidly away from the house. Running beside the horse was the great black dog I had met on the balcony the night before. I knew the man was Julian, and I envied him his escape, however brief, from the problems that had to be faced eventually. Had I been wiser, I might have realized that my failure to speak the truth about not knowing of my aunt's deception helped to precipitate the nightmare in which we were soon to be caught up. But I was not wise, only hurt and confused.

I was still out on the balcony when Mrs. Harmon knocked on the door and admitted herself.

"Dear, dear," she clucked solicitously, "you will catch your death of cold out there, Mrs. Synclair."

"Oh no, I like it. I had never seen the sea before. I find it fascinating," I replied, forcing my thoughts away from the scene in the library.

"Well, you be careful on the balcony—the wind can be strong."

"Was there something you wanted, Mrs. Harmon?" I asked.

"Well, Master Julian said I was to show you the house. You just let me know when you are ready."

"I'm ready now," I answered, glad for something to do to occupy myself.

We went out into the hall and turned left, Mrs. Harmon chattering as we walked. "We're going to the nursery wing now—I thought you might like to see that part first. Of course, it hasn't been used since Miss Dorcas and Master Julian and Master Norman were small, but now with two young ladies in the house, I suppose it will be filled in no time."

She looked at me slyly, and to my embarrassment, I flushed, thinking that if it were up to Julian to fill the nursery, the whole wing might as well be closed forever. But I said nothing, and fortunately Mrs. Harmon interpreted my silence as the natural reticence of a young bride in discussing such matters.

We climbed a short flight of stairs, and passed through a door into a hallway. Before us was another door, which, when Mrs. Harmon opened it, led into the nursery. A skylight shed bright light over one end of the room, and I could see small tables and chairs, scuffed with use, standing to one side. A bookcase was against the wall, filled with books that almost spilled out of the shelves, while a box of toys, much battered, had been placed next to a large rocking horse in the corner.

The rocking horse caught my attention and I walked over to it. It was very lifelike, even to the strands of real horsehair that made up the mane and tail. Its glass eyes, faded to a ghostly white, stared at me, and I stepped back uneasily, chiding myself for imagining that they were following my movements. Something was wrong about the horse; I realized that the eyes should have been brown, instead of that opaque paleness. Oh, what did it matter, I thought, irritated with myself for being disturbed at a child's toy. But I turned away a shade too hastily, and saw the housekeeper staring at me in surprise.

"Excuse me, Mrs. Synclair," she said anxiously, "but are you all right? You look so pale."

"Oh, it's nothing, Mrs. Harmon. I . . . I do not care for that toy, that is all." It was absurd, I told myself, to feel a sudden revulsion at the toy, but I said hastily, "I think we should be getting about the rest of the house."

I forced a smile to reassure her, and saw her glance from the toy horse back to me once more before she bustled out. I followed, suddenly anxious to leave the room. As I closed the door behind me, I glanced at the rocking horse again, and stopped with my hand frozen on the doorknob. Surely it was my imagination that the horse was rocking slightly? Ridiculous, I told myself—but the light glinted off those eyes at a tiny movement of the wooden body. The rocking horse seemed suddenly sinister, and I slammed the door, feeling my heart pound in my throat.

Mrs. Harmon was some distance down the hall, and at the noise from the door she turned and stared at me curiously. I took a deep breath, forcing myself to be calm—after all, it was ludicrous to be frightened of such a harmless toy, I assured myself. But I hurried after the housekeeper, glad of her comforting presence.

As we inspected the rest of the house, Mrs. Harmon chattered away, but under the trilling of her words, I could sense that she was curious about my reaction in the nursery. But as I felt ridiculous about explaining, and she was too well trained to ask, both of us pretended that nothing was wrong. At last we came to the occupied portion of the house, and I breathed more easily. In this wing, Dorcas and her husband and Mrs. St. John had their rooms. Julian and I occupied the other wing, so we were separated as though we lived in different houses. I was glad of this, thinking that perhaps I would not come into frequent contact with the other members of Julian's family. Norman had his rooms on the second floor overlooking the gallery.

As we paused on the balcony and looked down on the great expanse below, Mrs. Harmon said, "You should have seen it in the old days, my dear. Julian's father and Mrs. Dorothea used to give such parties that the whole gallery was filled. What a sight it was to stand here and look down on all the ladies and gentlemen in their finery. It looked like a garden, it did, with all the colors of the ladies' dresses, and the men so handsome in their evening dress. I was nursemaid to the children then, Miss Dorcas and Master Julian, and for a treat, we used to come here and watch. Sometimes Master Julian's father would catch sight of them and wave." She hesitated for a moment, then went on firmly, as though to convince me. "He was a great man, if I do say so. How everyone admired him—it was quite a blow when he . . . died."

She sighed, lost in her memories, and I wondered that Julian had never mentioned his father to me. But then, I amended, Julian had not discussed anything about his family with me.

I looked at the portraits lining the stairway, and asked Mrs. Harmon if Julian's father's was among them.

She shook her head. "No, the portrait was taken down when Master Julian inherited. It was hanging in the drawing room above the fireplace. I don't know where it is now." She sighed again, her eyes sad. "It was so awful for him, poor child. He went to his father, begging him to explain about that vicious slur against his mother, but his father was too far gone in his own troubles by that time. He died not long after that, and I don't think Master Julian ever forgave him for putting him off—"

She stopped, her eyes wide with embarrassment. "Oh, forgive me, Mrs. Synclair, I didn't mean . . . That is, I . . . Oh dear!"

The poor woman was almost in tears. Hurriedly, I assured her that I would say nothing to Julian, and she rushed off, her shoulders heaving with emotion. I looked after her, thinking angrily how unfair it was that such a vicious piece of gossip about Julian's mother should be alive after all these years. I had no great love for Dorothea St. John after our one meeting, but still, I couldn't help but feel sorry for her; unfounded rumors were so difficult to combat when innocence was one's only weapon, especially when it seemed so often that people would rather believe lies than the truth.

I was to think of this incident later, and to wish fervently that I had paid heed to my own thoughts at the time. But by then it was too late. . . .

That afternoon I was summoned—there was no other word for it—by Julian's mother to take tea with her in her rooms. I presented myself at her door and was admitted by Louisa, who vanished at once after letting me in.

Mrs. St. John's rooms were heavily ornate, with silver and dark-rose-striped wallpaper and dark furniture. But even the furnishings could not compete with the overpowering presence of the personality who occupied the apartment. I sat down on the sofa with some hesitation, and looked at Julian's mother.

She was dressed in unrelieved black silk, as though this were an occasion for mourning; a gold brooch pinned at the throat of her high-necked gown and a heavy gold ring were the only ornaments she wore today. I waited for her to speak.

She took her time in doing so, busying herself with the silver teapot and the delicate china cups in front of her. There was also a plate of biscuits, which she handed to me silently after pouring tea for both of us. I took the plate but found I had no appetite; her expression seemed more forbidding than the previous night, and I fought down an impulse to make my excuses and flee the room. I was determined not to be afraid of her.

At last she spoke, in that cold voice I already found myself disliking. "I wanted an opportunity to speak to you privately, Larissa," she said, picking up her own cup with a steady hand and even steadier gaze at me.

"I have talked with Julian, and as he seems adamant that this marriage of yours will be preserved, I have come to the conclusion that perhaps it would be best if we understood each other. I have no intention of relinquishing my authority here as the mistress of the house—if you have any notions of taking the reins yourself, I must disabuse you of the idea at once. You are far too young—and have no experience in such matters, I am sure."

She paused to take a sip of tea, as well as, I supposed, to allow me time to digest her words. I sat silently, unwilling to remind her that many young women who were newly married were required to assume the role of mistress of a large establishment. I did not remind her because the thought had not occurred to me that I would assume responsibility for Peregrine House; Julian had never mentioned it.

She seemed to be waiting for some response from me, so I said agreeably, "I'm sure you are right, Mrs. St. John; such a responsibility is of course beyond my capabilities—now."

She nodded as though she had been certain of my agreement, and then continued with a slightly distasteful expression, "I regret that the subject must be brought up once again, but I feel that I have the right to know how your marriage came about. Pray give me the details as briefly as you can."

Her expression angered me; I knew full well that Julian had discussed something of our marriage with his family because of their attitude toward me, and I did not intend to subject myself to any interrogation from the disdainful woman sitting opposite me. I said, more sharply than I intended, "Mrs. St. John, if you wish to know what arrangements were made, I suggest you ask your son. He is in a far better position to explain than I am."

"Do not be impertinent, miss," she said; "I asked for an explanation, and I intend that you shall give it to me."

"I'm afraid I do not know what it is that you wish me to tell you," I said stiffly.

Her eyes narrowed. "So, you claim innocence in a scheme to snare a rich husband by pretending to be an heiress yourself? I am afraid I cannot believe that you know nothing."

It was rare that I lost my temper, even at the provocation my aunt had provided, because I had learned early in life that my aunt would not tolerate any display of defense by her victims. But suddenly it was as though the years of quietly taking abuse had slipped away. I was angry at the attitude of the woman before me, as well as the rest of the members of Julian's family, and I did not stop to think of the consequences of my rashness.

"Mrs. St. John, I do not care what you choose to believe, since it is obvious that nothing I can say will sway you from your prior convictions. As much as you want to deny it, I am married to your son, and nothing you can do will alter that fact. And since Julian has chosen to bring me here, I suggest that we attempt to maintain some kind of civil relationship, as we are all forced to live in the same house. I will try to stay out of your way as much as possible, and that is all the solution I can offer you. Now, if you will excuse me?"

I rose on trembling legs, somewhat horrified at my outburst, but helpless to call back the words now that they were spoken. Mrs. St. John rose also and said scathingly, "I suspected as much—you have not even the saving factor of good breeding. I have never been subjected to such rudeness, and I will thank you never to speak to me in that manner again. As for maintaining a 'civil relationship,' I am afraid that will be impossible. I do not care to associate myself with persons of lower station than myself in a family atmosphere, whatever my son chooses to do. You may go."

I turned and left the room quickly. But my shame was to be prolonged, for as I came out of the room, Dorcas was standing in the hall. It was obvious that she had been listening to the conversation, for a smile of satisfaction played on her full lips, and her blue eyes turned on me a gaze full of mockery. I started to brush past her, but she stopped me with a firm grip on my arm. "So—you thought to play the grand lady with my mother, did you?" she said, laughing gaily. "You do not know my mother very well if you choose to stand against her, my dear sister-in-law!"

"Dorcas, let go of my arm," I said through clenched teeth.

It seemed that no matter where I turned, I was up against yet another enemy. I pulled my arm away from Dorcas' grasp and fled down the hall, trying to shut my ears to the mocking laughter that followed me.

I had to get out of the house. I had to be by myself, away from the oppressive atmosphere. I reached my room and snatched my cloak from the wardrobe. A few minutes later, I let myself out the front door.

The breeze from the sea was refreshing to my hot face and I walked over to the retaining wall that ran by the side of the cliff. As I looked down, I could see a series of stone steps cut into the face of the cliff and leading from a small gate I had not noticed before. The gate swung open easily at my touch, and I cautiously let myself through it. A wooden railing ran beside the steps and I held on to it as I went down, fearing that the wet steps would be slippery.

I reached the bottom and started walking on the sand, away from the house. The waves came rolling in to the shore, and I was fascinated by the way the late afternoon sunlight shone through the water as the wave formed, then turned over on itself and broke into white foam as it raced toward the beach. I walked until the house on the cliff was far behind me, then I sat on one of the rocks that littered the shore and looked out toward the sea. It was peaceful here, and I could almost forget the problems I had left behind. So absorbed was I in my study of the sea that I failed to notice the figure on horseback until it was almost upon me. The horse was cantering down the beach, spraying sand in its wake, and the girl, or woman, who rode it sat the saddle as though she were part of the horse. As she came up to me, I could see that she was beautiful in a bold sort of way; her pale blond hair streamed loosely out from under a small blue riding hat, and her riding habit of the same blue color fit her superb figure like a glove. She came riding up to where I was sitting and reined in her horse so sharply that I felt tiny grains of sand stinging my face as they were flung from the horse's hoofs. She sat the restive horse calmly, her gloved hands holding the reins with assurance as the horse pranced under her. She looked down at me with arrogance, and I could feel myself stiffening under her cool appraisal.

At last she said, "Do you know you are on a private beach? You have no right to be here."

I said stiffly, "I'm sorry, I did not know it was private. I only arrived yesterday." I rose from my position on the rock and saw her regarding me steadily.

"Who are you?" she demanded.

"My name is Larissa Synclair. My husband and I just arrived at Peregrine House last night," I answered, and then wondered why she took a sudden sharp breath when I mentioned my name. Her face seemed to lose some of its color as she digested this information, but before I could ask her her own identity, she wheeled the horse sharply about and gave him a smart tap with her crop that sent him speeding down the beach in the direction in which she had come. I stared after her, puzzled, but then forgot the incident as I realized it was later than I thought and I must be getting back to the house. Not that anyone would miss me, I though wryly. I bent down to shake the sand from my shoe, and started back.

When I let myself in the front door, I could hear angry voices from the direction of the drawing room. I did not stop to identify the voices, but hurried to my room wondering why it seemed that everyone in this house quarreled with one another.

Soon it would be time to dress for dinner and I went to my wardrobe to select a gown. Julian had spared no expense when he had chosen my wardrobe, and though I had to admit his taste was excellent, still I longed for the more tailored gowns that had been mine. I remembered that Julian had looked at them with distaste and had ordered everything thrown out after we went to the dressmaker. Tonight I would wear a pale green silk that was my favorite, though Julian had allowed me to have it only because the dressmaker had insisted that it complimented my hair and eyes. I hoped Louisa would not come to help me dress tonight. She made me nervous with her superior attitude, and I had the feeling that she was watching me, ready to report any bit of information to Mrs. St. John. I could manage well enough, I thought, considering that I had never had the luxury of a personal maid before in my life.

A knock on the door interrupted my thoughts, and I called permission to enter. A girl of about fifteen came in and stood nervously just inside the door.

I looked at her inquiringly and she said in a quavering voice, "If you please, Mrs. Synclair, the mistress said I was to be your maid. My name is Ellie."

I was surprised at this generosity on the part of Julian's mother. I looked at the girl, who bobbed a curtsy and stood with her eyes downcast, looking as though she were about to burst into tears at any moment.

"What is the matter?" I asked.

"Oh, Mrs. Synclair, I don't know how to be a lady's maid—I was just promoted from the kitchen, and I'm afraid I'll do everything wrong, and the mistress will find out and I'll be dismissed. . . ." The words came out in a rush, then she did break down into tears.

I could appreciate how she felt; it was difficult not to be overawed by the formidable Mrs. St. John, so I said briskly, "Well, I suppose we will have to learn together. I've never had a maid before, so we will just keep our mistakes to ourselves—it will be our secret."

"Oh, Mrs. Synclair, you are so kind!" Ellie said,

36

wiping her eyes with her apron. "I didn't know what to expect!"

I could not suppress a feeling of triumph over Mrs. St. John; I supposed the fact that she had sent a kitchenmaid to wait upon me was a sort of insult; how dismayed she would have been to discover that I much preferred someone like Ellie to the stiff Louisa or the bold Betsy. I said calmly, "I think I would like to take a bath before dinner. I had not realized that the salt spray from the sea can make one feel so grubby."

"Oh, yes, ma'am, I'll get the water right away." Ellie bustled off, almost tripping over the threshold in her eagerness to please me.

I smiled, thinking that perhaps I had found an ally in this house after all.

I had my bath, and found myself refreshed and composed for dinner with the family. Ellie helped me dress and then we both struggled with my hair, which, after my outing on the beach, showed an unfortunate tendency to escape from the smooth coil at the back of my neck into unruly curls around my face. I was almost ready when Julian came into the room.

Ellie and I had been laughing at her efforts to do my hair and I was pleased that her nervousness had almost disappeared, but when Julian entered, she gasped and moved back from the dressing table as though she were seeing some kind of monster. He looked at her with an inquiring gaze that seemed to unnerve her still further, and in her confusion she backed into a small table and knocked it over. Fortunately there was nothing of value on the table, so no damage was done, but Julian became angry at her clumsiness and ordered her from the room. She burst into tears and fled.

"You should not be so familiar with the servants," Julian admonished, looking at me as though I were a child to be chastised. "And I think we will make another choice for a maid for you—that girl does not seem to know what she is about."

Julian might wish to ignore the fact that I was his wife, but the least he could do was permit me a few of the rights to which I, as his wife, was entitled. I had found a possible friend in Ellie—the only one in this house who seemed to like me—and I did not want to lose her. "The girl is understandably nervous in her new position, but I think that in time she will make an excellent lady's maid. I propose to keep her with me. Surely, if I am to have a maid, I have the right to choose whoever pleases me."

Julian looked at me, startled out of his usual implacability. It was as though he were seeing me in a new light, and was disturbed at what he saw. For a moment I was afraid I had gone too far, but then he shrugged and said offhandedly, "If you wish to struggle with such a clumsy girl, that is your concern. Are you ready to go down?"

The Family—I had begun to think of them in that term—were just going into the dining room when we arrived. The conversation broke off as we entered, but Julian seemed unperturbed by what I thought was an obvious tension in the room. Calmly he escorted me to the foot of the table and held out the chair placed there. I looked up at him uncertainly, knowing full well that Mrs. St. John expected to be seated here, but he nodded at me coldly, and there was nothing I could do but seat myself. I dared not look at Julian's mother; it was as though everyone in the room were holding his breath, waiting for her anger at my usurping her place. But Julian went over to his mother, and offered his arm with such a set expression on his face that there was nothing for her to do but take it, or create a scene. Stiffly, her posture indicating her indignation, she allowed him to seat her at his right while he himself sat at the head of the table. The others took their cue from Mrs. St. John, and I felt absurdly relieved that at least one obstacle had been overcome without open warfare. I was soon proved to be mistaken.

I knew that by seating me at the foot of the table

Julian intended that this would establish my place in the house, but Mrs. St. John had made it clear to me this afternoon that she was to be mistress of the house, and would not relinquish her place to me. I appreciated Julian's effort, but I knew that this would cause more friction between his mother and me. I smiled apologetically at her, trying to convey that this was not my decision, but she turned coldly away and ignored me the rest of the meal.

I was silent during the first course, studying the members of Julian's family. A candelabrum had been placed at each end of the table with a centerpiece of hothouse flowers in the center. I felt I could observe those at the table through the screen they made without my scrutiny being noticed. Julian was at the opposite end from me, but fortunately the branches of the candelabra were turned in such a manner that I could see him clearly, while the others were slightly hidden by the candles. It turned out that I needn't have worried that the family would not care to be observed by me; they paid me no attention at all.

Two maids, each in a starched apron with a frilly white cap, began serving as soon as we were seated, but only when the maids withdrew after serving the soup did Mrs. St. John turn to Julian and say, "Julian, this is intolerable!"

He turned toward her and said calmly, "What do you mean, Mother?"

"You know very well what I mean! This house cannot have two mistresses—and I told Larissa that myself this afternoon!"

From where I sat, I could see Julian's eyes narrow as he looked at his mother. He said, "I believe we reached that conclusion this afternoon ourselves in the drawing room, did we not?"

He paused and his mother nodded triumphantly, already certain of her victory. But his next words brought an angry mottled flush to her cheeks when he said, "I have given the matter some thought, after our . . . conversation today. As you know, Dower House is empty now, and I thought that perhaps you would prefer to move your things there. Of course, it is slightly smaller than this house, but then, you would be able to manage it to your satisfaction without having to consult another woman as to its management."

I thought Mrs. St. John would have a stroke, so angry did she become at his suggestion. Her face turned crimson, then white, as she struggled to control her fury. Dorcas gasped in horror at her brother's calm assumption that of course their mother would step down from her position, and Norman spoke angrily.

"Julian, you can't possibly be serious! You can't turn your own mother out of her house—you can't do such a thing!"

Julian turned the full force of his gaze on Norman, who to his credit did not shrink from it, as I surely would have done. He stared calmly at Norman for a moment, then replied coolly, "It may have escaped your attention, dear brother, but Dower House is more than adequate. In fact, my grandmother spent many years there, following a similar situation when Mother came to Peregrine House with my father. Mother should be quite comfortable there with a full staff of servants. I should think you would accompany her also, so that she would not be lonely. After all, it was her suggestion that this house cannot have two mistresses. If she feels uncomfortable here, then by all means she should make her residence where there will be as little conflict as possible."

Dorcas entered the conversation at this point, having recovered her power of speech after her first shock. "Julian, I won't have it! Mother belongs here more than . . . than . . . that sly baggage you brought here as your wife!"

It was Dorcas' turn to come under Julian's fierce gaze. "I warned you once before that I will not allow you to speak of my wife in that manner. I don't think I have to remind you that you and your husband are here on sufferance, Dorcas. If you feel that I cannot manage my household to your satisfaction, then it is time that you and Mathew found yourselves another residence also. Perhaps Mother would be happy to accommodate you in Dower House if you are unable to establish your own household."

Mathew was obviously dismayed at the prospect of having to provide a home for himself and his wife. He spoke for the first time: "I say, Julian, there is no need to be hasty. I'm sure Dorcas did not mean to imply—"

"Be quiet, Mathew!" Dorcas said sharply. "I can handle this!"

"Dorcas," Mathew said placatingly, "you know that the legal business regarding my estate has yet to be settled. I'm afraid—"

"I said, be quiet. There is no need to discuss anything about your inheritance at the table." Dorcas turned angrily from her husband and confronted Julian again. "Julian, I know you relish the thought that we are all in your power, but you must have some consideration for our feelings."

Julian stared distastefully at his sister for a moment. "I have every consideration for your feelings, Dorcas. That is why I put this suggestion to you. The other alternative is, of course, that we try to live in this house amicably. Do I make myself clear?"

The tone in which these words were delivered indicated that for Julian, at least, the discussion was finished. The others had sufficient respect for—or fear of—him that they, too, subsided, although unwillingly. At last Dorcas threw down her napkin and left the table angrily without offering any excuses. Mathew followed in short order, presumably to comfort his wife, although I could see that Dorcas was far too angry to listen to reason at the moment.

The rest of the meal was finished in silence, with Mrs. St. John sitting ramrod-straight in her chair and refusing any of the dishes set before her. I noticed that although her control was admirable, considering the shock she had been dealt by Julian, her hand trembled as she put her wineglass to her lips. Norman merely scowled fiercely at the table while I, confused and bewildered at the atmosphere of hate generated at the table, sat toying with the meal before me.

Of all of us, Julian seemed the most composed, and when the meal was finished, he sent for the cook to compliment her on the roast that had been served. This gesture was too much for Mrs. St. John; she left the table in a flurry of purple skirts, slamming the door behind her.

When she had gone, Norman raised his glass to Julian in a mocking salute before downing the contents in one swallow. He rose and bowed jeeringly in my direction and followed his mother.

Julian and I were alone in the dining room.

CHAPTER THREE

I waited for Julian to speak. The silence that descended upon us as we were left alone seemed to be vibrating still with the angry voices that had been raised during dinner. Julian sat with his lips compressed, as though he were trying to control his anger. How little I knew him then; had I been more perceptive, I would have realized that the scene in which he and his family had engaged had wounded him deeply, but of course he was too proud to show it at the time.

At last he said, "I'm sorry you were subjected to disagreement among the members of my family. But I am determined that you will be treated with respect, as is due my wife."

"Julian, it is not really important to me to be mistress of the house. I am sure your mother is much more capable than I . . . and I know that this will only cause trouble between us. Can we not live in peace here?" I thought that by offering to be set aside, it would be a solution to the friction.

Julian stared at me, his eyes narrowed as he considered my proposal. I was too young, too immature, at the time to realize that he had gone against his family to preserve some dignity for me, and that, by refusing him, I had made his gesture worthless.

"No," he said finally, "Mother will have to make the choice. I have no objection to her living here, but she has to see that we must live in harmony." His lips twisted bitterly as he added, "If it is at all possible."

"But, Julian—"

"That is enough!" he exclaimed angrily. "I am weary of this whole discussion. It will not be mentioned again."

He poured himself another glass of wine and drank it quickly. Suddenly, he looked tired; there were lines in his forehead that I had not noticed before, and I wondered if the responsibility for all of us was taking its toll of him. After the scene at dinner tonight, I knew his family was no comfort to him; they argued and fought with him and among themselves. There was no harmony here, and it came to me that if I could not have a loving marriage, at least I could show my support of Julian by acceding to his wishes and trying to make things go smoothly for him. It was a noble thought, but one quite removed from my earlier desire to assert my rights as his wife, and I wondered that I should have such conflicting feelings for him.

Several days passed in a sort of uneasy truce. I tried to keep away from the others and began to take long walks on the beach. There were several small caves hidden among the rocks and I explored every one of them, feeling a delicious sense of freedom that I could do so without having to ask permission of anyone. Proper behavior according to a strict code had been my aunt's rule, and now several times I caught myself laughing gaily as I picked up my skirts and ran down the beach, or took off my shoes and stockings and felt the cool sand cover my bare feet. I knew if my aunt could have seen me, she would have been shocked at my behavior, and I felt like a child let out of school during my solitary walks on the beach. And if my thoughts turned every so often to Julian, I tried to ignore the reason why my heart pounded uncomfortably whenever he came to my room, or the thrill that ran through me as his hand carelessly brushed mine.

I never saw the woman on horseback again, though occasionally I would stare down the beach, hoping to see her riding toward me. I wondered who she was and how she came to be riding on this particular beach, for I had discovered that this property belonged to Julian. The next time I saw her, I would not be so quick to apologize for trespassing on my husband's property.

Julian did not concern himself with how I spent my days; in fact, we rarely saw each other. I assumed that he was occupied with business matters, for every morning he would ride out and return only in time for the evening meal. It was a lonely life for me, but I preferred being by myself; anything was better than the continual squabbling and quarreling among the members of Julian's family.

Then one day, while I was walking along the beach as usual, I saw the great dog that belonged to Julian. He was running along the sand, racing the waves as they came rolling in to shore. He looked as solitary a figure as I must have, and I felt a kinship with him. I called to him and he regarded me suspiciously for a moment before coming over to me and sniffing the hand I held out to him. After that, he would mysteriously appear whenever I was on the beach and we developed a sort of friendship between us. We took our walks together and occasionally he would condescend to fetch a piece of wood I would find on the shore and toss for him. We explored the caves together and I felt more secure when he was with me. The startling fact of his two differently colored eyes ceased to bother me, although sometimes when we sat on the sand together and he held his head to one side, regarding me, I had the uneasy feeling that he was aware of my thoughts.

I thought it best that I did not mention to Julian that Berus and I were becoming good friends; from his reaction that first night on the balcony, I thought he would not like it if he knew the dog was in my company and might even forbid me to take Berus with me on my walks. I did not feel that I was deceiving Julian, because I knew the reason he did not want me to associate with Berus was that he thought I might be injured by him. But as time went on, and Berus and I became better acquainted, I knew that the dog held no danger for me; in fact, it seemed as though Berus thought himself my protector, often looking anxiously back at me if I stopped to examine something and fell behind as he raced along the sand.

The only time I saw Julian's family was in the evenings, when we were all gathered for dinner. There was no mention of Julian's mother's moving from the house, and I continued to occupy uncomfortably the chair opposite Julian. Mrs. St. John had made no move to include me in the running of the household, and I was relieved the subject was ignored by both of us. I knew that, should I have attempted to try to help with the house, Mrs. St. John would have waited for me to make a mistake, which I surely would have done, and then she would be able to confront Julian with evidence of my incompetence. I convinced myself that I did not want Julian to be disturbed by any further display of friction between his mother and me, but to be truthful, I had to admit that I did not want Julian to see me in a more unfavorable light than he already did. At any rate, Mrs. St. John continued in her role as before, and I tried to occupy myself as best I could.

I began to be worried about Julian. He was thinner and more tired-looking as the days passed, with new lines of worry becoming etched in his face. I did not dare ask him what was the matter, as I was afraid I would anger him. So I merely watched silently, on the rare occasions that I saw him, and wished uselessly there was some way I could comfort him.

My feelings surprised me; where before I was content to maintain a surface relationship with Julian, as time went on I found myself more and more drawn to the man who was my husband in name only. I suppose it was due in part to the manner in which his family treated him that I became aware of the need I felt to support him. The conversations at dinner were a revelation to me. It seemed that Dorcas and Norman went out of their way to be condescending to him, and even to laugh at him behind his back. I soon found this intolerable because I knew Julian was aware of their attitude toward him and chose to do nothing about it.

For example, one night at dinner Dorcas broached the subject of having her own and Mathew's rooms done over.

Julian replied, "Dorcas, if I remember correctly, you had those rooms refurnished completely just last year. I am still paying the bills as the result of your extravagances."

"But, Julian," she said nastily, "I can't help it if this house is so gloomy. When I was shopping last week, I saw the most perfect silk wallpaper, with curtains to match. You cannot be so parsimonious that you begrudge me the least little pleasure."

"I can't manage it at this time, Dorcas," Julian replied quietly.

His sister appealed to her mother, as it seemed she always did when thwarted by Julian in some way. "Mother, you were with me—don't you agree that it would be little enough for Julian to do for me—for us," she added belatedly, looking at Mathew.

And as always, Mrs. St. John sided with her daughter against Julian. "Yes, Julian—after all, I did not notice you complaining when the bills for your wife's new wardrobe started coming in."

Julian looked at his mother, as though wondering how she had come by the knowledge of my new gowns, but he was silent. I could see his jaw tighten as he tried to control his impatience.

"Speaking of spending money," Norman said casually, "I'm afraid you must know sooner or later. I bought a new hunter—he really is a beauty, Julian—and since I was short of cash at the time, I had the bill sent to you. I knew you could afford it better than I. If you want to see him, I have him in the stables. Can't wait to try him out at Lord Effington's hunt next week."

Julian looked from one to the other and I knew what he would say: he would agree to their demands, not because he was weak, but because he was too impatient with their selfishness to debate further.

I wanted to stand up and shout at them that they had no right to assume that Julian would grant every selfish wish, every whim that caught their fancy. But then I thought: it is not for me to interfere; Julian is aware of what they are doing to him, and if he chooses to ignore it, then I must do so also. But it was becoming increasingly difficult to remain silent.

One night Dorcas brought up the subject of opening the house for a party. I could tell from the sly look on her face that she was up to some mischief, and that somehow I was to bear the brunt of it. I had had few words with Dorcas since that first day when she accused me of being an adventuress, preferring to stay out of the way of her acid tongue. But tonight she was all smiles as she talked gaily of a party, and I felt uneasy when I saw the glitter in her eyes as she looked briefly at me, then turned away to begin again her conversation with Julian.

"Julian, I think you really should—you know, to introduce your new bride to all our friends. It is only proper, after all—otherwise they might think you have something to hide," she finished maliciously.

Julian stiffened at this last remark, but before he had an opportunity to reply, Norman offered his encouragement: "I think it's an excellent idea, Julian. After all, Peregrine House has not had a party since . . . well, for a long time. And I'm sure everyone is waiting anxiously for a glimpse of Larissa." Norman turned to me and smiled, but behind that smile I thought he was challenging me to refuse the party. For some reason, it had become a contest of wills; Dorcas and Norman were waiting for Julian's reply a bit too anxiously, I thought.

I looked at Julian, awaiting his decision also. He stared back at me, and I thought he was debating the merits of the suggestion and wondering if I would be able to carry off the occasion among the friends and neighbors who were certain to be curious about us. I was right about his hesitation, but so wrong about his reasons. Had I known, I would have made some excuse for not having the party, but my selfish wish to prove myself to Julian was uppermost in my mind, and I scarcely noticed the look of remembered pain in his eyes. I nodded slightly, hoping to convey my eagerness to have the party; our eyes held for a moment, then he smiled grimly, and, with his eyes still on my face, said to Dorcas, "I think that is an excellent idea, Dorcas. We will have a ball to celebrate the occasion of my marriage to Larissa. I'm sure that you three women can get together and plan an affair that will be remembered."

He raised his glass in a mocking salute to me, and I did not know until a long time later what his agreement had cost him.

I scarcely listened to Dorcas' excited chatter concerning the party during the rest of the meal. Caught up in my own pleasant dreams of being such a success with Julian's friends that he would be forced to view me in a new light, I was too self-centered to note the withdrawn, almost pained expression on Julian's face as he looked around the table and listened to Dorcas and Norman interrupting each other with their own ideas for the party.

Daily, Ellie was growing in confidence as well as in her ability to serve as a lady's maid. I made a point of praising her often, for I knew how it felt to do one's best for someone and then receive no thanks in return. We began to experiment with my hair in the afternoons when I came back from my walks on the beach. Ellie brushed my hair until it shone, and became quite adept at pinning it up this way and that while we tried to decide which style suited me best. It was a pleasant way to occupy myself, for when I had offered to help with the preparations for the ball, Mrs. St. John had loftily informed me that everything would be taken care of without my assistance.

A dressmaker had been installed in the house, and Dorcas spent much time with her for fittings. I had accidentally entered the sewing room one day and Dorcas had flown at me, pushing me out into the hall, and saying that her gown was to be a surprise.

Mrs. Harmon bustled around the house, her plump little face alight with importance. She supervised the housemaids, who cleaned and polished every room until it shone, for it was expected that some of the guests might remain overnight. All the carpets were taken out and beaten with whisks until not a speck of dust dared remain; the whole house smelled of beeswax and turpentine as the floors were buffed and polished, and the furniture rubbed until it gleamed.

Harmon and several of the servants climbed up on ladders and dusted the high arched ceiling of the gallery, using feathers that had been tied to the ends of long poles; the crystal chandelier was taken down carefully and washed and polished. From the kitchen came delicious smells, as the cook and her staff made preparations for a feast.

In the midst of all this activity, I felt somewhat lost. It seemed as though I was in everyone's way as they hurried and bustled about, readying the house for the great night. Once I happened to meet Mrs. Harmon as she paused for breath and asked her if there was anything I could do. She looked at me in surprise, and I knew what she was thinking: it was not for the wife of the master to bother herself helping servants; but I could not help it. I felt so useless. After a moment, she nodded, as though confirming something in her mind, then she said, "I should think you can! I've told Mrs. St. John that the gardener is waiting for her to decide

49

on the flower arrangements, but of course she has so much on her mind. . . . Do you think you could go along and decide for her?"

I knew she had concocted this story at the last moment, but nevertheless I was grateful for her understanding. I told her I would be happy to talk to the gardener, if she could show me the way. She nodded happily and led me toward the back of the house. We went through a side door and I was amazed. There in front of me, sheltered by the house, was a long building with a curving roof of glass. The glass sparkled in the sunlight and I could see the dark green leaves of some tall plants inside pushing against the glass as though eager to be outside.

Mrs. Harmon opened the door, which was also made of glass, and called "Tom! Tom, Mrs. Synclair has come to talk to you about the flowers for the ball. Tom—where are you?"

"Here I am, Mrs. Harmon—you don't have to shout the place down. I'm not deaf yet!" came a gruff voice from somewhere in the back of all this greenery.

A man came hobbling around the corner, leaning heavily on a cane. It was obvious that he had a crippled leg, for, as he walked, it dragged slightly behind him. But he was not a man to accept pity; as he came toward us, I could see that his black eyes sparkled and his seamed face was lit with a smile of pleasure as his gaze rested on me. He reached up and pulled a battered felt hat from his head and said, "My name's Tom, Mrs. Synclair. It's a pleasure meeting you. I was hoping you would come sometime and see my plants."

"Thank you, Tom," I said, looking around at the profusion of greenery and blooms that seemed to fill every inch of space. "They are beautiful."

Tom looked pleased at my compliment and offered to show me his "treasures"; it was plain that he felt a great deal of pride in his work and I told him I was eager to see everything.

Mrs. Harmon said, "Will you be all right, Mrs. Synclair? If I don't go back and supervise those lazy girls of mine, not a thing will get done—and my, we have so much left to do!"

Mrs. Harmon rustled away and soon Tom and I were engaged in exploring the glasshouse—or at least, I was busily exploring; Tom followed me, explaining and answering questions as we walked along. We went up and down aisles of wooden trays, over which a fine layer of gravel had been spread—to control the moisture, Tom told me—and upon which had been placed pot after pot of blooming plants. There was a small stove at the back of the glasshouse with a comfortable chair beside it. "For the winter," Tom told me with a wink, "so the plants and I can stay warm."

Everywhere I looked were banks of flowering plants: roses of all colors, fluffy carnations, irises on their long stems. Rubber plants stood side by side with small fruit trees; graceful ferns nodded over pots filled with blooms I couldn't identify. The air was warm and humid; moisture condensed on the glass roof and dripped down onto the bricked pathways. I was enchanted: it was like being in a garden, but such a garden I had never seen before.

As we walked along, Tom spoke lovingly of his plants. "My father was a gardener, and his before him," he told me. "I remember helping my father when I was just a little tyke. I suppose that was when I learned to appreciate growing things, for my father hated to see anything die. He said it was like life continuing in a circle: spring comes and the green shoots appear, then they bloom, and in the winter they sleep, to wait for spring again. But not in here," he added proudly; "in here it's always spring. And that's something to say—this coast is harsh on growing things without the protection of the glass."

He showed me how a series of wires and pulleys had been arranged so that screens could be pulled over the roof for insulation in case the winter was too harsh, and how certain of the glass panes could be unhooked to admit fresh air. Only when I noticed that it was becoming dark outside did I realize how the afternoon had sped by, so fascinated was I listening to this little wizened man speak of his plants and his history.

"Thank you for a most interesting time, Tom," I said when it was time for me to go. "Perhaps I can come back and help you sometime, if you would be willing to teach me."

He looked at me with his bright little eyes. "Of course, Mrs. Synclair. You're not like some I could mention—I think you have a feeling for growing things, like I do. You have to remember plants is delicate creatures—they don't like to be pushed and pulled apart." He paused and added magnanimously, "Come any time you like."

I left, smiling at his proprietary manner. But when I turned back to look at the glasshouse before going into the house, I saw that he was standing by the glass door, regarding me with a look of sadness and—pity? —on his face. He saw me looking at him and hastily turned away, hobbling down the center aisle, shaking his head as he went.

I felt a vague moment of alarm—why should he stare at me with such a pitying expression, I wondered. But I would not allow myself to dwell on it; it was time to get dressed for dinner, and soon I would see Julian. The anticipation of seeing my husband blotted from my mind the strange look I had seen on Tom's face and I hurried up the stairs to my room.

As I entered—I was becoming accustomed to the overwhelming redness of the furnishings, though lately I had entertained heretical ideas of stripping the apartment bare and starting all over again—Ellie was waiting for me. One look at her excited face told me something momentous had occurred; she confirmed this by saying almost immediately, "Mrs. Synclair—have you heard the news yet?"

Cautiously I asked what she was talking about.

"Mrs. Arminta Rossmore is arriving with her son tomorrow!" she announced importantly.

"And who, pray, is Arminta Rossmore?" I asked,

52

feeling immediately out of sorts; even the servants seemed to know more than I did in this house.

"Mrs. Rossmore is Mrs. St. John's sister-in-law," Ellie continued. "She rarely visits because the master and Mr. Edward—Mrs. Rossmore's son—have no liking for one another. But I suppose they're coming especially to meet you—and for the ball, of course. Oh, Mr. Edward is so handsome—everyone wonders why he hasn't married—"

Ellie turned crimson at this slip of the tongue and stopped in confusion. I took the opportunity to reprimand her for gossiping, feeling hypocritical as I did so, for I was as eager to listen as she was to talk. But I knew Julian wouldn't approve of his servants and his wife gossiping together about members of his family, so I diverted her attention by requesting some hot water for a bath before dinner. Ellie went out, and I sat down at my dressing table, absently studying my reflection while I wondered how the arrival of Arminta Rossmore and her son would affect me.

I was still sitting there when the communicating door opened and Julian came in. He had not changed for dinner yet and I was surprised to see him so early in the afternoon. Usually he timed his appearances in my room just as the dinner gong sounded, as though he did not care to seek my company a moment before absolutely necessary.

I looked at him, forcing my expression into one of calm politeness, and hoped that he did not notice the pulse beginning to pound in my throat as my senses reacted toward him against my will. I wanted to go to him and touch the lock of hair that fell onto his forehead, smooth away the frown he wore today. He was coatless, wearing a white linen shirt with full sleeves ending in cuffs that banded his strong wrists; the neck of the shirt was partly open, exposing a tanned throat and part of his wide chest. Fawn-colored riding breeches met dark brown riding boots that showed a high gloss even underneath a spattering of mud. I lowered my eyes and focused my attention on the boots so that he could not read in my eyes the longing to touch him, to have his arms about me. I was very much aware of him as a man, and frightened at the feeling of desire that washed over me as he stood there.

"I thought you should know that my Aunt Arminta and her detestable son, Edward, will be arriving shortly," Julian informed me grimly. "I have no desire to inflict my cousin on you, but it seems that for courtesy's sake I must admit them for a short stay."

I didn't know what to reply to this, so I remained silent.

After a pause, he continued, "You might as well know that Edward and I have never been congenial, and I find him more of an insufferable bore now than I did when we were children. He has always had the absurd notion that Peregrine House should have belonged to him."

Julian paused again, and I wondered why he was telling me this; he had always been most secretive about his family, and I was surprised that he should be volunteering this information. In a burst of false confidence because he had confided in me, I said, "Why does he feel that Peregrine House should be his?"

Julian looked at me coldly, and I realized instantly that I had offended him. I wanted to call back my words, but of course it was too late. He said, "There is no need to go into that—it is past history and doesn't concern you."

With a great effort I remained silent; I wanted to shout at him and tell him that of course it concerned me—I was his wife, wasn't I? No, that wasn't quite true; I was his wife in name only, and he had made it clear that the situation would not change. I shrugged as though it were of no importance to me and turned blindly away from him; I did not want him to see the frustrated tears that came into my eyes. He stood a moment watching me—I could see his reflection in the mirror—then, to my surprise, he came over to me and put his hand on my shoulder. He said softly, "I'm sorry, Larissa, but there are things here that you do not understand, and I would prefer that you do not pry too closely into my family's affairs. It is for your own good, believe me."

Rebelliously, I thought that if I didn't understand anything about Peregrine House, my husband, or his family, it was because everyone seemed to go to great lengths to keep me in the dark. I did not trust myself to respond to him, and in a moment he turned and left the room.

I had an absurd desire to put my head in my arms and cry, but my vanity would not allow me to appear at dinner with swollen eyes, so I lifted my head defiantly and moved to the wardrobe to occupy myself by deciding what to wear for dinner.

My mood of defiance sustained me through Ellie's preparations as I dressed. At the last minute, before Julian came in, I went to my jewel box and pinned on the ram's-head brooch that had been my mother's. It looked incongruous on the lavender silk gown I was wearing, but I didn't care. I felt so alone tonight that I wanted something of my own to remind me that I had once been loved and surrounded by my own family. As a rule, I was not one to indulge in self-pity, but tonight I was going to allow myself that luxury.

Julian rejoined me and it wasn't until we approached the head of the stairs that we heard the commotion in the gallery below. Julian listened a moment, then, with a muttered oath, seized my arm and propelled me rapidly down the stairs. Just as we reached the bottom step, a high, autocratic voice rang out:

"Julian! I simply will not tolerate such rudeness from your servants! Speak to your butler at once!"

Such was my first introduction to Julian's Aunt Arminta. She was standing in the hall, surrounded by piles of baggage and gesturing furiously in poor Harmon's face. She wore a traveling outfit of some dark material, trimmed with fur. At the moment her outsized hat was bobbing ferociously with every word until I feared it would fly off her head with the force of her indignation. Arminta Rossmore was a tall woman, stoutly built, but with the narrow autocratic face of the true patrician. She was not beautiful, but she had such presence that one forgot the hooked nose, the thin-lipped mouth, and the high cheekbones and was fascinated instead by her commanding personality. At least, *I* was fascinated; Harmon looked overwhelmed, Julian merely impatient that such a scene should be taking place in the hall.

Julian went to her side, almost dragging me along in his hurry. "Aunt Arminta, we didn't expect you until tomorrow at the earliest."

Arminta Rossmore gave him a scorching look. "Well, as you can see, I have arrived today. And this imbecile"—she gestured again toward Harmon—"has the temerity to keep me standing in the hall while he blathers on about fetching your mother. I tell you, Julian, I wouldn't tolerate such insolence for one minute in my own household!"

Julian made some soothing remark to her but Arminta refused to be mollified. She glared at him again, and I was horrified when I almost giggled at his helpless expression. But my impulse to laugh was quickly stifled when I suddenly found myself impaled by a gimlet stare from Aunt Arminta.

"So," she said, looking me up and down, "this must be Larissa. Come here, girl, and let me have a look at you."

The command in her voice gave me no alternative. I came forward and curtsied while Julian performed the unnecessary introduction.

"Well, Julian," she said cryptically, "I see this time you have chosen a woman who is not vacuous and inclined to faint at the first sound of unpleasantness."

Julian made a choked sound, but quickly turned away and began issuing instructions to Harmon for removing the numerous parcels from the hall to the room that had been prepared for his aunt. Harmon gestured to two frightened-looking footmen lurking just outside the door. In seconds, bags, footmen, and Harmon had disappeared, and all the confusion of their removal left me no time to wonder about Arminta's remark and Julian's reaction to it.

"Where is your mother, Julian?" Arminta asked, giving Julian another withering glance. "Although I can't say I'm surprised that she is ashamed to face me if she cannot manage your household better than this!"

I found my tongue at last. "The family is in the dining room, Mrs. Rossmore. Would you care to join us there? Or perhaps you would prefer to retire to your room at once. I can order tea and a light supper while you rest, if you wish."

I was determined not to be frightened of this woman who was obviously accustomed to bullying people, but as she fixed me with one of her glacial stares, I had to fight down an impulse to retreat from her. I forced myself to stand my ground, not caring to wonder what Julian thought of my highhanded manner of taking over the situation. To my surprise, Arminta gave a bark of laughter and her expression toward me softened slightly as she said to Julian, "At least there is one member of your intolerable family who is concerned for my comfort. Well, my girl, I suppose there is nothing for it but to beard the old lioness in her dining room. Come along."

Her reference to Dorothea St. John was my undoing; to my immediate embarrassment, I laughed aloud. Arminta looked down at me—she was very tall for a woman—and I caught the glint of wicked amusement in her deep-set eyes. It was as though we were suddenly sharing a secret and, in that moment, I found I was no longer afraid of her. Julian was another matter; when I dared to look at him, I saw he was wearing his most glowering expression and I knew I had offended him by laughing. He had good reason to be angry with me, I had to admit; my lapse was inexcusable.

But Arminta looked at him and said, "Oh, come, Julian! Have you no sense of humor? No, I can see you do not. Well, no matter. Are you going to escort your aunt and your wife to the dining room, or are you going to stand there radiating your displeasure?"

* * *

Julian's family was waiting in the dining room; from their various expressions, I could tell they had been informed of Arminta Rossmore's arrival. Arminta sailed in and addressed her first remark to Mrs. St. John. "Dorothea! I knew you were anxiously awaiting my arrival, so I arranged especially to come a day early. Not an easy feat, considering that, in this part of the country, train schedules are almost nonexistent!"

Before Mrs. St. John had a chance to reply, Arminta had turned to Dorcas, who was glaring at her sullenly. "Dorcas, my dear—and Mathew—how are the two lovebirds? I imagine your nose is out of joint, Dorcas, since Larissa has taken your place as the new bride. Oh well, one can't stay in the limelight forever," she finished, giving me a wink and linking her arm through mine.

I was surprised at this generous gesture; more than any words, it conveyed that she was willing to accept me into the family and wanted to make sure that everyone else was aware of it.

I saw Mrs. St. John tighten her lips on an angry retort, and Dorcas flushed a furious crimson; Norman displayed his usual nonchalance, as though the quarrels of his family were beneath his notice, but Arminta decided to include him in the camaraderie. "Still here, Norman? I should have thought that you would have persuaded Julian to buy you a nice fat commission in the army—or is that passé for young men of impecunious means and good breeding?" She smiled sweetly at everyone, all of whom returned murderous looks, then she said, "As Larissa has been so kind as to offer to show me to my room, I think I shall retire for the night. I couldn't possibly be at my best until I have recovered from the difficulties of getting here; I shall so look forward to joining you tomorrow. Oh yes, Edward will arrive sometime tonight or tomorrow—I never know what he is about, he is so vague about details. Well, then, good night."

"Just a minute, Arminta," Dorothea St. John said.

"Larissa, please sit down to dinner. I will take Mrs. Rossmore up. Arminta, there is something I wish to discuss with you."

Arminta smiled. "I rather thought there would be, Dorothea. Well, I suppose it would be best to get it over with. . . ."

Arminta smiled again conspiratorially at me, though I had no idea what we were conspiring about, and the two women left the room. I sat down in the chair Julian held for me, and felt as though a whirlwind had just been through the room, scattering everything in its wake. If nothing else, Arminta Rossmore was not a woman to be intimidated by anyone, and I thought that her stay was going to be most interesting.

The two women had scarcely left the room before Dorcas said furiously to Julian, "I can't understand why you allowed her to come, Julian! You know what an interfering busybody she is—and she upsets Mama. Whatever were you thinking of?"

"I couldn't very well refuse her, could I, Dorcas?" Julian replied calmly. "After all, she is a member of this family."

"How can you say that?" Dorcas screeched. "I can't consider her my aunt after she drove poor Uncle Adrian to an early grave by her overbearing ways. And it is interesting to note that her second husband followed in short order," she added darkly.

"Come, Dorcas," Norman teased, "you can't blame Aunt Arminta for Percy Rossmore's untimely death. He did die from a broken neck after falling down the stairs."

"She probably pushed him, I wouldn't doubt," Dorcas muttered, picking up a fork to attack the fowl that had been set before her.

"That will be enough, Dorcas," Julian commanded, his eyes on the serving maid, who was all agog at this most interesting glimpse into the private lives of those she served.

Dorcas subsided unwillingly, remembering belatedly that her remarks were certain to be repeated and relished in the servants' hall as soon as the family left the dining room.

We had progressed to dessert—a lovely shortcake topped with strawberries no doubt coaxed to life by the warmth of Tom's glasshouse—when I heard shouting again in the hall and boots ringing loudly on the stone floor of the gallery.

"What the devil now?" Julian exclaimed, half rising from his chair just as the double doors to the dining room were flung open.

CHAPTER FOUR

A tall, blond young man stood on the threshold, panting slightly as though he had been running. He was dressed expensively, from the fine dark blue cloak to the gray suit with a blue satin vest. His hat was tipped rakishly on his handsome head, and as his eyes swept over us, I realized with shock that he had been drinking. He swayed in the doorway, and Norman jumped up from his place at the table to go to him and offer support.

"Edward! I say, it's nice to see you again!" Norman exclaimed, thumping him so hard on the back that Edward almost fell forward.

Edward looked blearily at Norman, then smiled crookedly. "I couldn't get here fast enough—although I had to stop in the village to meet an old friend," he said, winking at Norman, who gave a shout of laughter.

"Up to your old tricks again, Edward? The ladies always did find you something of a cad. Soon as possible, you and I will have to make a trip down there and you can introduce me!"

"Norman!" Julian said in a quietly sinister voice. "Have you forgotten what few manners you possess?

Take Edward upstairs at once. He is in no condition for the dining room."

Edward and Norman looked at Julian in surprise. Edward said owlishly, "Good old Julian—just as much the gentleman as always. My apologies to the ladies for appearing in this condition"—he swept off his hat and bowed, almost falling on his face in the process—"but at the time it seemed unavoidable."

"Harmon!" Julian shouted. The butler appeared as if by magic. "Harmon, take my cousin to his room— I don't think he is able to arrive there by himself. And, Edward, I will speak to you in the morning when you are more coherent."

Harmon grasped Edward's arm, but Edward, as though focusing on me for the first time, moved unsteadily away from him. He stumbled over to where I sat. I clutched the arms of my chair for support as he leered down at me. I wanted to turn my face away from the alcohol odor on his breath, but I was mesmerized by his eyes. They were pale gray and fringed with impossibly long, dark, curly lashes. I thought irrelevantly that many a girl would envy him for those lashes.

"Since no one has had the courtesy to introduce us, allow me. Edward Synclair, at your service. You, lovely lady, must be no other than Mrs. Julian Synclair. I suppose in a way that makes us cousins—or something."

I nodded briefly, wishing only that Harmon would come and take him away. He was looking at me with such a strange expression that for a moment I thought he was going to reach out and touch me. So tense were my nerves that I thought if he did I should surely scream. If I hadn't been aware of the antagonism between Julian and Edward, I wouldn't have been as nervous about being the cause of an unpleasant scene; as it was, I was afraid Julian would erupt at any moment, so I sat there, stiff with fright.

"Interesting piece of jewelry you're wearing, Mrs. Synclair," Edward murmured drunkenly, looking intently at the ram's-head brooch.

"It was my mother's," I answered faintly.

"Oh?" He seemed surprised, then his expression changed to one of calculation as he stared intently at me.

I attributed his absorption in the brooch to his drunken stupor; more than anything now, I only wanted him to leave the room before Julian threw him out. I said, hoping I sounded calmer than I felt, "I think you must be unwell, Mr. Synclair. Please allow Harmon to show you to your room."

"What? Oh yes. To be sure," he answered, swiveling his head around to look at Harmon. "Well, Harmon—it seems as though I'm in need of a strong arm to get me up the stairs. I just appointed you for the job."

"Yes, sir," Harmon answered, his face impassive as Edward lurched over to him. He took Edward's arm again while Norman supported him on the other side. I could hear exclamations and shouts of glee from the two young men as the trio retreated from the room, while the quieter tones of Harmon were lost in their hilarity.

"Well!" Dorcas exclaimed. "Edward has finally surpassed himself. I didn't think even he would be so gauche as to appear completely drunk the first night of his arrival. I can tell it will be another of those disastrous visits. But you have brought it upon yourself, dear brother, by inviting them here. I only hope they won't ruin the party."

Julian threw down his napkin and stood up. "Larissa, have you finished?" he asked tightly.

I stood up also, leaving my dessert untouched. The scene I had just witnessed had made me lose taste for the delicacy, and I wanted to be away from this room as soon as possible. I thought I could still see Edward lurching toward me with that calculating look on his face; I shuddered.

"Mary," Julian addressed the hovering serving girl. "Mrs. Synclair and I will have coffee in the library."

I tried to cover my surprise; Julian had never asked me to have coffee with him, preferring to retreat to his study alone after dinner while I was forced to linger in the drawing room for politeness' sake before making my escape to the privacy of my own room. But I went to Julian and put my arm through his as though taking coffee after dinner were a nightly ritual. I saw Dorcas' lip curl as she saw through my pretense, but I didn't care.

The library was a cozy, masculine room; the fire was burning cheerfully in the fireplace, and the deep leather chairs and shelves of books bound in leather gave it an aura of comfortableness. Julian gestured me to a chair and threw himself into the one opposite. He passed his hand over his eyes in a gesture of pain and I wanted to do something—anything—to comfort him. But I waited quietly, intuition telling me that he did not wish any empty words of comfort from me.

We sat silently until Mary brought in the tray with the coffee. I poured a cup for Julian, then one for myself, after dismissing her so that we could be alone. Julian put his cup on the table beside the chair, then sprang up and began to pace about the room. I watched him warily.

He stopped suddenly and looked down at me with an expression I was unable to read. "Larissa, I must apologize to you. I had no right bringing you here, even as my wife. It was unfair to expect you to cope with a situation that I could not see my way out of. I'm going to send you back to your aunt, or if you wish, I can set you up in a house of your own away from here. I will see that you never want for anything, but I think your going away will be the best thing under the circumstances."

I couldn't believe it; couldn't believe that he was going to dismiss me as his wife as easily as that. The petty humiliations I had suffered from his family, the loneliness I had endured, the longing to have Julian become my husband in every sense of the word, rose up in me as though I would choke. I wouldn't allow him to put me away, as though I were a toy that had been outgrown, a useless ornament that could be tossed aside at a whim.

Perhaps if I had not grown to love this man I would have been able to accept his decision with equanimity, would have acceded to his wish that I go away quietly. Perhaps if I had been older, or more mature, I would have been able to accept it with good grace, for it was plain that Julian regarded our marriage as a mistake. However, in spite of knowing his feelings, I did not agree that it had been a mistake; I loved Julian, and wanted to do whatever I could to bring him some peace of mind. Julian was haunted by something—something that made him cold and unfeeling at times—and in my immaturity, I thought that I could help him banish his ghost. At least I wanted the opportunity to try.

Mustering all the dignity I could, I tried an approach I thought might make him reconsider. "Julian, I am not going away. If nothing else, think of the scandal that would cause for you."

"Scandal? You think I care about that?"

"Your mother would," I said. He grimaced and turned away and I continued quickly, pressing home this dubious advantage: "Your mother would never forgive you. I know she is opposed to our marriage, but I think she would be even more opposed to being put in the position of having to explain why you suddenly chose to remove me from the house."

His reaction was completely out of proportion to what I had just said. He turned fiercely to me and grabbed me by the shoulders, lifting me to my feet. "What do you know about that? How did you find out? Has Dorcas been talking to you? If she has . . ." The unspoken threat hung heavily in the air between us.

"Julian!" I cried, alarmed at his furious expression. "Julian, please! You're hurting me." He let go of me so suddenly that I fell against the chair. I was really frightened now. Julian paced about the room like a caged animal, the rage that had been building in him threatening to explode.

"Well? Has anyone said anything to you?" he repeated savagely.

I swallowed, feeling that I was in some kind of nightmare. "No, Julian. I don't know what you're talking about. No one has said anything to me. Should they? About what?" I knew I was gibbering, but I was so horrified by his reaction that I scarcely knew what I was saying.

He looked at me intently, and, thankfully, something in my expression must have convinced him that I was telling the truth; he stopped his agitated striding about and came over to me. I shrank back from him and he turned abruptly away again.

Suddenly I was quite calm. Instinctively I realized that the appalling force of his anger was not directed at me; Julian was involved in something I knew nothing about, something that caused his inner fury, and perhaps a feeling of helplessness because he could do nothing about it. I wondered if it had something to do with his family; it seemed that Dorcas and Norman— even Dorothea St. John—held something over him. Why else would he bear their resentment and scorn in silence? Or could it be that he was trying to protect them? Why was he so anxious that no one said anything to me, and what was it I was not supposed to discover?

I decided that if I was to help Julian, I would have to find out what everyone at Peregrine House was determined to keep hidden. Perhaps then Julian would be free to be himself and we might even be able to make a new start with our marriage. In my anxiety and concern, I did not care to think further than that. And I certainly did not want to reveal my plans to Julian; if he was aware of my intention, I knew he would surely send me away. Somehow I had to convince him to let me stay.

Trying not to betray myself, I said, "Julian, please reconsider. The ball is to be held in a few days; you couldn't cancel all the arrangements in that short a time and disappoint so many people. After the ball, if you still feel I should go away, then I will accept your decision and go. We could contrive some sort of excuse then, I'm sure."

He looked at me strangely. "Is the ball so important to you, then?"

I hesitated. I had never been able to play the part of the coquette; it was not in my nature to be simpering and coy. But I thought that Julian might be convinced if I resorted to a purely feminine reaction. Hoping I sounded wistful, I said, "I have never been to a ball before. . . ." I paused and sighed. "I did so want to go."

Julian exclaimed impatiently, then looked at me for a long moment. At last he said, "Very well. You shall attend your first ball. I only hope it won't be as much of a disappointment as I fear."

I did not take time to decipher his last curious remark; I was too happy that he had allowed me to stay, for the ball at least. Perhaps, if I was successful in discovering what troubled him, I would have time later to convince him that my place was here, beside him.

I did not have much time to form a plan, I thought, as I got ready for bed that night. I dismissed Ellie early because her ready chatter distracted me, but even after she had gone and the room was silent, I could not think of what I should do. How could I, who knew absolutely nothing about the situation that existed here, find a solution that would relieve Julian of his burden? I turned out the lamp and lay in the darkness listening to the pounding of the surf below my window. It was a soothing sound and suddenly I was so tired that I decided to give up my fruitless speculations and go to sleep. Perhaps in the morning when I was refreshed I could think of a plan. A tenuous hope, but all I could think of at the moment.

I woke to a beautiful day. The early morning sun made the white-capped waves glisten as they rolled in toward the beach. A light breeze came in from the ocean as I stood by my open window and I decided that an early walk would clear my mind.

The air was crisp and clean and, as I walked, gulls soared and shrilled above my head, swooping down occasionally to make an awkward landing on the sand. The very normalcy of the scene restored my equilibrium. The dark shape of Berus came running toward me, barking joyously. It had been several days since I had been out walking, and he seemed glad to have my company. I stroked the shaggy head and his plumed tail waved back and forth in response.

"Come on, Berus," I said gaily, "I'll race you to the rock."

We ran along the sand, Berus bounding ahead for a few feet, then racing back to make sure I was coming. The "rock" was a flat stone set back slightly from the beach. It was an excellent vantage point because, once I had climbed upon it, I could see a great distance up and down the beach. Berus and I came here often—I to watch the always changing pattern of the waves, Berus to sit like a sentinel, the breeze ruffling his dark fur.

I don't know how long we had been sitting there when I heard Berus give a low growl. Startled out of my absorption with Julian's strange behavior, I looked around. Edward was walking slowly toward us. I had no wish to talk to him after the spectacle he had made of himself the night before, but when he called to me and began climbing to where I sat, I had no choice. Berus seemed agitated; he barked furiously at Edward and growled again and again. For a horrible moment I actually thought the dog might attack him. I wound my fingers through the thick fur on his neck and ordered him to be quiet. Berus subsided reluctantly and pressed close to me as Edward came up.

"What!" Edward exclaimed when he saw Berus. "Don't tell me you are a witch too!"

"What are you talking about?" I asked crossly.

"You—with that dog. Don't you know that no one can get near him? At least, no one but Julian—and now you. He's a killer, from what I've heard. One of the witching dogs who hypnotize you with that one blue eye before going for your throat. It's said that the only people who can control them are witches—or warlocks, as the case may be."

"How ridiculous!" I snapped, thoroughly put out by this nonsense, as well as by his intrusion on my privacy.

"Oh no, not at all," he replied earnestly, his eyes watching Berus warily. "You know why Julian called him Berus, don't you? Typical Julian, always the subtle one. 'Berus' is a contraction of 'Cerberus,' the mythical dog who guarded the gates of hell. An apt description, don't you think?" he asked, gesturing to the house on the cliff.

"I'm sure I don't know what you are talking about," I said stiffly. "And now, if you will excuse me?"

"Oh no, please. I want to apologize for last night. What I remember of it, that is. If it's any comfort to you, I'm paying dearly for my actions—my head feels as though it were about to fly off."

"I'm sure it is only what you deserve," I said acidly, thinking what a horrible young man he was.

"Mrs. Synclair—may I call you Larissa? You are perfectly right to be cross with me. But I understand; living in that house would make anyone cross."

"Living in that house, as you call it, has nothing to do with it!" I exclaimed angrily. "You behaved abominably, and that's the reason I—"

"Oh yes," he said sorrowfully. "I'm sorry, but it's such a strain for me to come . . . home . . . that I usually manage to make a fool of myself by drinking too much before I arrive."

"And why should it be such a strain?" I inquired icily.

He shook his head. "How would you feel, knowing that what was rightfully yours belongs to someone else? Julian had no right to inherit Peregrine House! Why, he isn't even—"

"Mr. Synclair," I interrupted angrily. "I do not choose to continue this discussion. Pray take your complaints to my husband, if you believe you have been wronged." I started to rise, furious with myself for having continued this ridiculous conversation as long as I had, but his next words stopped me in mid-flight.

"Oh yes, Julian," Edward said with a sneer. "Well, Julian has his own way of overcoming obstacles. . . ."

I said sharply, "What do you mean by that?"

"Oh, nothing," he replied, shading his eyes with one hand and looking out toward the sea.

"What did you mean?"

"It's ancient history. Nothing was ever proved, for all that."

"Mr. Synclair," I said, beginning to get really angry with him, "it's rude to lead into a subject as you did, then say no more. If you didn't intend to finish, why begin at all?"

"Please call me Edward. And I'm sorry if you thought I was rude. Oh dear, I seem to be doing nothing but offering apologies to you today. Very well, I shall tell you—but you probably know all about it anyway." He paused and looked at me. "Surely Julian told you about Saramary?"

"Who . . . who was Saramary?" I asked, stumbling slightly over the strange name.

Edward looked surprised for a moment, then shook his head ruefully. "Isn't that just like Julian? He was always the one to keep secrets—though I can't say I blame him over this one. If my wife died such a tragic death—and in such unpleasant circumstances—I wouldn't want to talk about it either. Especially to my second wife."

My mouth went dry. "Saramary was Julian's wife?" I asked faintly.

"Oh yes. A beautiful girl, too—and with a handsome dowry. I sometimes wondered which Julian loved more: the girl or her money. Of course, it wasn't until her untimely death that he inherited. But it was enough to put the estate on its feet again—these large estates do gobble money, you know."

"How did she die?" I whispered.

69

"Fell through the nursery-floor window. It was all very strange—very messy inquest since there was some suspicion that Julian himself might have been responsible. . . ."

I gasped.

Edward said hastily, "Of course, all the others were under suspicion; Dorcas had been seen with her moments before, and Julian's mother had had a violent quarrel with Saramary that day over the attentions Norman had been paying to her. But I suppose on the surface of it Julian had the best motive—after all, there was all that money he stood to inherit and, perhaps more important, no man would care to be cuckolded by his own brother." He broke off and looked at me keenly. "I say, are you all right? You look awfully white. I suppose I shouldn't have told you all that straight away. It must sound horrible hearing it for the first time."

I managed to nod.

He sprang up and meticulously dusted off his suit with one eye on Berus, who stiffened at the movement. "I shouldn't worry about it, though, Larissa. Julian got off scot-free and the scandal has died a natural death by now. After all, it was four years ago. Pity about the baby, though."

"What . . . baby?" I gasped, feeling as if I should faint if I heard any more.

"Saramary's baby, of course. She was with child at the time. Of course the baby died with her. But it did stick in the jury's mind—why would a woman, eagerly awaiting the birth of her first child, commit suicide by leaping out a third-floor window? Oh, well, I suppose we'll never know, will we? It might have been for the best after all, though. . . ."

"How can you say that?" I cried, horrified.

"Oh, not about Saramary. The baby, I mean. Julian's father went mad—oh, didn't you know—and they say insanity can be inherited."

I swayed, feeling waves of nausea rushing over me. Dimly I saw Edward reach out to catch me before I toppled over, but Berus snapped viciously at him and he drew back hastily. I managed to say, "I'll be all right, Edward. It's just that it was a shock...."

"Oh dear.... How could I have been so thoughtless.... I am sorry, my dear," Edward stammered, realizing at last what he had said. "But I thought that of course Julian would have told you—after all, you are directly concerned too, aren't you? I'm terribly sorry...." Apologizing abjectly, Edward climbed down off the rock and hurried back toward the house, leaving me alone.

When he had finally gone, I sat for a long time numb with the shock of what I had heard. My brain refused to take in all he had told me. Well, I had wanted to know the terrible secret that surrounded Peregrine House and its inhabitants, and now I knew. The knowledge made me slightly sick, and I felt a great pity for Julian, who had been through so much. It did not occur to me to wonder why Edward had been so anxious to impart this information to me when it was clear that the whole family had been together in a conspiracy of silence, but I supposed that he was the type of person who relished the thought of disaster in other people's lives. I decided that I did not care for Julian's cousin.

I thought I would consider one thing at a time. The first, of course, apart from Julian's father's madness, which I refused to think about at all, was the horrifying death of Saramary. Saramary. What a curious name. Edward had said that she had been beautiful, and I could picture my predecessor as a tall, ethereal young woman, who for some reason had been desperate enough to take her own life. Could it be that she had discovered the terrible fact of madness in the family, and consequently could not bear the thought that her unborn child might have been tainted with the same weakness? I wondered how I would have reacted in the same situation; somehow I did not think I would consider suicide the only alternative, but then I couldn't be sure. It was easy to think oneself strong until one was confronted with an appalling situation. Then, of course, there was the inquiry. The whole family had been under suspicion, so there was the possibility that Saramary had not taken her own life, but had been a victim.

I remembered Dorcas' reaction, and Julian's, even Mrs. St. John's, when they discovered that I was not an heiress at all. Was it possible that in Julian's second marriage the bride was supposed to bring more money to save the estate, and that was the reason Julian married me—because he thought I would have a large dowry? A chilling thought entered my mind: now that everyone knew I had no dowry, was I in danger? Was it possible that, like Saramary, I would be eliminated in order to make way for yet another bride—a bride who would be able to shore up the sagging foundations of Peregrine House? I couldn't believe that anyone would be so calculating and cold-hearted. But what did I know of the pride that existed in the Synclairs? Was it forceful enough for them to use any means of prolonging their tenuous hold on their birthright? And what of Julian himself? Was he responsible for Saramary's death in order to further his own ends? Or was he mad, as his father had been? I cringed away from the thought.

But why was I considering Julian a murderer? All the evidence had been considered in a court, and Julian found not guilty. If those wiser than I had not believed him guilty, why should the thought cross my mind? Because, a tiny voice inside me warned, Julian surely had enough influence to make sure only the evidence that would exonerate him would be brought to light—especially when the family closed ranks to insure that no outsiders found out what had really happened.

This is ridiculous, I told myself. Idle speculation. Here I was in a tizzy because of some careless words on Edward's part. Edward, who probably knew no more than I did, and was enough of an enemy of Julian's to want to make trouble. But perhaps Edward knew more than he was telling; perhaps in his own way he was trying to warn me. No, the only thing I could do was try to find out for myself. I had wanted to know the secret that haunted Julian, and now I knew. I would have to progress from there. But somehow all the determination I had felt the night before, all my confidence that I could help Julian, seemed to drain out of me as I sat there staring at the sea. One thing kept returning to my mind, no matter how I tried to banish the thought: was it possible that I was married to a murderer?

When I got back, I found I had missed the midday meal, but I wasn't hungry. I was too keyed up to eat. I decided that it was time to take up Tom's offer to help him in the glasshouse. Perhaps in the peace and stillness of Tom's garden I would be able to think about what I should do first.

Tom greeted me enthusiastically. "I didn't think you would come, Mrs. Synclair. I thought you would be too busy with your duties in the house to remember me and my plants."

I smiled wryly, wishing I did have some duties in the house that would keep me occupied and fill my thoughts with mundane household matters instead of unanswerable questions. "No, Tom, I told you I wanted to learn about growing things, and I thought this would be a good time to start. What shall I do first?"

"Well, I was going to transplant some of these chrysanthemums into special pots for the party. Perhaps you would like to watch—I don't want you to get your hands too dirty."

"Oh, but I want to do more than watch—how else can I learn? Besides, I brought gloves for the occasion," I said gaily, flourishing the pair I had brought with me.

Tom looked at me with satisfaction. "I knew you would be different from the rest. There's some that would think mucking about in the dirt beneath them, and maybe it is, to their way of thinking," he said grudgingly. "Well, let's start."

He showed me how to use a little shovel to pry the flower plants out of the dirt, being careful not to damage the roots. He added a few inches of soil to the bottom of the gilded pots that were to be used for decoration at the party, then carefully placed a plant inside each, adding more soil until the pot was full, and pressing the earth tight about the plant to give it support. After he showed me how to do it, he left me on my own, and I worked happily for a time alone. The flowers were beautiful: whites and golds and oranges with dark green leaves. The gilded pots displayed their brilliant colors to advantage and I knew they would add their own special touch to the party.

Tom came back after a while and seemed pleased with the results of my work. I thought it was time to try to find out what I could from Tom. Perhaps he knew something about Saramary's death. Keeping my tone light, I asked, "How long have you worked for the Synclairs, Tom?"

He squinted and pursed his mouth as though he were thinking. "Well, Mrs. Synclair, I can't rightly recall how long, but I can tell you I was here as a youngster. Must be about fifty years or so."

"Then you worked for Julian's—Mr. Synclair's—father."

His expression became guarded. "Aye," he said briefly.

"And you were here when Saramary—the first Mrs. Synclair—came."

His eyes became even more cautious. "Aye."

"Can you tell me about her?"

"It's a subject you should rightly take up with the young master, Mrs. Synclair."

"Oh yes, I know. But Julian . . . doesn't like to talk about it."

He nodded. "I can understand that. Terrible business."

"Please, Tom. I would like to find out something about her—perhaps I could make things easier for Julian if I knew. Can you understand that?"

His eyes softened. I knew I had no business discussing family matters, even with someone as trusted as an old retainer of the family, but I had to start somewhere, and I knew that Julian's family presented such a united front against me that I could hope for no information from them. "Please, Tom," I pleaded.

"You having a hard time of it, Mrs. Synclair? I thought you might. You are different from them, and I suppose they don't like it. Ah well, I'll tell you what I can. What do you want to know?"

"Well . . . what was Saramary like?"

He paused long enough to dredge a battered pipe from his pocket. After he had tamped down the tobacco and lit it, he put it between his teeth and said, "Saramary Synclair was like sunlight shining through the trees—a quiet kind of person, but one you would notice for all that. Slender, she was, and delicate. She had hair the color of pale gold, and sometimes she wore it loose so that it floated around her face like a cloud. . . ."

"She was beautiful, then?"

He sighed. "Ah yes, she was beautiful. A quiet kind of beauty, as I said. When she found out that she was going to have a baby, she was the happiest woman on earth, I think. She wanted to give Peregrine House an heir. . . ."

"But she . . . died."

I had made a mistake. His wrinkled face became a mask. "Aye. She died."

"Why do you think she would want to commit suicide? I mean, you just said she was so happy."

"I couldn't say, Mrs. Synclair. There are dark passages in every person's mind, and who is to say that what shows on the surface is true?" He paused, looked around, then whispered, "I shouldn't be telling you this, Mrs. Synclair, but I think you should be warned. I wouldn't want what happened to her happen to you." His voice became lower still. "Her death was no suicide—and it was no accident, either. I know—"

"Larissa, here you are. I've been looking for you."

Julian's voice interrupted us, and I could have screamed with frustration. Tom had been on the point of telling me something that I was certain was important, and now I would have to wait. I forced myself to turn and face my husband with a pleased expression. "Why, Julian. I didn't think you would be home so early. Tom has been showing me his garden, and I've been trying to learn something about growing plants." I knew I was talking too much, but I was shaken by the furious expression of Julian's face as he looked first at me, then at Tom.

"Good afternoon, sir," Tom said, touching the brim of his hat with a fingertip.

"Good afternoon, Tom," Julian said coldly.

I turned to Tom and said, "Thank you for the lesson, Tom. Perhaps we can continue at another time."

If Tom caught the double meaning of what I was trying to say, he gave no sign. He nodded to Julian and me, then turned and hobbled off a short distance, stopping to examine one of his plants.

"Larissa, Aunt Arminta wants to see you. She doesn't like to be kept waiting."

"Of course, Julian. Just let me go to my room and freshen up. I seem to have collected more dirt on my hands than I put in the pot." I tried to laugh gaily, but something in Julian's face stopped me. He was staring at Tom's retreating figure with a frightening expression on his face. It was as though he hated the old man.

CHAPTER FIVE

Arminta Rossmore was ensconced in the drawing room. At her right hand was a goblet of amber liquid, which she flourished at me as I entered. "Care to join me, my dear? I find that a slight bit of whiskey in the afternoon helps my occasional bout of arthritis. Especially when I have to contend with these drafty mansions by the sea."

I shook my head, slightly shocked; I had never known a woman who drank whiskey, but then, I had never known a woman like Arminta Rossmore.

"Come and sit down beside me, Larissa. I wanted a chance to get to know you when the others weren't around to stifle you with their oppressive personalities." She laughed. "With the exception of Julian, perhaps, who after all has to carry quite a load on his shoulders, I find every one of them exceedingly dull."

I didn't know what to reply to this; my experience had been the opposite—since my arrival I had felt there was constant turmoil in the house, with everyone at each other's throats.

"You don't agree with me, eh? Don't tell me you are enchanted with Julian's family, because I won't believe you."

"I will admit I have found it difficult to become acquainted with everyone in Julian's family," I began cautiously.

"And you have made the effort and been scorned, haven't you? Oh, don't bother to deny it. I know them too well. Dorothea is an embittered old woman who has succeeded in spoiling her daughter and one of her sons abominably. If it had been up to me, I would have packed Norman off long ago to fend for himself. It would have done him a world of good to find that not everyone will put up with his irresponsibility. And as for Dorcas, that sly miss needs a strong hand and a husband who will put her in her place. Mathew, unfortunately, has about as much assertiveness as a mushroom. Thank God they are not my children; I have enough trouble with Edward. Although if Adrian had lived, perhaps Edward might have turned out differently. Who is to say?"

I was fascinated by this conversation. Arminta Rossmore might have a sharp tongue, but her honesty was refreshing. Talking with her was like biting into a lemon: an experience one mightn't care to repeat too often, but nevertheless tingling to the senses.

I thought quickly. Arminta was in a garrulous mood; perhaps if I could learn more about the members of Julian's family, I would be able to fit the pieces of the puzzle of Saramary's death into place. I did not want Arminta to realize that any probing I might do was anything more than natural curiosity, so I asked casually, "When did Julian's mother marry again? The age difference between Julian and Norman is not so great. . . ."

I was surprised. A touch of fear showed briefly on Arminta's face and her hand trembled slightly as she raised her glass and drank. After a moment she seemed in control of herself, for she answered calmly, "Julian is almost nine years older than Norman, three years older than Dorcas. Dorcas and Julian have the same . . . father, and Norman is, of course, the son of Bernard St. John. I dare say no one has troubled to explain the family tree."

I shook my head and Arminta continued, somewhat sourly, "Julian's father—another Julian, since all the eldest sons in line for Peregrine House are named Julian—was . . . ill . . . for many years. When Julian was . . . let me see . . . about six years old, I think, Dorothea came to visit me, bringing Dorcas with her. Her own health was frail from the constant nursing she was obliged to give her husband, and I finally persuaded her to visit a specialist in London. The doctor there prescribed several months abroad in warmer climates, away from stress of any kind, so Dorothea took herself off to Italy and the Mediterranean. She and Dorcas were gone for almost a year. When news of her husband's death reached her, she collapsed." Arminta paused again when she realized my confusion.

"I don't understand," I said. "You don't mention Julian—my Julian—surely Mrs. St. John did not go and leave him behind for that length of time! Why, he was just a child."

"His father refused to let Julian out of his sight. There was nothing she could do. He was being groomed to accept the responsibility of the estate."

"But so young!"

"Yes," Arminta said shortly. "So young. Well, anyway, when Dorothea recovered from her collapse, and finally took it upon herself to return, she brought Bernard St. John with her. They were married at the end of her year of mourning. But apparently our English climate was too rigorous for him," Arminta said scornfully. "Consumption took him off five years later."

She paused and looked at me companionably. "I gather there was some upset when everyone found out you weren't the heiress you were reported to be," she said.

I was disconcerted at the abrupt change in conversation and, more, I was uncomfortable; I didn't want to talk about the deception of my aunt. I nodded silently.

"Well, don't worry about that, my dear. It's Julian's own fault that he didn't take time to investigate. In fact, I can't understand it; Julian is usually most thorough in business affairs. No, I have come to the conclusion that he married for love; the money didn't matter."

I laughed bitterly, thinking of all the nights when I had longed for Julian to come to me in my lonely bed; all the times when I had wanted to feel his arms about me. If he had married for love, he had a strange way of showing it.

"Ah. You are thinking that you could never compete with the incomparable Saramary."

I stiffened; until this morning, I had never heard of Saramary Synclair. Now it seemed that no matter whom I talked to, her name was mentioned. I had the uncomfortable feeling that her ghost was beginning to haunt me.

"You did know about Saramary, didn't you?"

"Yes," I said cautiously, not wanting to betray the fact that I had found out about Julian's first wife from his cousin and not himself.

"Well, as far as I'm concerned," Arminta said, "there's no comparison between the two of you. She was a troublemaker from the start, and I never did discover why Julian married her. Oh, I suppose he fancied himself in love with her. That is, until—" She stopped, reaching abruptly for the glass of whiskey by her side.

I couldn't help myself. I asked, "Until what? What do you mean?"

Arminta put the glass to her lips. I noticed with surprise that her hand was shaking, though she tried to hide it with a laugh and a shrug. "I'm an old woman, my dear. You shouldn't pay attention to me; I don't know what I'm saying sometimes."

"Oh, please," I said urgently. "I didn't mean to upset you."

Arminta reached across and patted my hand. "It wasn't your fault, Larissa. It's just that talking about Saramary brings back such hideous memories. I never could believe that she could take her own life. . . ."

"You don't think she was murdered?"

"Good heavens, child! I think no such thing!"

Arminta suddenly looked so frightened that I said, to soothe her, "Of course you don't, Mrs. Rossmore. I'm sorry I said that. After all, there was an investigation, wasn't there?"

"Call me Arminta—it doesn't make me sound so old. Yes, there was an investigation. Horrible business. The house turned upside down for days, everyone questioned, and poor Julian taking the brunt of it all. It wasn't enough that Saramary was dead—no, the police insisted that he accompany them to their headquarters. It seemed he was the prime suspect, or whatever it is that the police term it."

"Julian was in jail?" I heard my voice rise on a note of disbelief.

"Oh yes, but only for a few days. The police couldn't put together enough facts to prove anything. He was released in time for the funeral. But, of course, there was the inquest after that and everything started all over again."

"You were here at Peregrine House during that time?"

Arminta sighed. "Yes. Unfortunately, Edward and I had come for a visit. The police insisted that we stay until the whole business was concluded."

"And the verdict was suicide?"

"Yes, everyone could account for themselves when it happened, and so of course there was nothing left except that verdict. Dorothea had had a quarrel with Saramary that morning. It seems that Norman had been paying a great deal of attention to Saramary, and Saramary, in Dorothea's view, was not forceful enough in resisting his flirtation. At the time of Saramary's death, Dorothea and I were having it out in this very room. I was insisting that she shouldn't interfere with her son's marriage—Julian was quite capable of dealing with his wife without her assistance, I felt—and she was arguing back that Julian couldn't see what was going on right under his nose and it was her duty to warn Saramary of the consequences of her actions. Mathew and Dorcas were in their own apartment arguing about the same thing. It seems that Mathew was almost besotted by Saramary, who amused herself by flirting with him, too, and Dorcas was almost out of her mind with jealousy. The two of them never did get along—Dorcas and Saramary, I mean—and I admit, I did feel sorry for Dorcas at the time."

"Where was Norman?"

"He had ridden to the village, and had just arrived moments before we heard the news."

"And Edward?"

Arminta looked affronted that I should ask. "He was lying down in his room. I had insisted that he retire because he wasn't feeling well, and had even brought him a soothing draft myself to make him sleep. He is cursed with the most fearful headaches, and when he feels one coming on, there is nothing to do but rest and wait until it passes."

"How awful for him," I murmured. Then I asked

the question I had been dreading to ask, but had to know. "Where was Julian?"

Arminta hesitated, then put the glass to her lips and drank. I waited in an agony of suspense for her to speak. Finally she said, "Yes. Julian. He said he had been out on the beach with that accursed dog of his. He and Saramary had their own quarrel because . . . well, he never would reveal what the quarrel was about. He said he took a walk to clear his head—he wanted to think. Unfortunately, no one saw him go; no one saw him come back to the house. Suddenly, he was just here. And Saramary was dead."

I felt faint. Julian, of all the others, had no one to corroborate his story. I couldn't believe that, no matter what the provocation, Julian would resort to murdering his own wife. I had to hold on to the fact that the investigation had proved him innocent. I wouldn't believe that my husband was a murderer.

It was as though Arminta read my thoughts, for she leaned forward and touched me comfortingly on the arm. "I didn't mean to upset you, my dear. You must remember that the police believed Julian's story and he was exonerated." She looked at me carefully. She repeated, "You must remember that."

I nodded and managed a wavering smile.

"That's better. I knew you were not the sort to swoon over something unpleasant. And because of that, I wanted to ask you something. You know about Julian's father, don't you?" she asked softly.

"There is nothing she needs to know beyond the fact that he was ill," Dorothea St. John's voice came harshly from the doorway.

I turned and stared at her, slightly embarrassed in case she had heard us discussing her. She took no notice of me, but instead rounded on Arminta, who sat regarding her calmly.

"How dare you gossip about me!" she cried. "One time you'll go too far, Arminta."

"We were not gossiping about you, Dorothea. I merely thought Larissa should be aware of the history of her new family," Arminta answered imperturbably. "And there is no need to look so ferocious. You should calm yourself—a crimson complexion is definitely not your color, my dear."

Dorothea St. John sputtered with rage, unable to speak. I had never seen her so angry, so out of control. I excused myself as quickly as I could, not wanting to be caught in the cross fire, and left the room, carefully shutting the door. Even before I had closed it, however, I could hear the beginning of a quarrel that was certain to set the whole house on its ears. I winced and hurried up the stairs, wondering why Mrs. St. John should be so furious to find Arminta discussing Julian's father with me. But then, I conceded fairly, it was possible that remembering that time was painful for her, and she did not want to be reminded of it or have anyone else judging her. For, after all, who could say that they wouldn't have behaved similarly in the same circumstances? I thought that indeed the strain of being forced to stand helplessly by while someone you loved was going mad would be too much for any woman to bear.

When I reached my room, I poked up the fire, feeling suddenly chilled. I sat down in one of the overstuffed chairs to try to make some sense of the different stories I had heard today about the tragic figure of Saramary Synclair. Different snatches of conversation chased through my mind until my thoughts were so completely jumbled that my head began to ache. One thought kept occurring to me, however, in spite of my confusion: Arminta Rossmore knew a great deal more than she was willing to say, and for some reason, the knowledge was frightening to her. She had contradicted herself on several points concerning Saramary's character, and I wondered why. Also, she—and Tom, too—had implied that Saramary's death was not a suicide. That had to mean that someone in this house was responsible for murdering her. My mind shied away from the hideous word and all that it implied, and I tried to think calmly about what I had heard today.

I remembered that Tom had been interrupted just as he started to tell me what he knew of Saramary's death. Suddenly it was very important to me to hear what he had to say. It was almost dark now and Ellie would be coming soon to help me dress for dinner, but some urgency that I didn't quite dare to analyze prompted me to seek him out immediately. I hoped he was still puttering about in the glasshouse; I had no idea whether he lived somewhere on the estate or had a house of his own, and something inside me warned that I would have to talk to him tonight.

The hall was empty when I came out of my room; I met no one as I crept down the back stairs and let myself out the side door. I could hear muffled talk and laughter along with the clatter of pots and dishes as the kitchen help prepared dinner, but once I was outside, it was as though I were completely alone.

In front of me stood the bulk of the glasshouse, the light from the half moon shining thinly off the glass dome of the roof. Inside, three lamps burned brightly at intervals along the bricked walkway. I was relieved; perhaps Tom was still inside if the lamps were lit. I let myself through the glass door and tentatively called, "Tom? Tom, are you in here?"

The yellow lamplight gave an eerie effect as it reflected off the leaves of the bushy plants that lined the narrow walk. Green-black shadows, where the light was too faint to reach, seemed to close in on me, and I had to force myself to walk slowly down the path. I called again to Tom and stopped to listen. Absolute silence, except for the occasional plop of condensed moisture dripping from the roof to the bricks below. The stillness was beginning to affect my nerves; I began imagining that I was not alone, that someone was hiding in all this greenery watching me. The specter of Saramary rose up before me, and I remembered that perhaps her death was not her own choice but someone else's doing. Perhaps that someone was hiding in the shadows right now. I looked over my shoulder nervously, trying to calm my pounding heart by telling myself that I was being ridiculous, that my imagination was running away with my common sense.

I was just about to start down the path again when I heard a rustling noise to my left. I stopped, frozen. A scream gurgled at the back of my throat and died as I strained to hear the sound again. Silence. My hand went to my throat of its own volition and under my fingers I could feel my own pulse beating furiously. I swallowed, my throat suddenly dry with senseless fear, and waited. My eyes tried to probe the deep green shadows and in my fright I convinced myself that the leaves of the plants were moving as someone silently passed through them.

The rustling sound was closer now, a tiny clicking noise against the bricks of the pathway. My body poised for flight, I had no power to move. When something ran past the hem of my skirt I almost screamed again in terror until I saw a tiny furry animal disappearing through a crack in the floor. A mouse! I sagged against one of the shelves in relief. Only a mouse, and I had been terrified. I felt slightly ashamed of my faintheartedness and resolved that I would have to learn to control my vivid imagination. Feeling more courageous now that the noise was explained, I walked forward, calling to Tom again. When I finally found him, I would tell him of my silliness and we would laugh that such a harmless thing as a mouse could inspire such terror in me.

I came around the corner of the pathway and stopped, the smile freezing on my lips. The courage I had felt just moments before drained away from me as I saw what was lying half on, half off the brick walkway. Without thinking, I ran forward and knelt beside Tom's body. I didn't have to touch him to know that he was dead. No—not only dead. Murdered.

The back of his head was crushed, a heavy flowerpot lying in fragments beside him. Before I turned away to fight the sudden nausea that rose in me, I saw that the chrysanthemums that had been in the pot were strewn about the floor, their petals splashed with Tom's bright red blood. I would always remember the sight of those crimson-tinged flowers, and tears filled my eyes when I remembered Tom saying to me that very afternoon, "Oh yes, Mrs. Synclair, spring is always the best time of year. I can see my plants turning green and feel that I have helped a bit in the miracle of life. . . ." Well, I thought sadly, Tom would never see another of his plants flourishing under his tender care. Then I became angry; it didn't seem fair that Tom, who had loved to promote life, should have his own snatched so cruelly away from him. And why? Why?

A sudden gust of air rushed over me as the door to the glasshouse opened and then slammed shut. The fear that had receded when I discovered Tom's body came rushing over me as I realized that the murderer had been here hiding all this time. I could feel terror claiming me again as I forced myself to look in the direction of the door, not knowing whether I would have to defend myself or not. My hand went out and closed over a shard of pottery that lay broken beside me; I clutched it desperately, looking at the door. But a flash of white was all I saw; the murderer was gone.

My relief was so great that I could not move for a moment, but as my shocked mind comprehended the fact that Tom was truly dead, I could only think of telling Julian. I turned and ran back the way I had come, slapping branches and leaves out of the way as I brushed by, not stopping to wonder if the murderer was waiting for me outside. I was beyond all thought except finding Julian.

I ran into the house and up the back stairs, stumbling over skirts that seemed heavy and oppressive when I wanted to move freely. I reached my room, flung myself through the door and past Ellie's startled face, and continued on through the connecting door. Julian was standing by his dresser, fiddling with the cuff link on his white shirt as he dressed for dinner. At my unceremonious entrance he looked up and his face mirrored the surprise I had seen briefly in Ellie's.

Now that I had found him, I began to sob helplessly. The horror of finding Tom dead, with his head crushed in, came to me in full force; I could not speak the words that would tell Julian of the poor man's death.

Julian came over to me and I flung myself against him. As his arms closed about me, I felt safe and protected and the terror I had felt moments before abated. I sobbed against his immaculate shirt front, still unable to speak coherently, while he murmured something soothing. Suddenly, I remembered the flash of white I had seen and I pushed away from him in horror. I had been too upset when I entered the room to take much notice of the white shirt he was wearing, but now it seemed to stand out like a warning beacon. I put my hands out before me in a protective gesture, and when he started toward me, I backed away from him in terror.

"Larissa," he said sharply, "what's the matter with you? What is it?"

I opened my mouth to speak, but no words came. I wanted to believe that he had not been in the glasshouse that night, that he had not taken the heavy flowerpot and smashed it against Tom's unsuspecting head; but the immaculate white of his shirt seemed to obliterate all reason.

"Larissa, tell me what frightened you."

His voice held such a commanding note that my mind cleared of its unreasoning fear. I thought quickly. I didn't want him to know that I suspected him of killing Tom. But did I? In my state of mind right now, I wasn't certain what I thought. All I knew was that he must not suspect that I had seen that flash of white leaving the greenhouse. It might be the only thing that would save me. I thrust aside thoughts of my own danger and took a deep breath.

I said as calmly as I could, watching him carefully for his reaction, "I was just in the glasshouse, looking for Tom. He's dead, Julian. Someone killed him."

His face turned white. If he was acting, he was doing

excellently, I thought, watching his expression of disbelief. Finally he said, "What do you mean someone killed him? After all, he was an old man. . . ."

"Yes, Julian, he was an old man," I replied coldly. "But someone killed him. His head was crushed by a flowerpot. It was no accident."

"I'll have to see for myself. You stay here until I come back. I don't want you to leave this room for any reason. Do you hear me? Do not leave this room!"

"But, Julian—"

"Don't argue with me. I don't want you involved in this." An expression of pain showed briefly in his eyes, but was replaced by fury. He muttered something about "not getting away with it this time," then he was gone, locking the door behind him.

I sat down on the bed, my legs suddenly refusing to hold me any longer. Dear God, I thought, don't let it be Julian; I don't think I could stand it if it's Julian.

I waited nervously, springing up and pacing back and forth in Julian's apartment, scarcely noticing the furnishings of the room, which I had never entered before. I had an impression of heavy, masculine furniture, and saw a smoking jacket with silk lapels flung carelessly on a chair. I picked up the jacket aimlessly, holding it to me as though to seek comfort from it. I was just about to put it down when I felt something crackle in one of the pockets. My hand felt in the pocket of its own will; I knew I had no business seeking what was there, but for some reason I couldn't stop myself. I drew out a torn piece of paper. There was writing on it; and I went to the lamp and held it under the light. The words seemed to leap off the paper at me.

My dear Julian,

At your request, I have begun the investigation. Several puzzling facts have come to light, and I would like to discuss them at your earliest convenience. Regarding your wife, Larissa Hamilton Synclair, I have found

The paper was torn in two at that point, and there was nothing else written. I stared at it, thoroughly puzzled. What was Julian investigating—and what had it to do with me, I wondered. But I had no time to think further about it; footsteps sounded in the hall, and the key turned in the lock. I stuffed the paper back in the pocket of the smoking jacket and hurriedly put it back on the chair. By the time Julian entered the room, I was standing where he had left me.

Julian came over to me and took both my hands in his. What should have been a tender gesture—one of the first spontaneous gestures he had made to me—was spoiled by my suspicion of him. I wanted to withdraw my hands from his grasp, but I found I could not.

"Your hands are like ice," he said. "Come and sit by the fire. I have something to discuss with you."

I looked at him warily, distrusting the look of concern on his face, but I obeyed.

When he had taken the chair opposite me, he said quietly, "I know you have just had a shock, but there is something I must ask you. Do you feel up to it?"

I nodded.

"Tell me exactly how you found Tom."

I shuddered; the memory was still too fresh in my mind to be disassociated from the horror of that scene.

"I went to the glasshouse to . . . to ask him something," I faltered. "The lamps were lighted, so I thought he might still be there. I called, but there was no answer. I found him lying on the pathway at the back, near the stove."

"What exactly was the position of . . . the body?"

I looked at him in surprise. "But didn't you see for yourself?"

He nodded. "But I want you to tell me what you saw."

"Well, he was lying face down, half off the path—"

"Face down?" he repeated sharply.

"Yes. . . . The fragments of the flowerpot were scattered around him. . . . The flowers were spattered with blood." I shuddered at the memory.

"Larissa, I want you to listen carefully. When Harmon and I found him, he was lying against the stove. There was a dislodged brick that he must have tripped on, and he fell against the stove. There was no broken flowerpot, no scattered flowers. Larissa, are you certain of what you saw? After all, the shock of finding him dead might have caused you to see something that wasn't there."

I listened in mounting horror, unable to believe what he was telling me. I saw the look of concern in his eyes as he searched my face for an answer I couldn't give.

I shook my head violently in denial. "No. Julian, I know what I saw. When I found him he was lying on the brick path. He was murdered—and the weapon was that flowerpot!" I heard my voice rising on a note of hysteria, and fought for control. In a moment I would blurt out my suspicions about Julian. I bit my lip and looked away.

"All right. I believe you. But someone must have gone back to the glasshouse and rearranged the evidence to make it look as if it were an accident. Larissa, do you understand what I am saying?"

"But who could have done such a thing?" I whispered.

He shook his head. "I don't know. But I am going to find out. I've already sent someone for the police and when they arrive they will surely want to question you. What are you going to tell them?"

I looked at him, horrified that he should ask. "I'm going to tell them exactly what I saw, Julian. I must."

"Larissa, I know you have no reason to trust me, and I wish I could convince you that you must, but it's too late for that now. But you must believe me that you cannot tell the police what you saw."

"But—"

"No. Whoever killed Tom—and I believe you when you say that he was murdered—went to great trouble to come back afterward and arrange things to make it look like an accident. If you persist in making an accusation of murder, you will be placing yourself in great danger. Do you understand that?"

Dimly, I began to comprehend what he was saying. I was the only one who had found Tom's body on the path, the only one who had seen the murder weapon. By the time Harmon and Julian had gone to investigate, all traces had been taken away. If I told the police what I saw, and they believed me, there would be another investigation and the murderer, perhaps afraid that he would be found out, might take it upon himself to remove the only person who had reason to believe Tom's death was no accident. On the other hand . . .

I looked at Julian bleakly, wanting desperately to believe that he himself was not the person responsible. The sincerity in his eyes almost convinced me, but I was too unsure of him to give him my trust. I remembered that it had been he who interrupted us earlier that day just as Tom had been about to tell me what he knew of Saramary's death. He was the only one who knew Tom was going to tell me something. And if he had been responsible for the death of his first wife, he would not want Tom saying anything about it to me. It would be for his own protection that he would have to get rid of the old gardener. And if all this was true, it wasn't for my safety that he was concerned, but for his own. There was nothing to stop him and Harmon from rearranging the evidence themselves and saying nothing about it. I came to the inevitable conclusion: if Julian was the murderer, I would be in danger if I told the police what I knew; if he was not, I was still in danger from the person really responsible if I insisted that Tom's death was no accident.

I knew it was wrong to go along with the story of Tom's tripping and then falling against the stove, but I knew also that there was nothing I could do to prove otherwise. The murderer had returned and rearranged the evidence; any claim I might make to the contrary would be met with disbelief. The family would close ranks against me to protect themselves. I decided to agree, at least outwardly, with Julian, but my determination to find and expose the murderer grew. I did not know how I would do it; I would have to be very careful, assuming a cleverness I wasn't certain I possessed.

Finally, aware that Julian was watching me anxiously, I said, "Yes, Julian. I see what you mean. Very well, I will pretend that it was an accident. But if the police go away satisfied that Tom's death was an accident, what will happen to the person who murdered him? Is he allowed to go on, completely undiscovered and unpunished?" I heard the scorn in my voice, but was unable to erase it. I looked at Julian carefully. Was there a hint of relief in his eyes when I agreed? I couldn't be certain, for almost instantly his expression became grim.

He said, "He will not get away with it as before, that I can promise you, Larissa. I have already taken steps to make certain that will not happen."

I stood to leave. My head was aching; there were too many mysteries here that I couldn't begin to solve. Desperately, I wanted to believe that Julian was innocent, but I was forced to accept the fact that I couldn't trust my own husband. There was no one here who was my friend. I had never felt so alone.

CHAPTER SIX

The first guest arrived early the next day. I was surprised; in all the confusion and questioning by the police, as well as the too recent memory of finding Tom dead, I had forgotten the ball completely. I had decided that a walk on the beach might clear my mind and, when the knocker on the front door sounded, I was just crossing the gallery on my way out. I waited curiously while Harmon admitted a smartly dressed man about Julian's age. It was obvious that he was known at the house; he and Harmon greeted each other by name.

I walked over to him while he was taking off his outdoor things and asking about a groom to stable his horse.

"I'm Mrs. Synclair," I introduced myself.

"Jeremy Bluntridge, at your service," he replied, bowing over the hand I extended him.

He straightened and I could see he had merry blue eyes under straight reddish-blond brows. His hair was the same reddish color and was blown this way and that. He saw me looking at his head and raised a hand to try to smooth his hair down, laughing. I smiled; his laugh was infectious. I decided that I liked this man.

He was about to say something more to me when suddenly his eyes went over my head and his face lit up with another smile. "Julian—I've come at last! I think I winded my horse, pushing him so hard the last three miles in my hurry to get here and see you."

"Jerry . . ." Julian said anxiously. His manner was abrupt, completely in contrast to the cheerful demeanor of Mr. Bluntridge. I looked at Julian in surprise, but then I realized that he was probably still as upset about Tom's death as I was. His next words confirmed this. "Jerry, I am glad to see you. It's just that we had an accident here last night. The gardener was found dead. The whole household has been turned around by the police. . . ."

I could see beads of perspiration on Julian's forehead; it was as though he were trying to inform Mr. Bluntridge of something beyond his words. Mr. Bluntridge took the cue, for his manner became one of genuine concern. "How terrible for you," he said contritely. "And here I come in without a thought in the world." He turned to me with a slight bow. "My apologies, Mrs. Synclair."

"Of course, Mr. Bluntridge. You could not possibly have known," I murmured.

Julian said, "I would like to speak to you in the library, Jerry. Larissa, I'm sure you will excuse us?"

I was annoyed at Julian's abruptness; I had wanted the opportunity to become acquainted with Mr. Bluntridge. But then I realized that there would be another time; he obviously intended staying here for a while, as witnessed by the valise Harmon was just bringing in and carrying upstairs. I nodded, forcing down my resentment, and went out the front door.

I didn't see Mr. Bluntridge again until teatime. When I entered the drawing room, no one else was there. I had inquired after Arminta, but her maid told me she was resting. Dorcas and Mathew had gone to visit some friends, and no one ever knew where the elusive Norman and Edward were. I was glad to be alone, and hoped Mrs. St. John would take tea in her own rooms as she often did. I heard footsteps at the door and thought it would be so pleasant if Julian were to join me for tea, but when the door opened, I saw that it was not my husband but Jeremy Bluntridge instead.

Mr. Bluntridge came in, holding the door for the maid with the tea tray. He waited until she had gone and then, with a solemn expression, sat down opposite me and said, "I'm so sorry about Tom's death. Julian told me you found him. It must have been quite a shock. . . ."

I looked away from those steady blue eyes, willing myself not to think of poor Tom as I had found him, and murmured something I hoped was appropriate.

"Well, I suppose one consolation is that Tom lived to a great age," Mr. Bluntridge said quietly.

"But he could have lived longer, if only . . . !" I stopped, horrified at my outburst. What was I thinking of, to blurt out thoughtlessly that Tom had been murdered. I glanced quickly at Mr. Bluntridge, whose unwavering blue gaze held my own. "I . . . I mean . . . Yes, he was a very old man," I finished lamely.

"Julian was very upset," Mr. Blutridge continued. "Tom has been with the family for many years, and I'm sure Julian won't forget him. In fact, he mentioned that he is going to see that Tom's family will be taken care of. Tom's death won't go unnoticed, believe me."

Staring thoughtfully at Jeremy Bluntridge's smoothly impassive face, I wondered at the subtle emphasis in his last words. Was he trying to tell me something? Was he trying to assure me that Julian was innocent, that he would do everything he could to discover Tom's murderer? I wanted to believe that, but a tiny persistent voice at the back of my mind wondered if Julian had succeeded in deceiving Jeremy Bluntridge too. Our glance met and held, and as I looked into the steady blue eyes opposite me, I knew that this man would not be fooled easily.

I felt myself relax, and said the first thing that came into my head. "Have you and Julian known each other long?"

He laughed, and the tension that surrounded us was broken by that easy sound. "Oh yes. We were at school together. He was the young aristocrat and I the boy who had to scrape pennies together, but for all that, we became friends. Julian set the pace, and I followed along. We were always in trouble, but it was such fun!"

I looked at him in astonishment. "Julian in trouble?" I repeated stupidly. I could not imagine such a thing of my serious husband.

He laughed again. "Yes, Julian. He was quite a rake in his younger days. Although now the responsibility of the estate weighs too heavily on him for him to be as lighthearted as he used to be. And of course . . ."

I knew that he had been about to refer to the death of Julian's first wife and all the grief it had caused him, and suddenly the specter of Saramary rose up between us, creating a sudden tension. I looked away in confusion and busied myself with passing cups and plates of cakes back and forth for the next few minutes, hoping the strained silence between us would smooth away.

I became aware that Mr. Bluntridge was staring at me intently again; his scrutiny made me nervous, so I asked, in a prim tone that I immediately regretted, "What of your family, Mr. Bluntridge?"

He stared. "What? Oh yes. I'm afraid I have no family, Mrs. Synclair. My parents died some years back and I haven't made any effort to trace any relatives."

I murmured my sympathy, but Mr. Bluntridge shook his head. "Oh no. My mother and father had a full life, always traveling here and there. They always said when they went, they would go in style, and together, and so they did."

He made no mention of how they had died, and I did not ask. I saw him studying me again and I tried to sip my tea with a semblance of calm. Why was he staring so?

Finally he said, "Julian said that you are alone also, except for an aunt."

"Yes. My mother died four years ago; my father has been dead for some time. My father's Aunt Flora was kind enough to take my mother and me when my father . . . died, and she is the only relative I know about." I didn't want to talk about my aunt; my years under her mercenary care were not fond memories, and I could not help but blame her in part for Julian's attitude toward me now. I cast about for another subject of conversation, but Jeremy Bluntridge went on: "What about your mother's family? Surely there must have been someone?"

I shook my head. "I never knew my mother's family. You see, she eloped with my father and was immediately disowned by her family. In fact, I don't remember her ever mentioning them."

"How did your parents meet?"

"I . . . I don't know. My father died when I was very young, and my mother refused to talk about him."

"Oh? Perhaps she felt that, but for her marriage, she would not have been estranged from her family."

"But she loved my father," I said fiercely. "She loved him enough to run away with him and leave everything behind."

"Yes, she must have loved him very much, to go

against her own family. It must have been a difficult decision for her," he answered gravely. "But yet you know nothing about them—except that they disowned her?"

I shook my head again. I remembered the one time I had asked my mother about my maternal grandparents. Her bitterness toward them had been such that I had never asked about them again. The subject was never mentioned between us, even when she lay dying.

"What was your mother's name before she was married?"

I came back to the present with a start. "I don't know," I said, and continued hastily when I saw his look of astonishment, "I admit that sounds strange, but you have to remember that my mother suffered greatly over her family's rejection; she couldn't bear to be reminded of it."

"How unfortunate for you," he said sympathetically.

I was becoming agitated at the conversation, as well as slightly shocked that I could be saying such intimate things about my family to someone I had scarcely met. And it was curious that Jeremy Bluntridge would be so pressing about something that was none of his concern. Perhaps if I had been wiser, I would have questioned his reasons for probing into what was, after all, a very personal matter, but as it was, I was grateful that I had someone's interest and sympathy. I wondered if I dared talk to him about Julian, but even as I wondered, I knew it was too soon to be going on about the mystery that surrounded Peregrine House. Mr. Bluntridge was too new an acquaintance for me to blurt out my unhappiness and fears about my husband, even if it did appear that the two of them were old friends. I would just have to wait until an opportunity to speak presented itself.

Jeremy said smoothly, as though there had been no awkward pause, "Perhaps you are better off not knowing who your mother's family was. If they could be so callous about your mother, you might be well off without them."

I murmured an agreement, hoping to convey by my manner that I did not wish to pursue the subject any longer, and then changed the subject firmly. "How long can you stay with us, Mr. Bluntridge? I'm certain Julian would want you to extend your visit beyond the night of the party; he is usually so busy that I know your company would encourage him to take a much needed rest."

"I haven't decided that yet, Mrs. Synclair. But I thank you for your kind invitation. Perhaps the three of us can arrange an outing together; I haven't seen much of Julian since . . ."

Again I knew he had almost referred to Saramary. I began to resent her intrusion even into the most insignificant conversation. It was as though her ghost were beginning to follow me wherever I went, and I rebelled at the thought that even in death she had the ability to overshadow me. Her death was tragic, it was true, but I had no wish to be haunted by her as everyone else seemed to be.

I said calmly, "Since Saramary's death?"

He stiffened imperceptibly, his eyes taking on a steely coldness as he regarded me. This was my first glimpse of the real Jeremy Bluntridge, but I did not know it at the time. I realized that his gaiety was a façade, that underneath that exterior was a man who knew what he was about, a man to be reckoned with, but I did not wonder why he chose to hide behind such an exterior. I was too concerned with thoughts of my own.

I continued to look at him calmly while he seemed to be assessing my intentions in mentioning Saramary's name.

At last he relaxed and said, "So you know about Saramary? I thought that Julian, being such a discreet person, wouldn't have discussed his first wife with you. Especially since she died under such mysterious circumstances."

"I didn't find out about Saramary from Julian. He

has never mentioned her," I said flatly. Then, abandoning all caution, I said urgently, "Mr. Bluntridge, there is a mystery about Saramary's death, as you yourself have said. Some say it was not a suicide. I would like to help Julian discover the truth, but I don't know how. Can you help me?"

Again that steely glance. "How do you think I can help you?"

"Well, since you and Julian are such good friends, I thought . . . I thought . . ." I faltered to a stop under that cool blue gaze. I wondered if I had been mistaken in assuming that Jeremy was interested enough to help Julian. Or even if he was, he might not think that it was any of my affair. I had confessed that Julian had not told me himself; if Jeremy Bluntridge was truly Julian's friend, he would believe that Julian had good reason for not wanting me to be involved.

I felt like a fool. I said, "Forgive me, Mr. Bluntridge. I have been precipitous in discussing such private family matters with you. Will you have another cup of tea?"

Thankfully, he declined, and in a few minutes I was able to excuse myself. I fled to my room, my cheeks burning with humiliation that I had so freely confided my fears and concern over Julian to a perfect stranger. I wondered what he must think of me, that I could babble on about something that did not concern him. In the future, I resolved, I would be more careful.

That night, when I was dressing for dinner, I thought I would wear my mother's brooch again. Julian's ruby pendant was beautiful, but I did not feel that it was really mine. I knew Julian had given it to me because it was the expected thing to do, not because he wished me to have it as his wife. I opened the little jewel box; the only thing it contained was the pendant, shimmering against the felt lining. I gave an exclamation of dismay; I was sure I had put the brooch back after wearing it the night Edward and Arminta had arrived, but it wasn't there.

"Ellie, have you seen my brooch? It doesn't seem to be in my jewel box."

Ellie, eyes wide, shook her head. "No, ma'am. I haven't seen it."

I was more puzzled than alarmed. I thought I had returned it to the box, but perhaps I was mistaken. "The last time I wore it, I pinned it to my lavender gown. Would you see if it's still there?"

Ellie went to the wardrobe and searched for the lavender gown. She took it out and glanced at the bodice, shaking her head. I began to be irritated; the brooch was the only thing I had left of my mother. "Search the floor; it must be here somewhere."

Ellie went to her knees and felt around the floor of the wardrobe while I opened the drawers of my dressing table, taking everything out and feeling far back into the recesses of the drawers. The brooch was nowhere to be found.

Ellie and I searched the whole room twice before I was forced to admit that the brooch had disappeared. I looked at her in consternation. "I can't understand it. I know I returned it to my jewel box after wearing it that night."

Ellie looked at me with an expression close to terror on her face. "Oh, ma'am, I didn't take it. I didn't."

"I'm not blaming you, Ellie. Don't be ridiculous." I realized that, in my anxiety to find the brooch, I had sounded accusing; I said more kindly, "I know you wouldn't take it, Ellie. It's just that it was my mother's and the only thing I have to remember her by."

"When you're down to dinner, I'll search the room again," Ellie volunteered, her relief visible that I wasn't going to accuse her of stealing.

I nodded, and when Julian came in to escort me to the dining room, I thought it best not to tell him about the brooch. But I wondered who had taken it—someone must have done so, otherwise it would have surely turned up when Ellie and I searched the room. But who would want it? It wasn't valuable to anyone; only to me because it had been my mother's. If someone had

100

come into my room for the purpose of stealing something, surely they would have taken the ruby pendant, which was worth so much more. But no, the pendant had been in the jewel box; only the ram's-head brooch had been taken.

I was silent on the way downstairs, trying to think of reasons for the brooch's disappearance. Perhaps someone had taken it to spite me. But who disliked me sufficiently to do such a petty thing? I had to admit to myself that it could have been any one of them; they all disliked me in varying degrees. But I couldn't just announce at dinner that my brooch had been taken by one of them, and could I please have it back. I could just imagine the fury around the table when I made such an unfounded accusation. No, I couldn't openly accuse any of them. I thought the best course would be to say nothing; perhaps then the person who had taken it would be forced to put it back when he found that his little scheme to upset me had failed. I didn't really care who had taken it; the most important thing to me was having it returned.

When Julian and I entered the dining room, I found that only three places had been set. Only the two of us and Mr. Bluntridge were present, and Julian murmured some excuse for the absence of the rest of the family. I was slightly embarrassed to see Mr. Bluntridge again after the disastrous scene at tea this afternoon, but it became apparent that he and Julian were interested in talking about mutual acquaintances from their school days, and soon I was able to relax and enjoy myself watching Julian smile and laugh at Mr. Bluntridge's gift of mimicry as he elaborated on some of their youthful exploits. To my relief, I was not required to join in their conversation, although Mr. Bluntridge made an effort to include me, laughingly explaining who so-and-so was and what he was doing now.

I had never seen Julian so relaxed, and thought that it would be wonderful if Jeremy could stay at Peregrine House for an extended visit. The two men seemed to have a deep friendship, and far from being envious over their shared jokes and amusement, I was happy that Julian had such a friend.

After dessert had been served, I rose and left them to their after-dinner wine. I did not care to linger in the drawing room alone, so I went upstairs, to find Ellie weeping. Poor child, she hadn't been able to find the brooch and thought I would blame her for its loss. I assured her that it would be found in time, and that she wasn't to be upset about it. She left me then, in better spirits, and I found myself wishing I could feel the same. The fact that we had not been able to find it in my room made me certain that it wasn't lost, but stolen. I considered the other servants; perhaps one of the cleaning girls had seen it and taken a fancy to it. No, I knew that Julian would not employ anyone who would steal, and Mrs. Harmon would be horrified to learn that I would think any of her girls capable of doing such a thing. So it had to be someone in the family. But who? It was useless to speculate. I decided to accept the loss, as much as it hurt me to do so. The brooch had obviously meant something to my mother, for she had kept it all these years, and it meant something to me too, because she had treasured it so. But there was nothing to be done about it now.

The next morning I went out onto the beach and walked along the sand dejectedly. Even Berus did not appear today, and I was alone. I wondered if this was to be the pattern of my life: wandering about by myself, wasting my time with nothing to do but stay out of everyone's way. I tried to shake off the feeling of self-pity that threatened me, and told myself that I would have to learn to be more resourceful. How I would manage that, I didn't know, but I knew I couldn't simply waste time wishing things were changed without trying to do something to change them.

Norman came cantering along the beach on a magnificent horse—his new hunter, I thought immediately, remembering his casual announcement that one night at dinner. Such was my depression that I was almost glad to see him. He reined in where I sat and looked down at me.

"Well, what do you think, Larissa?" he asked, gesturing toward his horse.

"He is certainly beautiful," I said, admiring the long, clean lines of the animal. I stood up and stroked the velvety nose and was rewarded by the horse snuffling into my hand, seeking a treat that wasn't there.

"He should be. Julian paid enough for him," Norman answered, jumping down from the saddle. "But what are you doing out here alone?"

"I often come out to walk along the beach. I find it restful."

"I can imagine; the atmosphere in the house is not conducive to peace. Of course, it wasn't always that way. When Saramary . . ." he hesitated, and again I had that flash of irritation when her name was mentioned. It seemed that everyone held their breath when they inadvertently mentioned Saramary.

"Yes? When Saramary what?" I prompted.

"Well, I was going to say that when Saramary was alive, the house was not in such a turmoil. She had the ability to smooth things over. She was especially good for Julian. But now he has become bitter; angry all the time. It's very difficult."

He scowled and looked down at the ground. "What did you think of Saramary?" I asked softly.

"She was one of the most beautiful women I had ever seen," he answered dreamily. "She was so clever in keeping Julian amused. There were many times that I was in trouble with Julian over something or another, and she always managed to turn his anger from me. I loved her like a sister."

"Why do you think she killed herself?"

He looked at me in astonishment that I could be so blunt about it, but I was beyond caring about tact; I wanted to know as much as I could about her. "I don't think she killed herself," he answered shortly. "But no one will ever be able to prove it. Even the police couldn't make a case for murder. I remember that day—God, I will never forget it if I live to be a hundred. Mother had been on at me about an innocent flirtation with Saramary. She didn't think it was proper, Julian being my brother and Saramary my sister-in-law. But Saramary was the sort of woman who delighted in innocent compliments, having men admire her. We do not have many visitors at Peregrine House, and it was a way to pass the time. Well, at any rate, Mother and I had a first-rate quarrel about it, and in the end I went to find Saramary to tell her about it to see if she could pacify Mother. She was very good at that type of thing, as I said. I went to their apartment —hers and Julian's—and heard them quarreling about something. I didn't stay, because Julian was shouting, and I thought I wouldn't be able to control myself and would burst in on them. She didn't like any kind of unpleasantness, you know. To be honest, I was still smarting after Mother's remarks about my behavior, and I left the house. I went to the village to drown my sorrows, as it were, and when I returned, Saramary was dead. I've often thought that if I had interrupted Julian and Saramary, she might still be alive."

"You sound as though you believe Julian is responsible for her death."

A glint of fear showed briefly in his eyes. "I didn't say that," he muttered. "Saramary's death was a suicide; and whatever the reasons, they were her own." He swung himself abruptly into the saddle and, with a brief wave to me, cantered down the beach, leaving me standing more puzzled than before.

No matter who I talked to, in the end it all seemed to come back to Julian. Everyone implied that Julian was responsible, but, when pressed directly, denied it flatly. Suddenly it seemed to me that everyone was far too eager to implicate Julian. Could it be that they all were in some measure guilty of Saramary's death? Or was I simply refusing to see the obvious? Somehow I would have to find out more about the elusive Saramary. She seemed to have presented a different side of her character to everyone in the house. Who was the real Saramary?

Dorcas and Mathew had returned by the time I got back to the house. I had never seen Dorcas in such a gay mood; it seemed that their visit had done them some good. They had been shopping while they were gone, and to my surprise, Dorcas put her arm through mine and insisted that I come to her apartment to see her purchases. I was suspicious of her sudden friendliness, but thought I should make another effort to be friendly to her in return. So I went gladly, listening to her chatter all the way to her room.

I had never been in Dorcas' rooms before, and was surprised that they were so light and graceful. Scattered about the sitting room were little tables of a French design; the sofa and chairs were covered in pink- and white-striped silk, and all around were statuettes and bric-a-bac. A hutch stood in one corner of the room and was filled with delicate china cups and saucers that had been hand-painted. The decor of the room was an insight into an aspect of her character that I had not known existed. I would have thought that, Dorcas being so much like her mother, her rooms would be heavily ornate and oppressive, but that was certainly not the case. Paper-wrapped parcels had been deposited on the sofa and she went eagerly to these and began unwrapping them. Several lengths of velvet and satin appeared, as well as a new bonnet and fur-trimmed cape. I admired these, being honest in my compliments, for it was obvious that Dorcas had excellent taste. Her face was alight, and I had never seen her look so pretty.

"I thought it was about time to have something new and gay," she said, snatching up the bonnet and posturing in front of the mirror. "We have all been depressed for so long."

"That bonnet certainly becomes you," I said, thinking that the dark blue felt matched her eyes perfectly.

She looked at me curiously, as though wondering

whether or not I was mocking her. Satisfied that I was not, she turned to the mirror again and made a great business of arranging it to best advantage.

"I never should have thought it," she said suddenly. "After the way I have snubbed you, I should think you would have reason to do the same to me."

I was silent, wondering at her sudden change of attitude toward me.

"Mathew bought these things for me," she continued. "We went to Mathew's solicitor; it seems that he will have some good news for us in the near future—perhaps the tiring legal business of Mathew's estate will be solved. I can hardly wait!"

I knew then the reason for her gaiety; with Mathew coming into his inheritance, she would feel that she was her own mistress. I hoped this was so; this was a Dorcas I had never seen before, and if the thought of coming into an inheritance brought about the change, I was all for it.

I looked down at the material spread out on the sofa and ran my fingers over the luxurious velvet in a deep rose tone that I had always admired, but had never been able to wear. On Dorcas, however, with her black hair and fair skin, it would look beautiful. I said so.

She came over to the sofa and sat down, looking into my eyes. "I'm afraid I may have misjudged you," she said thoughtfully. "I don't really think you are an adventuress after all."

"Why don't you think so now, when before you were convinced that it was so?" I asked.

"I . . . I don't know. Let me just say that I have changed my mind. You know," she said in a burst of confidence, "Saramary would never have been so complimentary."

Here it was again, a reference to Saramary. But this time I was not irritated that she had intruded into the conversation. I was beginning to be eager to grasp every detail of Saramary's life; it had become very important to me to reconstruct the day she died.

"What do you mean?" I asked.

Dorcas gestured impatiently toward the rose velvet lying between us. "She would have said that it was too bold. She always thought that she had the best taste; that only she knew how to dress. She used to drive me to distraction with her pale colors and mincing attitude." She paused and looked at me again intently. "Oh, I know you are going to say that I misjudged her too. No one could believe that dear, kind Saramary would have a mean bone in her body. But that wasn't true. Oh, she wasn't vicious, I don't mean that—she was sly. I remember the day she died; we had a quarrel that day, too. I don't even remember what it was about; it seemed as though we were always quarreling about something. And then, after that, Mathew and I had a quarrel about her right in this very room. Mathew was just like the other men—he couldn't believe that *she* would ever cause any trouble. And then we heard that she was dead. I couldn't believe it—Saramary would never commit suicide. She had too much to live for; Julian wound around her little finger, the baby coming, everybody doting on her. Oh no, she wouldn't end it all when everything was going her way."

"Perhaps it was an accident," I ventured.

She looked at me impatiently, as though I refused to see the obvious. She said, "Oh, no. It wasn't an accident. I thought at first I would be blamed; after all, we had been quarreling that same day, and everyone knew that I disliked her. But I didn't dislike her enough to kill her. It was fortunate that Mathew was able to tell the police that we had been together when . . . it happened. Otherwise, I daren't think what would have happened to me." She paused thoughtfully. "But Julian had had words with her that day, too. And he didn't have anybody who could vouch for his whereabouts. . . ."

As her voice trailed off, I thought: here it is again, the implication that Julian was responsible. I wondered again at Dorcas' unaccustomed friendliness to me. Was it possible that she had brought me to her room for this purpose—to convince me of her innocence in Saramary's death? Suddenly, it seemed that everyone had done an about-face; where before they all refused to talk to me, now they were very eager that I should know of their individual innocence in Saramary's death. But why was it so important to convince me—why had I become the one person who should be persuaded that Julian was the guilty one? It was all very puzzling.

The day of the ball was at hand. The servants, supervised by Mrs. Harmon, were scurrying about giving finishing touches to the house in preparation for the festivities that night. Two long trestle tables had been set up in the gallery and covered with snowy linen cloths. The new gardener and two of the servants were busy arranging the flowers and greenery, and the floor was given a final polish. Later, the cook and her helpers would bring out all the dishes they had been so busy preparing for this night, and the tables would be filled with every conceivable delicacy, as well as great roasts, hams, pies, and pastries. The silver punch bowl had been placed in the center of one of the tables, with cups arranged all around it.

When I went up to start my own preparations for the night, I found Ellie in a state of great excitement. She had never been on hand before to help dress anyone for such an occasion, and I had to stop her from dashing about the room in her eagerness to do everything right. I took a long, leisurely bath that had been scented with bath crystals and rosemary, and had to keep a tight hold on myself to prevent myself being too nervous at the thought of meeting all Julian's friends for the first time. As I sat at my dressing table for Ellie to do my hair, I was surprised at my reflection; my eyes sparkled with excitement, and two spots of color glowed in my cheeks. For once my hair behaved perfectly, and I had to admit the style we had chosen for that night complimented me. Ellie had pulled my hair back from my face into a cascade of curls. A few wispy curls touched my forehead and cheeks, with the rest flowing down my back.

When it came time for Ellie to help me into my gown, she pulled it reverently from its padded hanger in the wardrobe. It was a beautiful gown—the most beautiful I had ever owned, and I owed it all to Julian, I thought, as I touched the heavy emerald green satin. The voluminous skirt had been embroidered with seed pearls, with a scattering of pearls across the bodice. I had been hesitant about wearing such flamboyant color, but by the time Ellie had hooked me into it, even I had to admit that the deep green complimented my complexion and reddish hair. Ellie adjusted the folds of the skirt so many times that finally I laughed and told her she would take out the crispness if she handled it any more. She smiled shyly, and I knew from her expression that I looked well. I only hoped Julian would think so.

I told Ellie she could leave me; I knew that in spite of her willingness to help me dress, she was anxious to be away and attend the little party that the servants were having to themselves on this grand occasion. With a final loving pat to my hair, and a last lingering glance at my gown, she left, humming happily. I went to my dressing table and took out the ruby pendant. With fingers shaking from excitement, I fastened the clasp and stood looking in the mirror. The ruby seemed to pulse with a life of its own as it lay against my throat, and I thought that it added its own touch to the beautiful gown I was wearing.

Julian came in just as I was turning away from the mirror. Our eyes caught and held, and I was shaken to see the admiration in his eyes as he looked at me. Suddenly the atmosphere in the room seemed charged with emotion; to cover my confusion I twirled before him gaily, ending with a deep curtsy that spread my skirts in a perfect circle around me. I lowered my eyes so that he wouldn't see any betraying emotion, but when he reached down and took my hand, pulling me to my feet, I could not help looking into his eyes once more.

"You . . ." he began, then cleared his throat. "You look beautiful, Larissa. I shall be proud to have you on my arm tonight."

I did not trust myself to respond, fearing that I would say something that would ruin this moment, so I nodded and took Julian's arm. I had the fleeting thought that, for tonight at least, I would forget the mystery surrounding Saramary's death; forget that Tom had died before he could tell me what he knew. I could think of nothing but the fact that Julian was proud of me. Tonight was going to be the most exciting night of my life.

As we walked toward the gallery, I could hear the musicians that had been hired to play for the ball. There was a hum of voices, and I was relieved that Mrs. St. John was receiving; she had insisted on acting as hostess, and I was content to bow to her wishes. I looked at Julian, walking so tall by my side, and thought again how handsome he was. His ruffled shirt, the black silk cravat, the satin lapels of his coat, emphasized his dark good looks, and I was proud to be walking beside him. Glancing up at the face I loved, I wondered how I could ever have possibly suspected this man of murder. His eyes, the set of his mouth, held no hint of cruelty, or of evil, but rather a memory of pain, and, perhaps, self-mockery. I wished again, with a sense of my own futility, that I could erase that pain from his eyes, bring a smiling response from that distant expression.

I sighed, and as if Julian could read my thoughts, he smiled briefly, and held out his hand, and we began walking down the stairs together. At once the murmur of voices ceased, and a hundred eyes turned to watch our descent. I was determined not to appear nervous, though my hand was shaking in Julian's steady one. Surprisingly, he gave my fingers a slight squeeze, and when I looked up at him, he smiled briefly again, giving me the reassurance I needed to raise my head and smile naturally at the crowd below.

Edward was standing at the foot of the stairs; as we passed him, he bowed and I nodded in his direction, my smile becoming a trifle fixed. But then Norman came up immediately and exclaimed, "My God, Larissa. You look enchanting! Don't forget to save a dance for me."

I laughed and said I wouldn't forget, and from that moment on I was so busy being introduced to the many people who crowded around us that I forgot to be nervous.

There were so many people that I can't remember all their names, but a few stand out in my memory: Lord and Lady Effington, both stout, both looking as though they would choke in all their finery and would much prefer to be in the out-of-doors with their horses and dogs; Colonel and Mrs. Huxley, who both stared, frankly curious, at Julian's new wife; Sir Thomas and Lady Pembroke, a saturnine couple whose obvious affection for Julian just missed including Julian's wife; and finally, Lord and Lady Ashton, an elderly couple who seemed taken aback when we were introduced. They both stared fixedly at me for some time, and I was just on the point of asking them what was the matter when Edward came up and maneuvered them away to the punch bowl. I saw them after that, staring at me, then putting their heads together and whispering. Lady Ashton shook her head, but Lord Ashton seemed determined to press his point, whatever it was, for the two of them walked some distance away and sat down on the little chairs ringing the room, still arguing and gesturing toward me. I was curious about their reaction, but, in the whirl of seemingly endless introductions, I forgot all about them.

At last the musicians began a waltz, and Julian led me out to the center of the floor to begin the first dance. As I stepped into his arms, I forgot that nearly everyone was staring at us, some of them with a sly smile on their faces, and gave myself up to the joy of being in Julian's arms. We whirled around the floor, and Julian bent his head to whisper in my ear, "You certainly have made a favorable impression, Larissa. Even my mother is surprised—have you seen her looking at you?"

I shook my head; I did not want to talk about his mother. I just wanted to luxuriate in the feeling of having Julian close to me. When his arm tightened about my waist, and he drew me nearer to him, I thought how wonderful it would be if he were ever to return my love. I looked up at him and was surprised to see tenderness in his face as he looked down at me. I almost said, "I love you, Julian," but stopped myself in time; I did not want to ruin our dance by making him angry with me. It was not the time to declare my feeling for him, no matter how happy I was.

After that, I danced with Edward and Norman; even Mathew came up to claim a dance from me. I danced with every man in the room, I think; all of them paying their respects to the new wife of Julian Synclair. I don't think I have ever felt so sure of myself, so proud that I justified Julian's confidence in me. But that feeling was short-lived.

I saw Dorcas talking with her mother, and went over to them during a lull in the dancing. Dorcas had on a sapphire blue silk gown and looked beautiful. But it wasn't until I came close to her that I saw that her eyes were overly brilliant and her expression strained. She drew me to one side, out of the way of the others, and said, "Larissa, I'm sorry. It was mean and cruel of me, and . . ."

Puzzled, I asked, "What are you talking about, Dorcas?"

She gestured at the crowded room. "This. When Norman and I were planning about the party, I could only think what a humiliation it would be for you. I didn't realize . . . I didn't know that I would change my mind about you. I wanted you to know that I'm sorry."

"Humiliation? What humiliation?" I asked, astonished.

But just then Mathew came over and Dorcas, with a last despairing look at me, went with him. I stood watching her, completely at a loss as to her behavior. Mrs. St. John, who had been standing close by, came over to my side. She said, "You are looking well tonight, Larissa. The ball is turning out better than I thought; perhaps all our friends and acquaintances have decided that we are not to be pariahs after all."

I thought this a curious remark, but my thoughts were still on Dorcas and her strange behavior. I nodded absently and Mrs. St. John drifted away. It was true, now that I thought about it, that I had seen some sly, knowing looks pass back and forth among the guests as Julian and I had taken a turn around the room, making sure to speak to everyone assembled there, but I thought at the time it was just conjecture on their part as to how happy a couple Julian and I were. I didn't think we had given anyone cause to gossip about that; Julian had seemed the perfect husband, concerned that I was not too tired, offering to bring me some refreshment. Whatever our private life —or lack of it—I thought we had presented ourselves as happy as any newly married couple could be. I had been determined that none of the people here would know any differently. But now it seemed as if there was some undercurrent that I couldn't quite grasp, some hidden meaning for those sideways glances I had noticed. I wondered what it was.

I saw Arminta standing alone across the room and went over to speak to her. Perhaps she could explain why I suddenly felt so uneasy.

"Well, my dear," she greeted me, "in spite of everything, you have succeeded in being the belle of the ball. Of course, I knew you would not have any trouble there, but all the same, I suppose there were those who might have wished otherwise."

"What do you mean?"

"Nothing. Just the foolish rambling of an old woman. Pay no attention to me," she said. "Tell, me, what do you think of the vultures gathered here tonight?"

I looked at her in surprise; her tone was bitter. "I didn't think of them as vultures, Arminta. In fact, I have met some very nice people."

"Oh yes. There are a few here—genuinely nice, I mean. But by far the majority came because they were curious about you, and interested to see what Julian had got himself into."

"Don't you think that's natural?"

"Yes, to some extent," she admitted. "But it never fails to surprise me that those you count as friends have a way of disappearing when there is trouble and appearing later on to gloat. I can't tolerate hypocrisy, and some of the people here abound in it."

I was about to reply, when suddenly there was a flurry at the door. A young woman was coming in— the same woman I had seen that time on the beach. She was unescorted, and as she paused on the threshold, I could not understand why. She was more beautiful than I remembered her; her fair hair shimmered in the candlelight, and her yellow satin gown was exquisite. She surveyed the room as though she owned it, and when Norman came up to her and bowed, the smile she bestowed on him was radiant. Taking the arm he offered her, she advanced regally into the room.

"Who is that?" I whispered to Arminta.

Arminta looked at me with a strange expression on her face. "Haven't you met her before?" I shook my head, declining to tell her of the time on the beach, and she continued, "That, my dear, is Rose Streitten, one of the richest and most eligible young women in this part of the country. She is reported to have men falling all over themselves for her favors."

I could well believe it; her beauty and haughty poise would make her the center of attention in any gathering. I watched Norman leading her across the room and could not help a stab of envy as she smiled and greeted the people she passed. She was so assured, so in control, that beside her I felt almost like a schoolgirl.

"Well, what do you think of your rival?" a voice said in my ear.

I turned and saw Edward standing beside me. "What do you mean, my rival?" I asked curtly.

I followed his glance and almost gasped in shock. Rose Streitten had reached Julian's side, and with a flick of her hand dismissed Norman, who had no choice but to leave her side. I saw Julian look down at her with an expression that I had never before seen in his eyes while Rose glanced up at him, a brilliant smile curving her full lips. Julian responded with a smile that made my heart turn over; how many times had I wished that he would look at me this way? Now I knew why Julian had never touched me; he had been bewitched by this woman. I had no claim to beauty myself, would never have any hope of looking as lovely as this woman did tonight, and the thought brought scalding tears to my eyes. In that moment when Julian and Rose Streitten stood looking at each other, I knew that to Julian I might never have existed. The realization brought with it a crushing humiliation; I knew any hope I might have had that I could make Julian love me had evaporated. All Rose Streitten had to do was walk into the room and Julian had no eyes for anyone but her. I was grateful that at least I had not made a total fool of myself by declaring my love to Julian; that would have been the final blow to my pride.

While I struggled to maintain my composure, Edward stood quietly by my side. Then he said, "Well, what are you going to do?"

"Do?" I asked coldly, summoning all my control. "What do you mean, Edward?"

"Well, I thought . . . I thought . . ." He paused and looked at me uncertainly.

"Yes, I know what you thought, Edward. Did you perhaps think I would become hysterical because Julian smiled at another woman? How childish you are! Excuse me, but I must attend to my duties and meet Miss Streitten. Oh, she has a lovely smile, don't you think?"

I walked away from him and had the satisfaction of knowing that he was completely puzzled by my behavior. I gave one look over my shoulder to where he was still standing; and, at the astonished expression on his face, I actually laughed. Not for worlds would anyone in this room discover what an effort it was to walk calmly across the room to where Julian and Rose Streitten were standing.

I could sense a thrill of anticipation from the people gathered in this room as I approached Julian. Out of the corner of my eye, I saw that many had stopped their conversation and were staring frankly; Arminta's description of vultures came to my mind and I raised my head higher. No one would be able to say afterward that I shrank from my competition. I nodded and smiled to the people I passed, and some had the grace to blush and turn away, pretending to resume their interrupted conversation. Others continued to stare, but it didn't bother me; my only concern was the couple I approached.

I came up to Julian and put my arm through his, a gesture of affection that was not lost on Miss Streitten. Her beautiful eyes narrowed, but she forced a smile; she was as aware of the interest of the crowd of people as I was.

"Julian," I said, "you have neglected to introduce me to this lovely young woman." Before he had a chance to reply, I turned to her and said, "I believe we have met before, but you forgot to give me your name. It was that time on the beach—do you remember? But of course, you were in such haste that you scarcely gave me time to reply to your charge of trespassing. What an amusing situation, do you not agree?"

Julian coughed—no, choked actually, and I repressed a smile at his discomfiture. Finally he managed to say, "Larissa, I would like you to meet Miss Rose Streitten, a neighbor of ours. But I gather that you have already met?"

I held out my hand. She was forced to take it or appear completely rude. I grasped the unwilling fingers lightly and murmured, "So pleased to meet you properly at last."

"Indeed, Mrs. Synclair," she said faintly.

"You may call me Larissa; it seems to pointless to stand on formality when we are such near neighbors. It would make things so awkward, don't you agree?"

I smiled at her and turned to Julian. "Julian, do you think we could have some refreshment? I know Cook would be disappointed if we did not sample her excellent table. You will excuse us, Miss Streitten?"

Thankfully, Julian did not resist when I began to move away. I was filled with a sense of victory that I had disappointed all the people who had been hoping for a scene between Rose Streitten and myself, but I was uneasy over Julian's reaction. I looked up at him, expecting to see anger in his eyes at my conduct, but to my surprise I saw that he was smiling down wryly at me, although he said nothing.

We were standing by the punch bowl when Lord and Lady Ashton, the couple who had stared at me so curiously when we were introduced, came up to where we were standing. Lord Ashton, a tall, gray-haired gentleman, bowed and commented upon the success of the ball. Lady Ashton, almost as tall as her husband, elaborately coifed and gowned and with a magnificent diamond necklace around her slender neck, looked down at me and smiled warmly. She said, "Forgive me, Mrs. Synclair, but I feel I must ask you . . ."

She hesitated, looking at her husband for guidance, but he was staring fixedly at me again, and did not see her glance for help.

"Let me begin again," she said when he did not respond. "If we seemed rude to you when we were first introduced, it was because you bear a startling resemblance to someone we once knew. It was as though we were seeing her again after a long absence. We thought surely we must have been mistaken, but the longer we watched you, the more we became convinced. Has anyone ever commented on the fact that you might resemble your mother? Perhaps it is she we are thinking of."

Lord Ashton's stare was unnerving. I replied, without looking directly at him, "I doubt that you would have been acquainted with my mother. We lived in London for many years—I was born there. But perhaps it was there . . . ?"

Lord Ashton spoke musingly. "No. We rarely visit London. But there is something. . . ." He hesitated, a puzzled frown on his face.

Just then Edward appeared at my elbow, saying gaily, "Here you are, Larissa! The musicians are just tuning up for the next dance—may I have the pleasure?"

Julian frowned at Edward and, when Edward took no notice of his warning look, said curtly, "Edward, you are interrupting."

Edward bowed politely. "So sorry, Lord and Lady Ashton. I confess my enthusiasm ran away with me. Did I interrupt something important?"

Lady Ashton replied quickly, "We were just discussing the fact that Mrs. Synclair bears an astonishing resemblance to someone we once knew. Surely you remember—"

Again Edward broke in, and I was surprised that he could be so rude. He said, "Perhaps Larissa has one of those faces that look familiar, even when you know it is not." He turned to me and continued, "We mustn't let the music go to waste, Larissa."

He held out his arm. I took it; one look at Julian's thunderous expression was enough to convince me to accept Edward's invitation before Julian exploded. As we moved away toward the dance floor, I sent an apologetic glance toward Lord and Lady Ashton, who stood staring after us as though unable to believe Edward's appalling behavior.

"Edward," I said through clenched teeth as we fell into a waltz step. "That was unbelievably rude. How *could* you?"

He replied airily, "Oh, the Ashtons are well acquainted with me. It is only what they would expect. And I did want to dance with you again."

I was furious with his casual attitude, but I knew he was capable of making an even more appalling scene if he chose, so I changed the subject, asking, "How are you and the Ashtons acquainted with one another? I thought they lived several miles from here."

"They do. But I became acquainted with their ward —a young man by the name of Timothy—while we were at school together. He invited me to stay with him during several holidays. So you see, I had an opportunity to get to know the Ashtons quite well. Rather stuffy couple, I must say."

I ignored his last comment and asked instead, "Where is Timothy now? I don't believe I have met him tonight."

"No, I dare say not." Edward grinned. "Poor Tim. He got himself involved in a brawl one night at school —it wasn't really his fault—and was knocked senseless. He never recovered."

There was something in his expression that was horrifying. It wasn't only his callous attitude about a friend's death; it was that he almost seemed to relish it. As I looked into his pale eyes, I wondered if anyone knew the real Edward; in that moment, he seemed evil somehow, and I shivered involuntarily.

He laughed. "Oh, I forgot. Ladies aren't supposed to listen to such dreadful tales. I thought you were above such delicate airs, Larissa; you seem too strong for your own good."

I wondered what he meant, but just then the dance ended and I did not have an opportunity to ask him to explain himself. I wasn't certain that I wanted to continue the conversation anyway; Edward seemed to find something amusing in putting people at a disadvantage.

As he led me from the floor, I saw Jeremy Bluntridge coming toward us. This was the first time I had seen Mr. Bluntridge that night; he was dressed correctly for the occasion in evening black, but even the formality of his attire could not suppress the unruly head of red hair. I fought down an impulse to laugh at the incongruity and smiled sedately instead. Beside me, Edward stiffened; it was obvious that he did not care for Jeremy Bluntridge, but Jeremy took no notice of his attitude.

"How beautiful you look, Mrs. Synclair," Jeremy said. I acknowledged the compliment with a nod of my head, and he continued, addressing Edward, "The Synclairs are doing themselves proud tonight, don't you think?"

"If you will excuse me, Larissa?" Edward said coldly. "I think I see someone I would like to talk to."

It was a direct insult to Mr. Bluntridge, and I gasped at the rudeness of it, looking quickly at Jeremy to determine his reaction. To my astonishment, Jeremy laughed as Edward walked away without a backward glance. "I don't worry about Edward, Mrs. Synclair," he said. "He has always been like that—rude and incorrigible, to say the least. It's a wonder that any woman as charming as Arminta Rossmore could have produced a son like Edward, who seems to delight in being as impossible as he can be."

"Do you find Mrs. Rossmore charming? I imagine some people find that her sharpness can be a bit overwhelming," I said, diverted by the thought of Arminta's astringent manner.

He laughed again. "I think that quality is what I most admire about her. You can be sure that whatever Arminta Rossmore says will be exactly what she has on her mind, regardless of the consequences."

I laughed with him, agreeing completely, and our shared laughter banished the strangeness I had felt in his presence ever since the day we had tea together.

"Would you care to dance? I'm not known for being light on my feet, but I am willing to try, if you are."

As we moved around the floor, I was inclined to agree with him that his strong suit was definitely not dancing, but his conversation was so amusing that I did not mind an occasional awkward movement. He sighed in comic relief when the dance was finished, and apologized for his clumsiness. When I assured him honestly that it was quite all right, he smiled at me and said, strangely, "I was not prepared to find Julian's wife so completely without airs and pretenses. I think that this time Julian has made quite the proper choice —you should make certain that he knows it, Mrs. Synclair."

I was so surprised at this remark that I said nothing for a moment, and by the time I had collected my wits, Julian was standing beside me, claiming me for the next dance, and Jeremy bowed and was gone.

When I stepped into Julian's arms, I hoped he was not going to take me to task for my behavior to Rose Streitten; I did not want to ruin the evening by quarreling with him, and I knew that I would have to defend myself should he bring up the subject. Instead, I was surprised when he said, "Jeremy seems to have taken to you. You should feel honored, since he has never had much use for women."

At my surprised look, he continued hastily, "It is only that he feels most women are empty-headed and too concerned with themselves—it makes him impatient."

"And do you feel the same way, Julian?" I asked.

"I'm beginning to wonder just what I feel," he said, frowning.

I said lightly, "It has occurred to me that perhaps men feel that way because men have never allowed women to be anything other than empty-headed and vain. Perhaps if you gave us an opportunity to be otherwise . . ." My voice trailed into silence at his expression.

I was astonished, then chagrined, when he laughed, his face breaking into a smile of such pure amusement that I was certain he was laughing at me. I could feel a flush of embarrassment spreading over my face, and felt even more uncomfortable when he noticed and laughed again.

"I see you have been talking to Aunt Arminta," he managed to say through another burst of laughter.

"On the contrary," I replied with what little dignity I could muster, "the thought was entirely my own. And I don't understand what you are laughing about."

"Never mind, it's not important. But I will say you continually surprise me, Larissa." Then he said a strange thing that I remembered long after for the surge of hope I felt when he said it: "Perhaps it's not too late, after all."

I was exhausted when at last the ball was over. Nervous excitement combined with the effort of meeting so many people left me tired and drained, especially when I learned that Mrs. Harmon's diligent efforts at house cleaning were to be wasted; many of the guests who had been invited to stay the night elected either to return to their own homes or to stay with other friends. As they all made their weak excuses, I watched Julian's face carefully to see if he was offended at their attitude, but if he was, he gave no sign of it beyond a tightening of his lips. Mrs. St. John stood silently by the door, her face strained and aloof with the effort of assuring everyone that she understood. For myself, I was angry that the same people who came eagerly to the ball, to drink his champagne and to eat his food, would offer Julian such an insult at the last. I was certain that the reason was the old scandal about Saramary. Oh, nothing was ever said openly about Saramary, but I had managed to catch a few whispered remarks that were not meant for my ears—and I knew some of these people would return home full of malicious gossip; I could see it on their faces. It was all I could do to accept their congratulations serenely.

There were a few exceptions, of course, true friends whose praise and good wishes were genuine. One such couple was Lord and Lady Ashton, who stopped for a moment with Julian and me while their carriage was brought around. They extended an invitation to dine with them in the near future, which I accepted immediately, not giving Julian an opportunity to refuse.

Rose Streitten came reluctantly before us to offer

her thanks. Julian smiled at her, while I gave her the barest of polite nods; I was too tired to wonder about the mute appeal in her eyes as she looked at Julian.

At last all the guests had gone. Julian disappeared in the direction of the library with Jeremy and I went upstairs to my room. Ellie was loyally waiting for me, curled up in a chair, fast asleep. I wakened her gently and told her I would manage by myself; it was very late. She went sleepily, hiding a yawn behind her hand.

As I undressed, I thought about the people I had met tonight. I wondered why some people seemed to revel in the disasters involving someone else; some of the men and women tonight, I knew, had come for the sole purpose of watching the Synclair family closely for any sign that something was amiss. I could only hope that we had not given them additional food for malicious gossip, and wished futilely that Rose Streitten had not come to the ball.

I yawned and got into bed, but once the lamp was out, I couldn't sleep, tired as I was. Rose Streitten's face came before me and I could see how beautiful she was. I wondered why Julian had not married her—Arminta had said that she was eligible and, more to the point, it seemed, had a great deal of money to her name. She obviously had some feeling for Julian from the way she immediately sought him out, but I could not decide how he felt about her. It was strange that her name had not been mentioned between us; I should have thought that if Julian were in love with her he would have been furious at me for my treatment of her. I decided not to dwell on that; I must remember that for whatever reason, Julian had married me. I remembered that Julian had seemed less aloof toward me tonight; perhaps that was a beginning, small as it was. With this comforting thought, I turned over and went to sleep.

CHAPTER SEVEN

I was awakened some time later by a murmur of voices in the next room. The house was silent, so I knew it must be on toward morning. Sleepily, I wondered who would still be up at this hour; then I realized that the voices were coming from Julian's room. Jerked out of sleep as I was, I did not stop to think that the conversation in the next room had nothing to do with me; I could only think that something had happened to Julian. I fumbled at the foot of the bed for my dressing gown and, pulling it around me, went to the connecting door.

The door was slightly ajar, which was why I could hear the voices so clearly. I heard Julian say something, then the deep tones of Jeremy Bluntridge came through. Sighing in relief, I was about to turn away when my name caught my attention. Feeling like the eavesdropper I was, I put my ear closer to the door and listened; I would feel like a complete fool if Julian caught me, but their low conversation aroused my curiosity. I listened unashamedly.

Julian was speaking. I caught the end of the sentence: ". . . must be some way to find out. That idiot Edward is well on his way to charming her, and he doesn't do anything without a good reason. I tell you, I don't like it."

"I don't either, Julian," Jeremy answered, "but I tried to find out what I could before coming here. As you know—"

Julian interrupted, "Yes, yes. But Edward seems to know something about it. Why else would he be so attentive? You might try the Ashtons—they seemed to feel they knew Larissa from somewhere. We must be sure. . . . Now about the other thing. I want to make certain that the business of Saramary is closed once and for all. I refuse to live under the shadow any longer. I'm sure you noticed some of Mother's so-called friends licking their lips tonight—what did they expect? That I would turn into a maniac right in front of their eyes? Tom's death was no help—although I'm sure Larissa isn't telling me everything on that score. You don't think he told her something he shouldn't have, do you?"

"I don't know. It seems likely, and if so, Larissa mustn't realize how much danger she is in. We have to move fast, Julian."

Julian murmured an agreement, then I heard the clink of glass as though a toast were being raised. I crept away from the door, terrified that I should make some noise and Julian would discover that I had been listening.

I got into bed and pulled the covers up to my chin in an effort to stop my sudden shivering. It was unbelievable that Julian and Jeremy could so calmly discuss Tom's death as though it had been at best a minor inconvenience. And what did Edward have to do with anything? How little Julian knew me if he thought that I was being charmed by Edward. The opposite was true; I had the uneasy feeling that there was something basically evil about Edward, and I wanted to stay as far away from him as possible. I remembered Julian saying something about closing the business of Saramary once and for all—did that mean he wanted to contrive some evidence that would put him in the clear? Was that why he needed Jeremy's help? And for that matter, who exactly was Jeremy Bluntridge?

Another chilling thought struck me: Jeremy had said that I must not realize how much danger I was in. Danger from whom? Julian? Jeremy? Throughout the rest of the night, I sat terrified in my bed, certain that I was surrounded by evil on all sides. I did not know whom to trust—if anyone—and the realization struck a chilling note in my heart. Who was telling the truth about Saramary's death? Was I in danger because I wanted to learn the secret of what had happened that tragic day? Was my curiosity about to lead me into the same dangerous course that had ended Saramary's life? I felt there was only one thing to do—I had to know the sequence of events that led up to the day Saramary fell, or was pushed, out of the nursery-floor window. For my own peace of mind, I had to find out for myself. I was becoming obsessed with Saramary's death, and no matter what the cost to me, I had to find out.

Dawn came, sending fingers of light into my room. For some reason, I thought of the nursery. Saramary had thrown herself, or had been deliberately pushed, out of the nursery window. My legs seemed to move of their own volition; I climbed the stairs and found myself going through the nursery-floor door. I hesitated, remembering the rocking horse that had frightened me for some reason the day Mrs. Harmon and I had come here. But I was determined not to go away now that I had come, and, trying to calm my pounding heart, I opened the door and went in.

Everything was as I remembered it: the scuffed tables and chairs, the overflowing bookshelves, and the horrible rocking horse standing in the corner. Trying not to look at the sinister toy, I went to the windows first and looked out. It seemed the purest folly to have the nursery facing the sheer drop of the cliff, especially since the windows weren't barred, and the distance to the pounding surf below made me feel slightly queasy.

I stepped back and looked around the room once more. Everything seemed as it should; but what did I expect? Saramary's ghost to appear before me wailing about the injustice of being accused of suicide? No, I would have to search further if I wanted to find any clues that might have been missed.

There was a cupboard built into the wall beside me. I wandered absently over to it, my mind still taken up with the horrible idea of leaping to one's death down on those sharp and dangerous rocks below. I opened the door, tugging at it, since it was stuck on the hinges, and looked inside. Nothing. Apparently it had been used to fix chocolate for the children, since it had shelves and a small grate; it was empty now, and I moved to close the door again when a spider dropped down in front of my face. It startled me so that I stepped back too hastily and half fell against the overflowing bookcase. Immediately, the haphazardly piled books on one of the shelves fell to the floor with a crash that sounded deafening in the empty room. I froze, certain that the whole household could hear the thunderous noise and would rush up to discover what had caused it. I waited, trying to think of a valid excuse for being here in case I was found, but after a few minutes it became apparent that the heavy baize door to the nursery floor muffled all sound. Of course it would, I reassured myself; the household would not want to be bothered with the noise of children playing, why else would the nursery be so far away from the rest of the house?

I hurriedly bent and started to retrieve the fallen books and then stopped with my hand frozen in midair. There in the space where the books had been was a small door; dazed, I looked first at the little door, then at the books scattered over the floor. I remembered that the shelves had been piled carelessly, as though someone had been in a hurry to replace the books and tried to force them into some semblance of order.

Could it have been Saramary, I wondered with a thrill. Then I dismissed the thought as preposterous. Why should she use this secret compartment in the nursery? It had probably been put there for the children's amusement; children liked to feel that they had some secret place of their own for their little treasures. But there had been no children in this house since Julian and Dorcas and Norman were young. Had this room remained untouched for all that time? I put my hand out and felt around in the small spaces for a means of opening the door. It was flush with the wall, with no protruding knob or pull to open it. I sat back on my heels and studied it, absently tucking a lock of hair into place where it had fallen during my struggle with the cupboard door. My fingers touched a hairpin. Of course! How could I be so stupid, I thought, irritated with myself. I pulled the hairpin from my hair and pushed it into the crack with all my strength, bending it double, and had the satisfaction of hearing a tiny click. The door swung open.

Steeling myself, I put my hand into the dark hole and grimaced when my fingers felt the gritty interior. I was certain that I would be bitten by a spider, or something worse, and was just about to withdraw my hand when my fingers touched something flat, a book. I drew it out excitedly and saw that it appeared to be a journal of some kind.

As I traced the faded gold lettering on the cover, I had the feeling that someone was watching me. Quickly I whirled around and glanced over the room. No one was there. Then why was I certain I felt another presence?

I slipped the journal into my pocket, my feeling of being watched increasing my uneasiness; I was certain that unseen eyes were watching my every movement. The urge to get out of the nursery was overwhelming; it was as though, by staying, I was in danger, but danger from what I couldn't explain. I closed the secret door and hurriedly put the scattered books back into place; even in my hurry, I couldn't leave evidence that someone had been here. I took one last look around the room and my eye fell on the rocking horse. It seemed to stare at me malevolently and I shuddered, wondering why an inanimate object should seem so evil. The glass eyes stared at me, but I knew it was not those eyes I had felt on me a moment ago. I almost ran from the room, pulling the heavy door to the nursery closed behind me, and went downstairs.

It was fortunate that I had left the nursery when I did, for when I reached the second floor, I met Julian. He looked at me, startled, and said, "Good heavens, Larissa. What have you been doing? You're covered with dirt!" He reached up and rubbed at a streak of dirt along my cheek while I fumbled with my handkerchief and an answer to his question. I had been in such a hurry to leave the nursery that I had forgotten I was covered with dust from my explorations. Fortunately, he was too concerned with his own affairs to listen to an explanation, and he continued, "I've been looking for you. It seems that you made such a favorable impression on Lord and Lady Ashton that they have sent an invitation to you to be their houseguest for several days this coming week."

He handed me a heavy sheet of embossed paper upon which the invitation was written.

"Why . . . how nice," I murmured, still shaken that he had found me in such a condition, wandering the halls in a nightdress and wrapper.

"Do you want to go? I should think that it would be a relief to get away from all of us for a few days," Julian replied, looking at me closely.

"Do you want me to go, Julian?"

"I think it would be a nice change for you—after all, you have not been away since we arrived."

"Well, I don't know," I said doubtfully. "If you think I should . . ."

"Good. Then that's settled," Julian said crisply. But before I had time to wonder at the relief in his voice, he went on, "I'll send them an acceptance right now. Their messenger is waiting in the hall."

He turned away before I could say more, or ask him why he should be so anxious to have me away from the house for a few days. I went to my room to wash the grime from my face and hands, my pleasure in staying with the Ashtons dimmed considerably by his attitude of wanting to get rid of me even for such a short time.

The next few days were spent getting ready for my visit with Lord and Lady Ashton. It was decided that Ellie should go with me as my personal maid, and she was so excited at the thought that she could hardly speak. She turned my wardrobe inside out, washing and pressing and folding the clothing I was to take more times than I could count. I could not share her excitement; I was happy to be going on a visit, but I could not get out of my mind the eagerness in Julian's face when he had pressed me to accept the invitation. It seemed that I had been overly optimistic when I had thought that the night of the ball Julian seemed to warm to me. I wondered, and hated myself for it, if the reason he was so anxious to have me gone had anything to do with Rose Streitten. With my hindering presence out of the way, he might feel free to visit her. The thought was galling, but even more so was the thought of the triumph Rose Streitten would feel over such a victory.

It seemed that I had not had any time to myself since the invitation to the Ashton's was extended; I had not forgotten the little book I had found in the nursery, but each night I was too tired to take it out and read it. I tucked it into the bottom of my hand trunk and hoped that there would be time to read it when I was visiting the Ashtons. It seemed that I could not concentrate on anything but my obsessive belief that Julian was involved with Rose Streitten; even the mystery of Saramary had gone out of my mind for the time being. I hated to admit it, but I was jealous. In the several months that Julian and I had been married, he had been courteous to a fault, considerate for my comfort—but he had never once touched me, or indicated that he thought I was in any way desirable. I couldn't get it out of my mind that the reason was Rose Streitten. It was poor consolation that I could point to the fact that Julian had married me—of what use was that when my days and nights were so lonely?

The night before Ellie and I were to leave, I lay awake; tired as I was, I could not sleep. The house was quiet; I knew it was late and I should try to sleep or I would be a poor guest tomorrow when we arrived at the Ashton's, but, obstinately, sleep refused to come. I tossed and turned, fluffing the pillow and then pounding it in exasperation. At last I gave up the effort and got out of bed. The moon was full that night; I could see it shining whitely through the curtains. I thought that perhaps a breath of fresh air would clear my mind and make me sleepy, so I put on my dressing gown and went out onto the balcony, leaving the door open behind me. The sea murmured below me and I could see moonlight shining through the waves as they came rushing in to shore. I rested my arms on the flat stone of the balcony wall and leaned over the edge, fascinated with the play of light on water. It was a beautiful night: one of those rare times when there was no fog to obscure the beach below.

The continual sound of the surf was soothing; I thought dreamily how nice it would be if Julian were here by my side to enjoy it with me. And when strong hands closed on my arms from behind, I thought for a moment that Julian had appeared in answer to my dream. I was about to turn my head to speak to him when something heavy was thrown over my head; the hands tightened their grip. I was jerked out of the dream and into a nightmare reality. Someone was trying to force me over the edge of the balcony! The soothing sound of the waves became crashing, frightening, mingling with my scream of terror as I tried to claw the suffocating blanket away. The hands had a vise-like grip on my arms, pushing me over the edge of the balcony. The thought flashed through my mind that the beach was far, far below me; I struggled desperately to move back from the edge.

Then suddenly I felt the stone of the rail scraping my arms as the hands started to force me over. With the pain brought the realization that I was going to die. I did not think after that, could not think of anything except fighting for my life. I fought against those unrelenting hands, my breath coming in painful gasps from lack of air. My head felt light, my senses clouding over, I knew I was going to faint. I panicked at the thought, twisting away desperately, and flailing out with what little strength I had left. The vise-like grip loosened for a moment; I snatched the advantage and pushed as hard as I could.

I hit something solid, heard a grunt of pain and then the tinkle of glass breaking. Muffled footsteps moved away from me as I clawed the blanket off my face and breathed in great drafts of air. My lungs felt as though they were on fire and my arms were numb. I looked around quickly, but my attacker was gone. Staggering back into my room, I lit the lamp with shaking hands. The tiny flame was comforting after the black darkness of the blanket over my head, and I bent over it as though it were my only security. Suddenly, my legs felt like water, and I sank to the floor in a heap, gasping. My eyes went toward the door and I saw that it was open. The attacker could be outside in the hall looking in at me right now. With a great effort, I pulled myself to my feet and stumbled over to the door. As I shot the bolt, I gave a gasp of relief that I was safe. I leaned against the comforting solidity of the door and tried to think, but terror was uppermost in my mind, and my only thought was that someone had just tried to kill me.

CHAPTER EIGHT

I did not sleep all that night, but sat huddled in a chair by the dying fire, my mind blank with the horror of what had happened on the balcony. My experience took on a nightmarish quality; I was almost convinced that I had been dreaming until I saw the dark bruises already forming on my arms. Desperately, I needed to confide in someone. But who? With the exception of Arminta Rossmore, there was no one in this house I felt I could trust, and I wasn't even certain I could trust her. I was suspicious of everyone, and with good reason, I felt. There was no one to turn to, no one to rely on but myself. I had succeeded in driving away the attacker once—but what if it happened again? I shuddered at the thought and huddled deeper in the chair.

I thought of Julian's eagerness to have me away from the house for a few days. Was it possible that I had misinterpreted the conversation I had overheard between Julian and Jeremy Bluntridge? Could it be that Julian was truly concerned for my safety, that he realized it was dangerous for me here and wanted to protect me? Or could it be that his concern was a pose, so that when something happened to me he could safely say that he had tried to take me away for my own protection? But why was it so dangerous for me here? I wanted to believe in Julian; anything but that I was in danger from whatever plan he had formed with Jeremy. But then I remembered that Jeremy had said they would have to move fast. Against whom? Me? And for what reason? How could I possibly be dangerous to Julian?

But even as I asked myself the last question, I knew the answer. My interest in Saramary's death was the reason. If Julian was responsible for Saramary's death, if there was still some evidence that could point to him as the murderer, and he believed that I knew about it, then that certainly meant he would have to get rid of me.

But I didn't know anything, I thought despairingly. Why would Julian believe I did? And then I thought of Tom. Tom had died—no, I corrected myself: Tom had been murdered—before he could tell me whatever it was he knew. But Julian couldn't be certain of that; if he was guilty, he couldn't take the chance that Tom had died, leaving me in ignorance of his secret.

All right, then, I told myself fiercely; if Julian was truly guilty, why had he tried to throw me over the balcony tonight? He certainly wasn't stupid enough to believe that the authorities wouldn't be suspicious if both his wives had committed suicide by leaping out of windows. If Julian wanted me dead, he obviously would choose a different method than trying to throw me off the balcony, something that would turn suspicion away from him, something that would appear . . . accidental. And two suicides by leaping out of windows certainly wouldn't be accidental, no matter which way one looked at it.

So. My attacker tonight hadn't been Julian. But if it wasn't Julian—who was it? Norman, with whom Saramary had flirted, and whom she had then cast aside in boredom? Mathew, trying to protect Dorcas, who had admitted disliking Saramary so intensely? Jeremy, the unknown, trying to help Julian clear his name? Or Edward, who believed that Peregrine House should be his? Their faces swam before my eyes, and I conceded that it could have been any one of them. Each had a motive, no matter how weak-sounding it was, and I knew instinctively that whoever had tried to kill me on the balcony tonight was responsible for Saramary's—and Tom's—death. And would have been responsible for mine, had not my terror given me the strength to drive him off.

Springing out of the chair, I paced the room, trying to decide what to do. The obvious thing, of course, was to leave the house immediately and never return. At least that way I would be safe. But would I? What would prevent the murderer from coming after me to make certain I would never be able to reveal what I knew about Saramary's death? It would be useless to insist that I knew nothing; whoever it was couldn't take the chance that I was telling the truth.

So, I couldn't go, and I couldn't stay. I sank down into the chair again, facing the terrifying knowledge that whoever was trying to kill me would try again. The next time, and I knew with a dreadful certainty that there would be a next time, he might succeed.

Trying to fight down the unreasoning terror my thoughts invoked, I tried to decide what to do. My only protection, slim as it was, was to discover the real reason Saramary had died. Once I knew why, I should be able to unmask the murderer, and thus protect myself. It was my only hope, and even as I thought about it, I had to admit that my chances for discovering the murderer before he acted again were so frail as to be almost nonexistent.

At six o'clock I heard the servants stirring and knew that Ellie would soon come in to light the fire and bring me hot water. I wanted to be dressed and ready when she came; I didn't feel up to concocting an explanation for the bruises on my arms, which she would be certain to notice. I forced myself out of the chair and bathed hurriedly in the cold water from the pitcher on the dresser. The icy water on my face revived me and I was just buttoning my gown when she came in.

"Mrs. Synclair!" she exclaimed when she saw me.

"Good morning, Ellie," I said calmly, marveling that I could speak at all. "Please bring my chocolate; we don't want to be late."

"Is . . . is something the matter, Mrs. Synclair?" she asked, looking at me anxiously.

I hoped my expression did not betray my nervousness. I turned to her, with what I hoped was surprise. "No. Why do you ask?"

"You look so pale. Aren't you feeling well? Perhaps we shouldn't go."

Her face fell as she thought about not going on the trip she had so looked forward to, and I had to laugh at her downcast expression. "What nonsense. Of course we shall go. But not if you keep standing there with that empty smile on your face. Hurry, Ellie. I want to be ready when the trap is brought around."

She bobbed a quick curtsy and rushed away to fetch the chocolate. I thought that the first hurdle had been overcome. If I could deceive Ellie, who knew me so well, into believing that nothing was wrong, I could deceive the rest of the family also. There would be only one person besides myself who was aware of what happened last night; I was certain that I would be able to discover who it was. After all, someone had tried to murder me; by all rights, I should be at the least hysterical with terror. Instead, here I was, calmly preparing to visit the Ashtons as though nothing had happened. The person responsible need not know that it was taking all my self-control to appear calm; I hoped that my attitude would be sufficient to throw him into confusion and betray himself without thinking.

I left Ellie to make certain that my small trunk was taken downstairs and went down to the dining room. I hoped that the family would be gathered there and that I would be able to pass the next test. I was disappointed; only Edward was there.

"Good morning, Edward," I said coldly. I had still not forgiven him for his outrageous behavior the night of the party.

"Good morning, Larissa," he replied, standing up as I came into the room.

I went to the sideboard and, under cover of pouring myself a cup of coffee, watched him carefully. He did not seem nervous. His hand was steady as he put a cup to his lips, and when he turned to look at me, his gaze was just as steady. Try as I might, I could find no trace of guilt or surprise in his expression. Either he was an excellent actor or he was innocent; I was forced to believe the latter. Disappointed, I looked away.

"I hope you don't find the Ashtons too much of a bore," he said after a short silence.

"What do you mean?"

"Well, after all, they are almost in their dotage. I wonder that they invited you. What could you possibly have in common?"

"Sometimes you can be most unkind, Edward," I informed him icily. "I did enjoy what little I saw of them at the ball, and am looking forward to seeing them again, dotage or not. Now, if you will be kind enough to see if the trap is ready? It's almost time for me to go."

He bowed mockingly and went to the door. "If you find that you want to come home, send a message and I will be most happy to come and fetch you," he said.

"I'm sure that won't be necessary, Edward."

"Well, just remember that I offered."

Ellie was in the hall, waiting for me with my cloak and bonnet. As I put them on, I thought that Edward was a most irritating young man, so cynical and disturbing. I thought rebelliously that even if I was bored to tears at the Ashtons', which I certainly did not expect to be, I would never send a message to him. I would never give him that satisfaction.

The trap was brought around and I waited on the steps while my trunk was secured to the back. Just as the driver was handing me in, Julian appeared from the side of the house. His hair was disheveled, his face ruddy, as though he had been running. He came up to the trap and took my hand in his. I was surprised; Julian rarely volunteered to touch me. I looked at him and was further surprised to see the look of concern in his eyes.

He said, "Lord and Lady Ashton have invited me for dinner one night; I will ride over then. But if you need me before that, just send a message by one of their stable boys. Do you understand?"

I wondered about all this talk of messages; first Edward, now Julian. Was it genuine concern on their part, or something else I didn't understand? Julian bent to kiss my cheek, the affectionate husband who would miss his wife while she was gone for a few days. I looked toward the house and knew the reason for this display; Dorcas and her mother were standing by one of the windows, looking down at us. I waved briefly and Dorcas waved back. I couldn't see her expression and I wondered why everyone seemed so interested in seeing us off. Then I shrugged; perhaps they were as relieved to be rid of me for a few days as I was to be gone from them.

The driver clucked to the horse and we were off down the road that wound away from the house. I looked back once to see Julian still standing on the steps, a worried expression on his handsome face. Suddenly, I wanted to turn back and tell him about what had happened last night. In the light of day, I just couldn't believe that Julian would harm me in any way. But Ellie was chattering brightly, excited to be included, feeling important that she had been chosen to accompany me. Her chatter distracted me, and I forced my thoughts away from Julian and all the mysteries that surrounded Peregrine House.

The road followed the cliff for a few miles; through the trees and bushes along the road, we could see the ocean shining as the sunlight danced through the waves. The air was crisp and clean, and soon I forgot about everything but the pleasure of being driven along on such a beautiful day. The smartly stepping gray mare in front of us seemed to be affected by the beautiful day and our sudden gaiety, for I noticed the driver had his hands full trying to keep her at a steady pace; she wanted to run. I wanted to run too; I wanted to throw off my bonnet and let the breeze whip my hair about my face. It seemed that the oppressiveness the house imposed on me was gone; I was happy as I hadn't been for a long time.

We were passing through a stand of trees when it happened. Ellie was laughingly telling me a story about one of her sisters, when we heard a shot. At first I didn't know what had happened, but suddenly the driver shouted for us to hold on; the mare, who had been fidgety earlier, was now in a panic and the driver was using all his skill to hold her back. At a second shot, she bolted. The trap swayed from side to side as we pounded down the road, which suddenly ran closer and closer to the cliff. Ellie screamed in pure terror and I had to use all my control not to scream too. We were thrown from side to side in the trap, our hands uselessly trying to grab onto the handholds and slipping away as we were thrown to the other side.

The horse was now completely out of control. I saw the driver make an effort to gather up the reins when one of them snapped and came off the bridle. There was no way to guide the horse now; the driver pulled on the remaining rein with all his might, but only succeeded in turning her closer to the cliff. Ellie screamed again and covered her eyes with one hand. I put my arms around her and clung with all my strength. I could see the edge of the cliff close to our right wheel and prayed that somehow the horse would recognize the danger and move away of her own accord. But she was beyond seeing the danger; with Ellie screaming and the driver shouting, she raced blindly on. Wind whistled past my ears and the ground seemed to flash by. I thought surely we would be shaken to pieces, if not dashed down the steep cliff.

I closed my eyes and waited for death; then, as though afraid of what I couldn't see, opened them and saw with horror a tree fallen across the road. If the horse and trap ran into that we should surely all be killed. I screamed to the driver, but he had seen it also and was standing up in the seat. I thought for a moment he was going to jump, but then I realized that he was going to try to leap onto the back of the mare and attempt to guide her that way. I screamed at him not to be a fool, but he shouted back something that I couldn't hear. With fresh terror, I saw him begin to jump as the trap hit a large stone in the road; the driver was thrown off balance and hurled from the trap. I saw his face as we flashed by, the eyes wide with a horrified kind of surprise as he fell, then we were pounding on toward the tree. The crazed mare saw the tree at the last minute; with disbelief I saw that she was going to try to jump over it.

Dimly, I felt Ellie sag in my arms and knew she had fainted; I wished I had too. I saw the mare begin to gather herself. The last thing I heard was the scream of the mare as one of the branches pierced her side; the last thing I remembered was wondering why the useless piece of rein that dangled from her bridle looked as though it had been sliced through. Then blackness descended on me.

Voices. I could hear voices. I wanted to open my eyes, but the effort seemed too much to make. I lay silent, listening. The voices stopped. There was a rustling sound, and I felt a hand on my forehead. I wanted to reach up and push the hand away, my head hurt so; I couldn't move my arms. I tried to speak and heard my voice an unintelligible mumble. The voices began again. I could make out a few words: ". . . quite a shock to her system . . . must be kept quiet. I think she will be all right. . . ."

I wanted to tell the voice that I wouldn't be all right; every bone in my body hurt; I couldn't move. But the effort was too much. I said nothing.

Another voice. In my dreamlike state, I thought it was Julian's. But it couldn't be. What would Julian be doing here on the road? Dimly I remembered now: the accident, the horse bolting and trying to jump the tree in the road. Julian's voice, and not Julian's voice, because he said: ". . . my darling. . . ."

I sank into a dreamless sleep; it was so comforting not to think about what had happened. Sometime I would ask why, but not now; I only wanted to sleep. To forget.

More voices. The light hurt my eyes; I turned my face away from it. The light went away. Was that Julian beside me? No, it couldn't be. Why would Julian be here with me? Julian didn't love me; he loved Rose Streitten. ". . . No, darling. I love you. I love you. I love you. . . ." I was dreaming; I wanted to shake my head, to deny the dream words I was hearing, but again the effort was too much. It was so much easier to lie here and sleep.

The light came again; it pressed on my eyelids, hurting them with its brightness. I murmured irritably. Darkness again. And the voices, insistent now. "Larissa . . . Larissa." Who was Larissa, I wondered. "Larissa, you must wake up. Larissa, do you hear me?" To please the voice, I nodded my head. Perhaps the real Larissa would come in and tell them who she was; then they would go away.

"Larissa!"

I opened my eyes; Julian was standing over me. I

smiled cunningly; he could not fool me with that concerned look, that anxious expression. "Go find Larissa," I murmured, "if you want her so much." I thought myself quite clever; now he would leave to find that girl and I would be alone in my blessed silence. I closed my eyes and opened them again, expecting to find him gone. He was still here, turned away from me, talking to someone beside the bed. I heard him, as though from a great distance, ". . . but, Doctor, it's been over a week. Can't you do something? She doesn't even know who she is!" His voice rose in anger. It seemed to echo inside my head: ". . . doesn't even know who she is. . . ." Of course I knew, I thought tiredly. I'm . . . I'm . . . But the effort was more than I could handle. I went to sleep again.

Another voice. A strong voice, no nonsense. "Larissa, do you hear me? Answer me!"

I opened my eyes. A woman sitting beside the bed; for I knew I was in a bed now, a soft comfortable bed that I never wanted to leave.

"Go away," I said.

"Larissa, you must get hold of yourself," the woman said. "Do you remember me? Look at me!" Commandingly.

I struggled to concentrate. Where was I? What had happened? The accident, I thought. Where was Ellie?

Silence. I opened my eyes and looked at her. I remembered her: Arminta Rossmore. I tried to sit up. She pushed me gently back into the pillows. Through a heavy haze of pain, I asked again, "Where is Ellie?" Everything was becoming clearer to me now.

"First tell me who you are," Arminta said quietly.

"I'm . . . I'm . . ." I stopped in confusion. Why was it so difficult to think? "I'm Larissa . . . Hamilton. No. Larissa Synclair," I answered, feeling ridiculously proud of myself for dredging up the information.

"Quite right," Arminta said with satisfaction. She got up from the chair and started moving away.

"Where are you going?" I cried, frightened that I

would be left alone to fight the blackness that was about to descend upon me.

"I'll be right back," she promised.

She didn't come back; Julian did. I turned my face away from him. I felt so tired; I didn't want to see him.

He took my hands. I had no resistance to pull away from him. Weak tears slid down my cheeks and I didn't have the strength to wipe them away. Julian took out his handkerchief and gently patted my face. "Larissa, I've been so worried. You've been very ill, darling. But you're going to be better now."

Why was he calling me darling? It was too late for that; I was going to get better without him.

I said, "You don't have to pretend, Julian. Tell me about Ellie."

Again that dreadful silence. I didn't want to look at him; I knew what the answer would be. I forced myself to search his face. "She's dead, isn't she, Julian? And the driver? Is he all right?"

"The driver only had a few bruises. As for Ellie . . . I'm sorry, Larissa."

I heard the coldness in my voice, and wondered why I was so sure. I said, "It was no accident, Julian. Do you know that? It was no accident!"

I heard a voice screaming again and again. Could it be mine? Suddenly, people were rushing around me, something was forced between my lips, then a blessed feeling of lethargy came over me. I sank back into sleep.

Julian was beside me when I woke. I looked at him through half-closed eyes. His face appeared haggard; there were purplish shadows under his eyes. I wondered why he felt it necessary to continue the charade of a loving husband. What was the matter with me? Why was I suddenly so cynical toward him? I should be grateful for his concern, I thought. Then I remembered the deliberately cut bridle rein. Of course; he had to appear concerned and worried. No one would suspect a husband of trying to murder his wife if he seemed half out of his mind with worry.

I said quite clearly, "Julian."

He woke from a light sleep instantly. "Larissa? How do you feel?"

He bent over me anxiously. I turned away from him. "I feel weak and tired, Julian. How long have I been here—and where am I?"

"You are at the home of Lord and Lady Ashton, darling. We thought it would be easier to bring you here after the accident, since it was closer. You've been very ill for some time. But now you're going to be all right."

No thanks to you, I thought bitterly. But he proved correct; daily, I felt stronger. I was getting better in spite of myself. I knew now why I had preferred the oblivion of unconsciousness: my mind refused to accept the fact that my husband had tried to kill me. I had tried to fight that awareness and almost succeeded; the doctor informed me later that I had almost died. Poor man; I had to allow his delusion that Julian's love and my own will to live had pulled me through. The truth, I suspected, was more that I refused to follow Saramary by dying according to plan. I had not known I possessed such stubbornness.

When the doctor felt I was strong enough to know, he told me about poor Ellie. She had been sitting on the right side of the trap, closest to the edge of the cliff. When the horse, in a panic, had tried to jump the tree, the trap broke in two, throwing me to the left and Ellie over the cliff. When they had found her, it was too late. I had fallen among the tree branches. A severe blow to the side of my head had caused my partial amnesia; for the rest, I had numerous cuts and bruises, but I was fortunate that it was not more serious.

Poor Ellie; she had been so young, so eager to please. I was grieved over her death, the more so because I knew it had been no accident. Ellie had died when it had been intended that I should. I sent a note of condolence to her family along with a year of her wages and a wreath of flowers, and knew that it was not nearly enough. I was more determined than before to discover who was responsible.

My mind shrank from the final accusation of my husband, but, lying in bed during my convalescence, I had time to think. I remembered the day Ellie and I had set out so gaily for a visit with Lord and Lady Ashton. Julian had come running up to the trap at the last minute. He looked flushed, as though he had been running. Could it be that he had been down to the stables and cut the bridle rein deliberately, knowing that, when he fired the gun, the highly-strung mare would bolt and the driver would have to hold her in more firmly than usual? Had he planned it so that the rein would break with pressure and the driver lose control? Had he placed the tree across the road, hoping that the horse in her panic, out of control, would run straight into it, killing us all? All these questions ran through my head, over and over again, until I thought I would lose my mind.

Julian was by my bedside often; to all appearances, he was the concerned, dedicated husband. But was he? Was it all a plot to deceive everyone? I watched him carefully for any sign that he was disappointed with the failure of his plan, but I could find none. Sometimes I wished I had the courage to confront him with what I knew, but I could not make myself accuse him aloud. I tried to deny the love I felt for him, tried to convince myself that he had tried to murder me, but it was useless. I just couldn't believe that he was responsible. But if he wasn't—who was?

A few days later, the doctor announced that if I felt up to it, I might have a visitor. I nodded, thoroughly bored with my own company, and was pleased when Lady Ashton came in.

"How do you feel, my dear?" she asked as she seated herself in the chair by my bedside.

"Oh, so much better, Lady Ashton. The doctor says I may get out of bed in a few days. I don't want to presume on your hospitality any longer; you have been so kind."

"You mustn't concern yourself with leaving so soon. Why, John and I were horrified when we learned what had happened. After all, you were coming to visit us at our own invitation—we felt responsible."

"Please don't," I assured her earnestly. "It could have happened to anyone." I did not say that I knew it had been no accident.

She smiled and said, "John and I were only too happy to do what we could. But now you must rest. We will have a talk later. I have something to tell you that I think will be most interesting to you."

She rose to go, but I said quickly, "Please don't go. Can't you tell me now? I really am feeling much better."

She looked at me closely, then smiled gaily. "All right. I don't think we can wait much longer either. When John and I discovered it, we couldn't believe it ourselves. I'll be back shortly."

She left the room quickly and I settled back into the pillows wondering what could bring such a look of excitement to her eyes. She returned with Lord Ashton, who was holding something behind his back.

Lord Ashton bowed to me and asked how I was feeling. Manners first, I thought, although I could see that he was just as excited as Lady Ashton was. Then Lord Ashton came toward the bed and I saw that he was holding a picture behind his back. With a great flourish he set it on the chair and turned it around so that I could look at it.

I gasped. The woman in the portrait could have been myself. She had the same reddish hair, the same dark eyes in an oval face. The woman was much prettier than I, but had I been a little older, we could have been taken for sisters.

The woman in the portrait sat composedly on a quilted settee, one small slippered foot set slightly in front of the other, hands folded in her lap. She looked out of the picture with a smile curving her lips, eyes glowing with pleasure. And pinned to the bodice of her gown was the ram's-head brooch that she—and later I—had treasured for so many years. The brooch was lost now, but in its place I had found something infinitely more precious—my mother as a lovely young woman. I could not take my eyes from the portrait.

I looked in silence at Lady Ashton. She had tears in her eyes. "Yes," she said, "you see the resemblance yourself. That was why John and I stared so when we first met you. We couldn't believe it."

I looked again at the portrait. Was my mother ever that beautiful? I remembered her as drawn and thin, a bitter expression around her mouth, her hair prematurely gray. Had the years away from her family ravaged her to such an extent that it was difficult to believe she and this young woman in the portrait were the same? Tears sprang into my own eyes at the thought and I felt a deep pity for my mother, who had become old before her time.

I blinked away the tears and looked at Lord and Lady Ashton. They were standing by the portrait, staring sorrowfully at it as I was. They could not have known how bitterness aged my mother, but I knew they were thinking, as I was, of the lost years when my mother had deliberately cut them out of her life as though they didn't exist.

At last, Lady Ashton looked at me and said, "You know, don't you? The young woman in the portrait is our daughter, Alicia. Your mother." She dabbed at her eyes with a lace handkerchief and continued, "We could not be certain, even after seeing you at the party, but the very next day a young man by the name of Jeremy Bluntridge asked to see us. We pieced together the bits of information we had, and now John and I are convinced that you are our granddaughter."

She bent and embraced me, and then sat by my bedside holding my hand tightly. I was convinced at last. Smiling through my tears, I grasped her hand and held out the other to Lord Ashton. He took it gladly and together we looked at the softly smiling portrait of the woman who had been my mother. I was no longer alone; I had my own family.

We talked for some time. I learned that Lord and Lady Ashton—I must remember to call them my grandparents, but it was too unfamiliar for now—had tried to convince their daughter, my mother, not to marry my father. Lord Ashton knew that he was a spendthrift—this with an apologetic glance at me—and thought my mother would come to grief if she married him. She had been surrounded by luxury all her life, he said, and did not know what privation was. She thought it romantic, he added, shaking his head sorrowfully; nothing would do but that she should marry my father. There had been bitter words; my mother had left, saying she would never return. My grandparents had searched for her, but my mother had disappeared. I learned that my father's name had not been Hamilton, but Riverton, which was why they had never succeeded in their search; my father had taken a different name so that they could not be traced. Lord and Lady Ashton had given up hope that they would ever see their daughter again to ask for her forgiveness; they had worried constantly about her, but as the years passed, and every hope died, they had tried to resign themselves that their daughter was lost to them. Then they had met me at the party and tried to convince themselves that my resemblance to their daughter was coincidental; they couldn't believe that after all these years they had found a link to their daughter.

I took up the story at that point, saying firmly that my father had always been kind and loving to my mother and me. I had been too young to realize fully the disaster that my father had brought upon his family, but I wanted them to know that my mother and he had loved each other until the day he died. I glossed over my father's suicide, and, thankfully, the Ashtons did not press the point. I stressed the fact that my mother had been happy with my father, and I think they believed me.

When I had finished, Lady Ashton said, "You have lifted a great weight from us, my dear. It was our only hope that Alicia would be happy, and you have said that she was. John and I have often had the futile wish that we had simply agreed to Alicia's desire to marry your father, but we thought we were protecting her from something she would be sorry for later. Can you ever forgive us, Larissa?" She looked at me anxiously.

I thought of all the wasted years when we could have been together. Perhaps my mother had had a reason for her bitterness toward her family, but I thought that now she would agree with me when I said, "I have always wondered about my grandparents. My life didn't seem complete somehow. I can't believe that even now we have found each other. Can you accept me as your granddaughter after all this time?"

After they had gone, insisting that I should rest, I basked in the delight of having a family of my own once again. Lord and Lady Ashton. My grandparents. It was too wonderful to believe.

I would have to seek out Jeremy Bluntridge and thank him for the part he had played in bringing us together. Whatever else he was, I had to be grateful to him for that. I was too happy to wonder how he had known enough about me to convince Lord and Lady Ashton that I was their granddaughter.

I tried to ignore the little warning voice inside me that insistently asked about Julian. Was this why Julian had suddenly become so attentive? Lord and Lady Ashton had told me that I was their only grandchild. And Lord Ashton had gone on at length about stocks and investments and land holdings—all things of which I knew little or nothing, though I realized that they involved a great deal of money—until Lady Ashton had insisted that there would be time later on to talk of such things. But Julian knew; he knew that Lord and Lady Ashton were wealthy. Perhaps now Julian wanted to make up for lost time, to convince me of his love now that he knew I would have money behind my name. Anger boiled up in me the longer I thought about it. Well, Julian Synclair, it's too late for sudden declarations of love, I thought. Julian would soon discover that I was not one of those empty-headed women he and Jeremy talked about. I would learn to be as cold-hearted as he was, and as calculating. Two can play that game, I told myself angrily, and furiously dashed away the treacherous tears that told me I was only fooling myself.

CHAPTER NINE

Julian knocked on my door after Lord and Lady Ashton had gone. As I gave him permission to enter, I wondered at the calm steadiness in my voice and thought with satisfaction that I would soon learn to dissemble as well as my husband. I looked at him from under my lashes as he entered and thought grimly: he knows about my new-found grandparents. Why else would his normally taciturn features be drawn into such a tender, loving expression? For an instant, I had the most unladylike impulse to slap him.

I said demurely, looking down at my folded hands, "Why, Julian. You must be reading my mind. I was going to send for you. I have the most wonderful news!"

He came eagerly to my bedside and grasped my hands. His touch, which only a short time ago would have set me trembling with pleasure, now repulsed me. How dare he think me so simple that I would swoon at the first sign of affection! I put out of my mind the hours he had spent hovering over me while it was unknown whether I would live or die; that concern was hypocritical, I knew now. If he had been truly concerned, it had been for the loss of the substantial amount of money he would lose if I died before Lord and Lady Ashton had identified me as their granddaughter. How chagrined he must have been to find that his plan to murder me had almost succeeded; had he known that I was truly an heiress, he would rather have wrapped me in cotton to insure that nothing would happen to me—and the money I suddenly represented.

His voice startled me; I had been so preoccupied with these thoughts I had almost forgotten that he was here. "Yes, darling, I know. It's unbelievable, isn't it? I mean, your finding each other after all these years. How happy you must be!"

He bent and kissed my forehead, and I, who had longed for his kiss, fought down an impulse to rake his smooth, handsome face with my nails.

"Oh yes, Julian. I can scarcely believe it yet. There is so much to talk about, so many years to catch up to. But I'm afraid it will have to wait. I'm going home tomorrow."

"Tomorrow!" He was shocked. "But you can't. The doctor says you won't be able to travel for two weeks at least!"

No more was I going to be the shy, willing, eager-to-please Larissa. I had been through two terrifying experiences and had somehow managed to remain alive through both of them; I had suddenly found that I was not without family support of my own, and most important—I knew this would make me safe from Julian and his plots—I was suddenly, unbelievably, an heiress. And if Julian thought he could easily manipulate me by pretending love and devotion, then he was sadly mistaken!

"Two weeks?" I said, smiling sweetly. "Nonsense. No, I must return to Peregrine House without delay."

"But—"

"Julian, it's not like you to fuss," I said, and had the satisfaction of watching that particular shaft hit home as he winced. I made a great pretense of examining my nails. "Besides, I've been thinking. I think it's time for your mother to move into Dower House. One house can't have two mistresses, as you yourself have said, and I think she would be happier with a home of her own—especially since we will have painters and workmen swarming all over."

"Painters and workmen?" he managed to choke out.

I ignored his amazed, outraged, and horrified expression and yawned delicately behind my hand. "Of course," I said calmly. "Do take that vacant expression off your face, Julian. I intend redoing that hideous red room as soon as I return. What do you think? I thought perhaps yellow and white, but then . . . oh, I don't know yet. But the red definitely must go. What is the matter, Julian? Well, never mind, we can discuss the details later. I find that all this excitement has left me exhausted. It's not every day that I find I am not alone in the world. Imagine! Lord and Lady Ashton my grandparents—what a turn-around for us all!"

"Larissa . . ." Julian began. He looked aghast, as well he might, I thought furiously. What a shock it must be to find that I could be as cruel to him as he had been to me in the past. I had intended the remark I made about not being alone in the world to hit home, and I saw with satisfaction that it had. But my feeling of elation in successfully striking back at Julian for all the hurt he had caused me evaporated when I saw his expression change to one of silent pain. I had succeeded in wounding him at last; why then did I want to throw myself into his arms and beg his forgiveness?

I steeled myself against such a weak display of emotion and closed my eyes instead. Trying to control the tremble in my voice, I said faintly, "If you will excuse me, Julian? Suddenly I feel so tired."

Julian said nothing more; in a moment I heard the door open, then close softly. I was alone with my triumph over him. I had never felt so wretched in my life.

The next day, over the vehement protestations of the doctor and the pleading of Lord and Lady Ashton, I insisted on getting up and dressing. Finally, when my grandmother realized I would not be swayed, she sent her maid to assist me. I was glad of the girl's help; my brief burst of defiance had left me weak and trembling after so long in bed, and I was not certain I could negotiate my way around the room, much less down the stairs and into the carriage.

The maid, Nora, clucked sympathetically as I sat down weakly in front of the dressing table so she could do my hair. "Oh, ma'am," she said, "you look so pale. Perhaps it would be better . . ."

I gave her a ferocious look and she subsided. I knew she was concerned for me, but I did not care for sympathy; I could not afford to weaken now.

I glanced in the mirror and was horrified. A yellow and green bruise was just now fading from the side of my face; there were purplish circles under my eyes, and my cheeks were hollow. My eyes seemed darker than ever, staring bleakly out of a white, gaunt face I could hardly recognize as my own. I looked like a distorted rainbow.

I muttered disgustedly, but Nora, mistaking the sound for distress at the temporary ruin of my face, said quickly, "I am very clever with the hair, madam. If I pull it forward—so—you will not even know the bruise is there. Is that not better?"

I pulled myself together, smiling wryly into the mirror. "Yes, Nora. That is much better. But what do we do about the rest of it? I would look better with a sack over my head for the next few weeks!"

Nora looked horrified, and I realized my little attempt at a joke was lost on her. "No, no, madam," she said earnestly. "A little rice powder, a little rouge, and no one will know."

She bustled around me, dabbing powder and color onto my face, and when she stepped back with a flourish, obviously proud of her handiwork, I was hard-pressed not to laugh hysterically: now I looked like a ghost with red cheeks. Oh, what did it matter, I thought. Julian was lost to me anyway; why should I pretend that it mattered at all how I looked?

* * *

The carriage ride home was a nightmare. Even though Julian had curtly issued instructions to the coachman to avoid every pebble and pothole, and had surrounded me with numerous pillows and blankets for my comfort, I felt as though I was being shaken to pieces. A thunderous pounding at my temples forced me to close my eyes and pray I would not faint. Julian sat silently by my side, and only by reminding myself constantly of his treachery was I able to avoid leaning against him for support. At last, when I was certain that one more jolt would cause me to put aside my pride and beg him to halt the coach, I felt the carriage slow and then stop.

Proudly ignoring Julian's outstretched hand, I forced myself to step out of the carriage unaided. Suddenly the ground began to move under my feet, the house in front of me tilted crazily, and Julian swept me into his arms before I could fall flat on my face. Thus, ignominiously carried, and fighting back tears of helpless anger at my weakness, I returned home.

A far cry, I thought later, from the proud entrance I had planned: sweeping gracefully up the steps, nodding coolly to Harmon as he held the door, and smiling graciously at Dorothea St. John, who was to be overwhelmed at the sudden change in her daughter-in-law.

Settled amid lavender-scented sheets and embroidered pillowcases, I had to smile at the incongruity of my dramatic plans and the humiliating reality of what had actually happened. Well. No matter. I would soon be strong enough to carry through my charade. No one need ever know that I had once longed for Julian's love. It had been a bitter blow to my pride to discover that Julian thought I was so stupid as to believe that the sudden tenderness, the concerned love he had shown during my illness, was genuine, when, before, he could scarcely take the time to look at me. Gone was my schoolgirlish belief that Julian would come to love me for myself. I vowed he would never know I had once cherished the dream of loving him and having that love returned. The ugly emotion of pride had reared its head and I fostered it greedily; it was to be my strength in the empty years to come.

I spent a week in my room, refusing to remain in bed as the doctor had ordered. My only concession to his dire predictions of a serious relapse was the acquisition of a chaise longue which I had brought in and placed before the fire. I rested there in the afternoons, spending the mornings alternately walking about in my room to regain my strength, or standing on the balcony watching the always fascinating sea. I had to force myself that first morning to walk out to the balcony; the memory of those horrifying moments when I had been helpless in the fierce grip of my attacker while he tried to force me over the rail was still too fresh in my mind for me to be completely at ease. But I rationalized that nothing could happen to me in broad daylight, and it was true that the sea air was invigorating. By the end of the week I was feeling more myself and had planned my first encounter with Dorothea St. John.

Mrs. Harmon had come to tell me that she had found several panes of broken glass from the door to the balcony. Did I know how it had happened? I replied haughtily that I had no idea how they came to be broken, and wasn't it fortunate she had had the foresight to have them repaired.

She looked at me in such surprise that I almost relented; after all, she had been kind to me when no one else had. But her goggle-eyed expression indicated, more than words, her shock at finding such a change in me, and I was surprised myself to find I could play the lady of the manor so easily. Of course, I could have told her, it was not difficult to adopt a cold-hearted manner when one realized that the alternative was exposure as a fool. She curtsied hesitantly and went out, shaking her head in puzzlement. I knew it would be reported below-stairs that the young Mrs. Synclair, who had always been so meek and shy, had suddenly, inexplicably, become hard and unfeeling. I thought it just as well; there would be less conjecture after the battle with my mother-in-law, and the servants could nod knowingly and assure each other that they had known all along that I was just like the rest. It would make things so much easier.

I emerged from my room at the end of the week. The house was curiously silent, as though it sensed something unpleasant was about to happen. And it was. I had told Mrs. Harmon to inform Mrs. St. John that I would like to talk to her at teatime today. Even now I had to smile at the horrified expression on Mrs. Harmon's face when I told her my request. I was sure she thought I had lost my mind; no one would be so bold as to request Dorothea St. John's precious time. But I was, I thought grimly; I might as well get it over with quickly now that I had decided on my course of action.

To my surprise, Julian was waiting for me in the drawing room. I had not seen much of him since our return, making excuses that I was still not feeling well whenever he came to my door. I hadn't wanted to see him until I was fully recovered; it would never do to betray myself through some lingering weakness. But now I was well again. I could face him calmly.

"Julian," I said, admirably erasing the dismay from my voice as I thought how difficult the interview with Mrs. St. John was going to be with Julian present, "are you going to join us for tea? How nice." I sat down in Mrs. St. John's favorite chair, a high winged-back affair that resembled a throne; I knew that was why she preferred it. But today I must contrive to have the upper hand and I hoped this would give me some subtle advantage over her. I tried to ignore the flutter of nervousness I felt at the thought of trying to outwit Julian's mother, but I knew it had to be done; one less enemy in this house would distinctly be to my advantage.

I noticed that Julian was fidgeting, moving around the room, picking up something and examining it as though he had never seen it before, then putting the object down and moving to another. How unlike him, I thought; Julian was usually so controlled.

Abruptly he turned to me and said, "Larissa..." but at that moment the maid came in with the tea and he tightened his lips and waited impatiently for her to leave the room. The maid sensed a tension in the air and, after taking one look at Julian's set face, bobbed such a quick curtsy that she nearly fell and then almost ran from the room.

I busied myself with the tea tray, meanwhile watching Julian covertly as he opened his mouth to speak several times, then closed it again each time as though he was finding it difficult to say what he wanted to say. I had no intention of making it any easier for him; in fact, I found I was enjoying his discomfiture. Let him squirm, I thought nastily; I had done so often enough in *his* presence. Vengeance might be empty, I reflected, but nevertheless it did have its petty satisfactions.

"You were saying?" I inquired innocently, holding out a cup and saucer to him.

He was forced to take it and sat down impatiently across from me. "Larissa, I don't understand—"

"Milk?" I interrupted sweetly.

He shook his head curtly. "Larissa—"

"Sugar?"

He lost his temper. "Damn it, Larissa! I'm trying to say something to you!"

"There is no need to swear," I replied primly. "It's not my fault that I don't know your preferences for tea. After all, we so seldom share this hour."

"Larissa," he said between clenched teeth, "what I have to say is, I think, more important than discussing whether or not I prefer milk or sugar in the confounded tea! Are you prepared to listen to me now?"

I inclined my head graciously, as though unaware of the building fury in him, and set my face into an expression of polite interest that infuriated him all the more. I thought scornfully that it was about time Julian learned that not everyone trembled in fear of him, but I took care that my expression did not betray my thoughts. Actually, it was gratifying to learn that I had the power to move Julian to emotion, any emotion. Rage was perhaps not the pleasantest of emotions to be subjected to, but it was far more satisfying than Julian's former indifference, I thought, as I watched him struggling to regain his composure.

"Now," he said, in a tightly controlled voice, "I don't begin to understand the drastic change in you since . . . since the accident. Even less do I understand your sudden desire to remove Mother from this house, when before you were perfectly content to allow things as they were. But I would like to know what I have done to earn your sudden animosity. You were not like this before. . . ."

He stopped and looked away. I had no sympathy with the anxious look in his eyes, the knowledge of what this effort had cost him in terms of pride; I was far too angry. How dare he play me for the fool! As if he didn't know why I had every reason to hate him! Wasn't it enough that first he had tried to kill me, and when by some miracle I had survived, had done an about-face and pretended suddenly to love me? All my careful plans vanished in the face of a fury I had never known before. I stood up so quickly that I almost upset the tea tray. The delicate china and silver clattered alarmingly on the tray, but I was too enraged to care.

"How dare you ask me that!" I said, my voice shaking with fury. "Do you think me so stupid that I cannot see through your little schemes? Well, you may congratulate yourself on your cleverness, Julian Synclair, but pray do not expect me to sing your praises also. Hate? You flatter yourself that you could arouse such an emotion in me! No, I despise you. Do you hear me? I . . ."

His face had an appalled expression that would have been comical in other circumstances; it was difficult to believe he was acting. He interrupted me quickly. "What are you talking about? What schemes?"

"Oh, so now that I have confronted you with your own duplicity, you have the gall to try to play innocent!" I said scathingly. "Well, it's too late for that, Julian."

"Larissa, I demand to know what you are talking about."

"All right!" I cried, my fury betraying me, making me say things I had resolved to keep to myself. "Let me refresh your memory! Don't tell me that you have forgotten poor Tom—Tom, who was murdered because he dared try to tell me something about your precious Saramary! What have you done about that, Julian? Have you conveniently put his death out of your mind—have you succeeded in convincing yourself, as you have convinced everyone else, that his death was an accident? Well, let me tell you, Julian, that I haven't forgotten! I know what I saw that night —and what I saw was a murder! You can't—"

Julian's face was white, his lips a tight line when he said, "Larissa! Do you want the whole house to hear?"

But I didn't care if the whole house heard me or not. I was beyond caring about anything except flinging my accusations into his face. I rushed on, heedless of the consequences. "Fine," I said scathingly, "I will leave the subject of Tom for one that is closer to me. Have you forgotten so quickly the night on the balcony when you tried to force me over the edge? Yes, I can see you have difficulty remembering. Perhaps because you failed so dismally to be rid of me as easily as you rid yourself of Tom. No ones likes to be reminded of his failures, least of all Julian Synclair, so you moved on to your next plan: causing the accident with the trap. But again you were unsuccessful. Much to your chagrin, I imagine, I survived again. But of course you quickly learned that was to your advantage, did you not? Suddenly, I became the granddaughter of Lord and Lady Ashton and, as such, in line for an inheritance. How pleased you must have been with yourself. You had the opportunity to turn your failures into a success and immediately set about trying to prove you loved me after all. Did you really think I would be such a fool as to believe this sudden reversal in our relationship?"

I stopped for breath, noticing for the first time the stricken look on his face as he stood appalled at my outburst. His expression goaded my fury; to my immediate horror, I slapped him as hard as I could.

I stepped back, aghast. Julian's face was white; the only color the crimson imprint of my hand on his cheek. The sudden silence was absolute; I found I had nothing more to say.

Julian did not move for a moment. Then he said quietly, "I'm sorry you believe such things of me, Larissa. It seems we have nothing further to say to each other." He bowed with meticulous politeness and left the room without looking back.

I stood frozen in the same position I had taken when I stepped back from him. Dear God, I thought: what have I done?

CHAPTER TEN

For a few days after that appalling scene with Julian I was numb. I spent much of my time walking on the beach, Berus by my side, trying to decide what I should do. A hard knot of despair inside me said that I had lost Julian forever. That thought, which had meant so little to me during the days of my convalescence when I had been so furious with him, now caused an almost unbearable pain. And added to that was the constant pounding doubt that if Julian was innocent of all I had accused him of, why hadn't he denied it? Why, *why*? How could I possibly love someone who had tried to kill me? I asked myself that question a thousand times, and each time I answered, ignoring the evidence before me, speaking only from my heart: I loved him, no matter what he had done. I loved him, and I had driven him away by exactly the same cruelty I had deplored in him. It was bittery ironic, and exactly what I deserved for my lack of faith in him.

I was walking on the beach, making myself thoroughly miserable by these thoughts, when I saw Edward walking toward me. Berus was off somewhere on a chase of his own, and so lonely was I for companionship that I even welcomed Edward's company.

"Hello, Larissa," he said as he came up to me. "It's a beautiful day, isn't it?"

I was about to reply sourly that indeed it was not, but then he looked down at me and smiled engagingly. His eyes crinkled at the corners as he squinted in the strong morning light, and for a moment I was caught off guard. Edward could make himself very agreeable when he chose, and his smile seemed to soften the tension in me for some reason. I smiled slightly in return.

"Why are you walking on the beach by yourself?" he asked. "Is Julian so concerned with affairs of his own that he can't be bothered to accompany his wife?"

"I have no idea what Julian is doing," I replied stiffly, wishing Edward had not mentioned my husband.

To my surprise, Edward linked his arm through mine. I looked up at him and he smiled again. "Will you accept me as your escort for today? I fear Mama and I must leave soon, so I won't have the opportunity to be much longer in your delightful company."

"When are you leaving?" The question slipped out before I realized how it would sound.

He laughed. "Are you so anxious to have us gone?"

I flushed, embarrassed that he should be able to read my thoughts so easily. "Of course not," I lied. I didn't mean that at all."

"Good. I realize that I've been appallingly rude to everyone on occasion, but I just can't seem to help myself. Julian and I have never got on, as you might have guessed. I just can't seem to please him."

His little-boy-misunderstood attitude irritated me. I

said shortly, "Why do you have to please Julian? Do you not have a life of your own?"

He pretended not to notice my sharpness, but said smoothly, "Of course. It's just that Julian and I are much the same age—in fact, almost exactly the same age. We grew up together, in a manner of speaking, since Mama and I were so often at Peregrine House when I was young. From the time I was a little boy, I have always looked upon Julian as a sort of brother. Unfortunately, Julian does not view the situation in the same light." He sighed, and again I felt that flash of irritation; one never knew when talking to Edward whether he was dissembling or not. It was difficult for me to sympathize with him.

Edward's relationship with Julian was none of my affair, but it was pleasant to address myself to someone else's problems with Julian for a change, so I asked casually, "And why is that?"

Edward looked surprised at the question. "Why?" he repeated. He seemed to consider for a moment, then said, "I suppose it is because Julian really doesn't feel secure in his position here. He never has, even when we were boys together."

"What do you mean?" I could feel myself becoming angry with Edward again; I always hated it when he spoke in innuendo, especially where Julian was concerned.

"Oh, I'm sure you've heard the rumor about Julian's illegitimacy," Edward said offhandedly. "I've never thought much about it myself, but it seemed to make such a difference to Julian."

Oh, but it does make a difference to you, Edward, I thought savagely, with a flash of insight; that's why you feel Peregrine House should be yours, instead of belonging to Julian.

So strong was my feeling of sudden revulsion for this man walking beside me that I almost snatched my arm away from him. But some instinct saved me from that gesture; I didn't want Edward to know of my suspicions just yet. I would need more time to clarify my feelings in my mind before I said anything, and until that time I would pretend a friendship that I didn't feel, but that was necessary in dealing with Edward, who was so calculating himself.

"Yes, I've heard that rumor," I said calmly. "Personally, I despise gossips who have nothing better to do than to perpetrate such vicious lies. Don't you?" I looked up at him guilelessly, and he was forced to agree.

"Yes, I suppose so." Edward shrugged. "Although it's unfortunate that the gossips do find something of the truth in what they say. For example, it wasn't gossip that Julian's . . . father . . . hanged himself because he couldn't face the reason for that particular rumor."

"I won't—" I began furiously.

"Won't believe it?" Edward finished for me. "As you like. But don't forget Saramary. I'm sure that she found out something about Julian's father and confronted him with it. After all, she was going to have his child; she had a right to know the truth."

"The truth?" I repeated stupidly.

Edward shrugged again. "Was Julian's father mad, as they say? Or was it something else that caused him to take his own life? We'll never know, I guess. Julian certainly won't say. Will he?"

It was his turn to look guilelessly at me, and I was forced to admit I didn't know. But secretly, I still held on to my belief that Julian had been the innocent victim. Even after all that had happened to me, I could not believe such terrible things of him.

We were still standing there, Edward composed and unruffled as he looked toward the sea, I staring fixedly at the sand beneath my feet as though the answer to Julian's guilt or innocence were written there, when Julian himself came riding down the beach toward us. Instantly, my thoughts were diverted, and I had the suspicion that he had been with Rose Streitten. I had taken care to discover that she lived in the direction from which he was riding; and for an instant, I was furious that he should be coming from a visit with her. Then I realized that I had absolutely no reason to be jealous; I had assured by my own actions that Julian had no reason to consider my feelings about anything. Edward and I waited for him to ride up to us, and I tried to arrange my features into a modicum of composure while my jealousy raged inside me.

Julian reined in his horse as he reached us, and I could see that he was furious that Edward and I should be together. I remembered a fragment of conversation that I had overheard between him and Jeremy to the effect that Edward had succeeded in charming me, and I knew this was the reason he was angry. He looked witheringly at Edward, who had the audacity to bow politely and ask if he was having a nice ride.

"Not that it's any of your concern," Julian said curtly, "but I have been on estate business. I do not have time to idle away the days as you do, Edward."

I felt Edward stiffen by my side, but he said lazily, "Oh, forgive me, Julian. I thought that since Rose Streitten lives farther on down the beach, you might have been visiting her. I understand that she has been asking your advice on certain matters. . . ."

"Edward!" Julian shouted. "Some day you'll go too far!" He was beside himself with rage at the implication of Edward's remark. I was shocked myself that Edward could be so blatant in front of me, but even more alarmed when Julian threw himself out of the saddle and advanced toward Edward. "I've had enough of your insinuations, Edward," he said threateningly. "You will apologize to Larissa for your unfortunate remark."

He waited, slapping his riding crop against his leg as though he would not hesitate to use it if Edward did not comply immediately. I could see by the way that Edward backed away slightly from him that he had no desire to engage in a battle with Julian. He turned to me and said quietly, "Forgive me, Larissa. I did not mean to imply anything indecorous. Julian has the most unfortunate habit of turning an innocent remark into a slight against him. Forgive me if I have precipitated an unpleasant scene." He turned and walked quickly back toward the house, leaving Julian and me alone on the beach.

Abruptly, Julian swung up onto his horse. He looked down at me angrily and said, "I would prefer it if you did not seek Edward's company, Larissa."

I did not care for the contemptuous look on his face; I answered immediately, "I don't know why not, Julian. It seems harmless enough for me to talk to Edward when you are likewise engaged with Rose Streitten." And I turned away also, leaving Julian sitting on his horse as though he were going to explode with rage. I turned back in a moment, though, and asked him, "Will you arrange for the workmen to come this week? I am anxious to begin redecorating the red room as soon as possible."

He bowed jeeringly from the saddle. "As you wish, Mrs. Sinclair," he said so sarcastically that I almost winced. But my pride was just as strong as his, I had found, and I was able to look at him calmly and say, "Thank you, Julian. Would you care to help me select the colors? After all, I would not like to do anything without your express consent."

The barb hit home; his face turned crimson with the effort to control his anger. He replied curtly, "I'm sure you are able to decide such things on your own. And if not, perhaps Mother would be happy to advise you. That is, before she moves to Dower House."

I tried to conceal my surprise. "Oh, have you consulted her about moving?" I asked stupidly.

"Yes. To my surprise and your gratification, she has agreed to move within the month. Perhaps you two can share workmen, as she will be redecorating also. Is there anything further I can do?" he added mockingly.

I shook my head, as unable to believe that Dorothea St. John had actually consented to move away from Peregrine House as that Julian had actually asked her to do so. For an instant, I wanted to cry out that she could stay, that he could do anything he wanted to, but that please, could we stop this constant battle. But of course, I did no such thing; my pride would not allow me to beg Julian for a reconciliation.

Julian spurred his horse with unnecessary violence and galloped off down the beach. I sank foolishly onto the sand and burst into tears.

After the encounter on the beach with Julian, I threw myself into redecorating my room. I was determined to show Julian and his mother that I could do something properly, and forced myself to concentrate, terrified that I would make a mistake and ruin the whole thing. But, slowly, the room was transformed. All the ugly red velvet draperies came down; the heavy furniture was removed, and the crimson carpet taken up. They were replaced by a green and white flocked wallpaper, cream-colored draperies, and a deep green carpet that was so thick I felt as though I sank at least two inches into its luxuriousness whenever I walked upon it. The dark furniture gave way to a lighter oak, which was rubbed and polished to a satiny glow by two of the housemaids. When it was finally finished, I looked at it with satisfaction, and thought that, no matter how dreary the day, my apartment would always be light and cheerful. I don't know why redoing the room was so important to me; perhaps I felt that at least in here I was removed from the oppressiveness of the rest of the house. And also, I had to admit, I had proved to myself that I could do something with talent; the room *was* beautiful. Even Dorcas exclaimed when she saw it, and Mrs. St. John admitted sourly that it was better than she expected.

The subject of her moving from the house was not mentioned between us; as the time approached, I began to feel that I had been unjust in insisting that she be the one to leave. It was obvious to everyone, I thought, that she had more right to live here than I did, but I was determined not to give way. I had set out on a course to prove my independence, and no matter how foolish I felt now, my pride would not allow me to change it.

Strangely, Norman and Dorcas were silent on the subject also, although when the moving day finally arrived, Dorcas embraced her mother on the steps, surrounded by piles of boxes and trunks, and tearfully assured her mother that she would come to visit her every day.

Mrs. St. John was assisted into the carriage by Julian, and as the coachman raised his whip to the horses, she looked at me and said, "If you have difficulties in your new position, and I am certain that you will, you have only to ask Mrs. Harmon. I have trained her thoroughly; she has promised to do her best for you. I don't care to have the household suffer through your inexperience."

I could feel my face flame at this none-too-subtle rebuke, but I nodded silently, knowing that everyone was waiting to hear what my answer would be, and determined not to give anyone the satisfaction of seeing me quail before that cold blue-eyed stare. She looked at me a moment longer, while I lifted my chin defiantly and looked back into her eyes. Finally, she gave the coachman the signal to leave and the carriage leaped forward. I saw her looking back at me with a satisfied smile on her lips and wondered who had really won our silent battle. I knew she expected me to fail miserably, and I was just as determined not to give her the satisfaction of knowing she had been right.

When the carriage had gone around the turn in the road and was out of sight, Dorcas gave me a fierce look before bursting into tears again, and the always silent Mathew put an arm around her shoulders and led her away into the house. Norman, who had been on hand to see his mother off, slouched away toward the stables and Edward, who had been lurking by the doorway, came over to me and whispered. "Well done, Larissa. I never thought you would be successful in removing the old dragon to another lair. With her out of your hair, things should be easier for you, don't you think?"

Feeling close to tears myself, and not certain of the reason why, I snapped, "Oh, do be quiet, Edward!" before gathering up my skirts and running into the house.

With Mrs. St. John gone, I found that my responsibilities in managing the household were frightening. But again my pride came to the rescue, and after numerous consultations with Mrs. Harmon, who soon proved to be invaluable, I was at last able to handle the never-ending details, if not with ease, then with some degree of competency. I went over the house from top to bottom again, spent time with Cook in the kitchen discussing meals, and supervised the servants in their various tasks. Finally, Mrs. Harmon came to me one day and said hesitantly, "Mrs. Synclair, I don't mean to be presumptuous, but if you keep on like this, you'll be exhausted. If you'll just tell me every morning what you want done, I can manage well enough, I think."

After that, things were easier, and I had some time to myself. Mrs. Harmon came to me every morning and together we discussed what should be done that day. I found to my surprise that I could manage the household just as well as Mrs. St. John, and although I knew I could not have done without Mrs. Harmon, presently I was able to feel that I did not need to lean so heavily upon her for assistance. Soon I knew that not even Julian could take exception to the way I managed Peregrine House. It was a source of pride to me that everything ran so smoothly, but I should have known that such tranquillity could not last forever.

I was in the sitting room one morning, going over the household accounts and smiling to myself at the panic I used to feel when I opened the ledgers and everything seemed a jumble. Now, after Mrs. Harmon's expert tutelage, I was at least able to make sense out of them, and spent part of every morning adding up columns of figures and trying to decide where it would be best to practice economy and where it would be advisable not to.

We had begun to entertain a little; I had talked to Julian about the advisability of at least keeping up appearances and he had reluctantly agreed, so we had given a small dinner party or two. Lord and Lady Ashton—I still found it difficult to think of them as my grandparents, but they were very dear to me—had come once or twice, and the week before, we had entertained Colonel and Mrs. Huxley, whom I had met at the party, and who, to my secret amusement, were horrified to learn that Julian had not given me a horse immediately so that I could join the hunt. In point of fact, the thought had not occurred to me; I kept well away from the stables because I had never learned to ride properly. But I could see that my lack of riding ability was a detriment in the country; some day I would have to speak to Julian about it.

I was learning to be a gracious hostess, and was pleased at the compliments I had received after our little dinners. Arminta had told me more than once how happy she was to find that I was able to manage so well. She and Edward showed no sign of leaving, and I was glad Arminta, at least, chose to extend her visit. Julian, I knew, was impatient to be rid of Edward, but I enjoyed Arminta's company and found that she was able to give me some excellent advice upon occasion. Surprisingly, she made no reference to the obvious icy politeness between Julian and myself, and I was grateful that she had chosen to abandon her usual scathing honesty in our case. Sometimes I felt that I was walking a tightrope of nerves; had she made any comment about our strained relationship, I was certain I would give way completely to my utter misery, and such lack of control was to be avoided at all costs.

At any rate, I was just going over the menu for the week when Norman burst in on me unannounced. I looked up in surprise; I did not see much of Norman, for he spent most of his time either riding his horses or staying with friends, much to his mother's disapproval, I knew. This morning, however, he seemed distraught, with a wild-eyed look that was totally unlike him. My first thought was that something had happened to Julian, and I said, in alarm, "Norman, what is the matter? Has something happened?"

He nodded and said wildly, "Larissa, I must talk to you. Please!"

"Sit down, Norman," I said as calmly as I could. "Shall I ring for something?"

He shook his head and then covered his face with his hands.

Thoroughly alarmed now, I got up and went over to him. "Norman," I said sharply, "tell me what is wrong!"

He groaned. "Everything. Everything is wrong!" Suddenly, he grabbed both my hands and said urgently, "Larissa, you've got to help me. You must talk to Julian!"

"I can't help you unless you tell me what is the matter. Norman, let go of my hands and stop being so melodramatic!" I was beside myself with fear for Julian now, and it was all I could do not to shake him to make him tell me what had happened.

He gulped and took a breath. Then he said, "You know Rose Streitten? Of course you do—you met her at the party. Well . . ."

I felt a pang of fear; what had Julian done that involved Rose Streitten, I wondered wildly. All sorts of terrible thoughts rushed through my mind: Julian, finally deciding the situation here was more than he could tolerate and running off with her; Julian filing for divorce so that he could marry her . . . I could not go on. I said, more sharply than I intended, "What about her?"

Norman looked at me curiously for a moment, startled out of his own misery at the sudden fear in my voice. He said hastily, "I've been seeing Rose against Julian's wishes for some time now. We . . . I . . .

169

have finally persuaded her to marry me. Oh, Larissa, we love each other, but if Julian finds out, he'll be furious. What am I to do?"

I felt a wild impulse to laugh hysterically. Rose Streitten and Norman St. John. I couldn't believe it. And all this time, I had imagined that Julian and Rose . . . oh no, it was really funny, I thought. But then I looked at Norman's miserable face and sobered immediately. "Why should Julian be furious?" I asked.

"Oh, Larissa, you've got to talk to him! You're the only one he would listen to!"

I had my private doubts about how much Julian would be willing to listen to me, but I ignored that and replied instead, reasonably, "I'll be happy to talk to him, Norman. But I don't think I will make much sense unless you tell me why he should be so furious to find that you and Miss Streitten are in love."

Norman hesitated. Then he said, "It's a long story, but I suppose you should know. When Julian's father died, Gerald Streitten was vocal in denouncing him: I don't know the reason why—it really doesn't matter any more, anyway, I suppose. But Julian felt his father's name had been unjustly smeared—he was devoted to his father at one time, Larissa—and he resolved never to have anything to do with the Streitten family again. He only consented to allow Rose to attend the ball because I practically went down on my knees and begged him. I thought if Rose could talk to Julian at the party, she could smooth the way for me when I told him I was going to marry her." He stopped and put his head into his hands again.

I was beginning to make some sense out of the confused jumble of Norman's story. I said gently, "And did you tell Julian of your intentions?"

"Good God, no!" Norman exclaimed, taking his hands from his face in horror. "That's what the problem is—why you must talk to Julian! It was the most appalling piece of bad luck that Julian saw Rose with me today at the beach. It was innocent, I tell you! Rose isn't . . . that is, all I did was kiss her, but then Julian came storming up the beach like the wrath of God and ordered me home when he saw us. He's on his way here now and so furious that I know he won't listen to reason. He never has thought much of me—and maybe I haven't given him reason to think otherwise—but I swear to you, Larissa, nothing happened between Rose and me. And if I can't marry her, I don't know what I'll do!"

He paused dramatically. I knew the anguish he was feeling was real, but I thought he had overestimated the fury of Julian's reaction. After all, the quarrel with the Streitten family had happened so long ago; why should it possibly matter now?

Eventually I calmed Norman by promising him I would talk to Julian. He was just about to leave the room when the front door slammed and we both knew Julian was home. Norman turned white and almost ran out of the room, and I was left to face Julian as he came storming into the sitting room looking like the devil incarnate.

He looked around the room, and then fiercely at me, as though certain I was hiding Norman behind my skirts, and asked curtly, "Where is he? Have you seen him?"

I nodded, but before he had a chance to say anything further, I went to the bell rope and, when the maid came in, ordered whiskey. "Julian," I said calmly, "please sit down. I want to talk to you."

"I haven't the time. I must find Norman."

"There will be time enough to talk to Norman later, Julian. Please."

He threw himself into a chair and scowled furiously down at the floor. When the maid brought a decanter and glass, I poured a generous measure and handed it to him. He took a drink, then demanded, "Well, what is so important that you have to talk to me right now?"

I held on to my temper; I always hated it when Julian reminded me that I had no place in his life, no claim on his time, even if it was true. "I wanted to talk to you about Norman," I said quietly.

"What about him? Has he already been here, whinning that he is not responsible for his outrageous behavior today? It's time he learned to face up to his actions. If you know where he is, you would be well advised to tell me immediately."

"Julian, I don't care for that tone of voice," I said, trying in vain to keep my temper. "Yes, Norman was here. He told me the incident was completely innocent."

Julian snorted derisively, but I continued as though I hadn't heard. "I believe him, Julian. He wants to marry her."

"What!" he shouted. "How dare he think I would ever sanction such a thing! He must be out of his mind! And you too, for taking his side over something you know nothing about. I suppose he forgot to tell you that the two families aren't on speaking terms, much less about to consider a marriage between us? No, it's impossible. I won't have it!"

"But, Julian, wouldn't it be better to patch up the quarrel between the Streittens and the Synclairs? After all, it happened so long ago. Suppose Norman and Rose decided to elope? Would you want the same thing to happen to them as happened to my own mother and father? My mother died without ever reconciling herself with her family. Imagine all the pain and anguish everyone involved suffered in consequence. Would you want to be responsible for that?"

"It's not the same situation," he snapped.

"Why not?"

"I don't know why I should bother to tell you all this, since it doesn't concern you, but Gerald Streitten was responsible for inventing numerous slanders about my father. I've resolved never to have anything to do with that man again. And that is final!"

"But, Julian, it happened so long ago. . . ."

"I refuse to discuss it further. Norman is living under my roof, enjoying his life at my expense, and while he does so, he will do as I say. And I say that he will not marry Rose Streitten!"

The tiny doubt I had about Julian and Rose Streitten suddenly blossomed into such an ugly suspicion that I uttered it without thinking. I cried, "I think the real reason you don't want Norman to marry her is that you wish you had her to yourself. My rival, as Edward has so unfortunately put it!"

Julian slammed the glass of whiskey onto the table so fiercely that the liquid splashed over the side. He towered over me as he stood, so enraged that he couldn't speak for a moment. I stood my ground before his furious expression, knowing I had gone too far, but realizing also that I had voiced my unspoken fear about Rose Streitten and wanted, no matter the cost to me, to know the answer. Our eyes held for a long moment, and I clenched my teeth together to stop my lips from shaking. At last he said, "I will not dignify that ridiculous statement with an explanation. You don't deserve one."

I heard his boots ringing on the floor of the gallery as he made his way toward the stairs, and in a few minutes, I heard one of the upstairs doors slam. He had gone to Norman's room, and God only knew what would happen now. I sank down in my chair and put my head in my hands. What was it about Julian and me that we always spoke the very words that were destined to drive us further and further apart?

Dinner that night was a tense affair. Norman, to his credit, was present, but sat in his chair with a white face, refusing everything set before him. Dorcas, too, was aware of the quarrel between Julian and Norman, and was subdued, confining herself to a few murderous glances in Julian's direction, which he ignored. Mathew made a few innocuous remarks from time to time, but subsided after Julian remarked cuttingly on the chatter at the table. I was silent also, watching Julian throughout the meal, wishing there were something I could say to relieve the tension. It was a relief when dessert had been served and we were free to go.

Everyone left the table except Julian, and I paused

by the door to look back at him. He was staring blackly at his wineglass, which had been refilled too often this evening, and suddenly I wanted to go to him and tell him how foolish I had been. I made a move to rejoin him, but he looked at me with narrowed eyes and said, "If you have any intention of bringing up the subject of Norman's foolishness, I have nothing to say to you. I think you have interfered sufficiently, don't you, Larissa?"

There was nothing I could do but leave the room. Norman met me in the hall; I shook my head and he turned away angrily. A few minutes later, I heard the front door slam and knew he had gone to drown his sorrows somewhere in the village. I only wished I had a similar means available to do the same.

I went upstairs to write a note to Jeremy Bluntridge, who had gone back to London while I had been so ill. I had finally prized his address from Julian, telling him merely that I wished to thank him for his part in reuniting me with my grandparents. Julian had ungraciously given it to me, but I had not had the time to write before. I sat at the small writing desk and tried to compose a suitable note of thanks, but the words would not come. My thoughts kept returning to the quarrel between Julian and Norman, and my own disastrous part in it, and finally, unable to concentrate, I threw down my pen and got ready for bed.

I was awakened from a restless sleep by a slight noise. I lay in the darkness listening, wondering what it was that woke me. Then I heard a whisper, "Lari . . . ssssa." The syllables of my name were drawn out on a long sigh, and I felt the hair on the back of my neck prickle. "Who's there?" I said sharply, trying to control the sudden tremble in my voice. There was no answer for a few moments, then the whisper came again: "Lari . . . ssa." I strained my eyes looking around the room. For an instant, I could see nothing, but as my eyes became used to the darkness, I saw an object by the side of my bed. It seemed to be moving, and for one terrible moment, I thought the person who had tried to force me over the balcony had returned. I caught my breath sharply, unable to move.

"Larissa . . . I'm going to kill you. . . ." Again the long-drawn-out whisper. My eyes were riveted on the object moving by the side of my bed, and as it came closer, I could see the gleam of pale eyes nodding up and down . . . up and down. . . . The object came closer and closer, and I was helpless to move. I raised my hands to ward off the final blow, and then screamed as something thumped the side of the bed. I screamed again in pure terror, covering my eyes with my hands to shut out the sight of those pale eyes moving back and forth as though they were suspended in the darkness.

Unbelievably, I felt a sudden draft of air from the balcony as the curtains billowed out into the room with the breeze from the ocean, and then the connecting door was thrown open and lamplight shone into the room. I screamed again at Julian's sudden appearance, and heard him shout, "What the devil!"

Someone was pounding on the door; with an angry exclamation, Julian stepped over to it and tore it open. I took my hands from my face and saw Mrs. Harmon, her nightcap all askew, standing there with a frightened expression on her round face. Behind her were several other servants, staring goggle-eyed into the room. Then Edward, his hair tousled from sleep, came forward and pushed his way in.

"For God's sake!" he exclaimed. "What's happened?"

I forced myself to look toward the foot of the bed, certain that the terrible monster I had half seen in the darkness was still crouching there, and then choked back another scream. The rocking horse from the nursery was rocking gently by the bed, all the more terrifying because it seemed to be rocking with a life of its own. I sobbed again and turned my face away; I could not bear to look at those pale, ghostly eyes any longer.

175

"Who is responsible for this?" Julian thundered, staring fiercely at the crowd in the doorway.

There was a murmur of denial and astonishment, then Julian shouted for someone to remove the rocking horse immediately. I saw Edward step gingerly to where the thing stood and pick it up, carrying it quickly from the room. After it was removed, I was able to draw a shuddering breath and smile shakily at Mrs. Harmon, who was beginning to fuss over me. Julian ordered the servants back to bed, adding ominously that he would talk to them in the morning, and we waited in silence until Mrs. Harmon returned with a cup of hastily made tea, which I accepted gratefully. As she turned to leave, I wanted to call out to her and beg her to stay; I only stopped myself from doing just that by the thought that she would think it strange indeed if I was afraid to be alone with my husband. And, glancing at Julian's furious expression, I had to admit that I was afraid of him, afraid that it had been he who had brought the rocking horse into my room, afraid that he was the one who had frightened me so thoroughly, afraid that he had threatened to . . . But I wouldn't think of that just yet.

Finally, Julian spoke, and when he did, I was startled so badly that I almost spilled the tea. "What happened?" he demanded.

Fighting down hysteria, I told him how I had been awakened by a voice whispering my name. But I could not tell him how those pale eyes, catching what little light was in the room, had seemed to have a life of their own, had seemed evil to me. Now that I was somewhat calmer, I could almost feel ridiculous that such a thing as a toy could inspire such terror in me.

He listened in silence, his jaw tightening in anger as I recited my story. Finally, when I had stopped, he said, "Did you recognize the voice?"

I shook my head. It could have been anyone, I thought desperately. It didn't have to be Julian—for surely I would have recognized his voice, frightened as I was, wouldn't I?

I looked at Julian. Was he relieved that I was unable to identify the owner of the voice? He didn't seem to be relieved; on the contrary, he seemed angrier than before. He paced back and forth across the room while I watched him warily. At last he threw himself into a chair, drumming his fingers impatiently on the arm as he stared into the fire that Mrs. Harmon had stirred up before leaving.

The tea was making me sleepy; I wondered if Mrs. Harmon had put something into it to make me sleep. Finally, unable to fight the drowsiness that was stealing over me, I closed my eyes, my last clear recollection of that horrible experience the sight of Julian, his head in his hands, his whole attitude that of defeat.

Julian was gone when I woke up in the morning. My new maid, Jean, was bustling around the room, building up the fire and bringing me hot water to bathe. She said nothing, but several times I caught her looking at me with a strange expression. Of course, I thought; the news of the night's events would have spread through the servants' hall by now. I should be prepared to endure such looks all day.

I decided it was best to say nothing, to act as though nothing had happened; but I was determined to be on my guard. The rocking horse in my room was not as serious, of course, as the two incidents on the balcony and in the trap, but it was clear that whoever was trying to kill me was still very much interested in doing so. The question was: how was this person so certain that the rocking horse would inspire such terror in me? To my knowledge, no one knew I had taken such an aversion to the toy when I had visited the nursery; I had done so the first week I had arrived. No one knew of my second visit when I had found the diary.

The diary! I had forgotten all about it! Oh, how could I be so stupid? My discovery had completely slipped my mind. Suddenly it seemed very important for me to find it.

I threw back the covers and leaped out of bed. Jean

177

stared at me, astonished. "Jean, when you were unpacking my trunk after I came back from the Ashtons', did you find a little book—a diary—at the bottom of the trunk?"

She shook her head, wide-eyed. "No, madam. There wasn't anything in it but your clothes."

"But there must have been! Jean, I need that little book. Bring me the trunk immediately!"

She went out hastily; I knew that she was wondering what sort of madness possessed the mistress now, but I didn't care. I must find that book!

Harmon knocked on my door a few minutes later, after I had waited in a fever of impatience while he brought the trunk down from the attic. I almost snatched it out of his hands, and, with shaking fingers, opened it. As Jean had said, it was completely empty. I felt around the edges, unable to believe that the book had disappeared. Harmon stared at me as though I had lost my mind before I remembered to dismiss him. He left, shaking his head, but I was too impatient to think about the latest piece of gossip he would be sure to deliver to the servants' hall. Instead, I turned to Jean and demanded, "Did you unpack the trunk when I came home?"

She nodded uneasily. "But there wasn't no book, Mrs. Sinclair. I swear it!"

"Did anyone have access to the trunk before you unpacked it?"

"No, Mrs. Sinclair. Just Harmon when he carried it up to your room."

The poor girl looked ready to burst into tears at any moment. With a great effort at self-control, I said, "Never mind, Jean. I'm sure I will find it later."

She bobbed a quick curtsy and left hurriedly, no doubt eager to be away from a mistress who was almost in tears herself from the loss of a little book.

I was just finishing dressing when Julian knocked discreetly on my door.

"How do you feel this morning, Larissa?" he asked cautiously as he came in.

"Foolish," I replied, with a small attempt at a smile. "I can't think why I became so hysterical at the sight of a toy from the nursery."

We both knew that the rocking horse alone had not caused my terror the night before, but as Julian looked closely at me, I pleaded silently with him not to continue the subject. He opened his mouth to speak, changed his mind, and frowned instead. With a sigh of relief, I turned away. My silence raised the barrier between us that much higher, but I knew that if he spoke further of the incident the night before I would not be able to stop myself from voicing my suspicion of him. And I must not accuse him, I told myself grimly; he mustn't know that I suspected him or I would be in even greater danger than before.

The silence between us lengthened until I felt I would scream from tension, and then, finally, he asked quietly, "Are you certain you are all right?"

I turned back to him, again forcing a smile. "Oh, yes," I replied, with an attempt at lightness. "Thank you for your concern, Julian."

He stiffened. I had irritated him by the deliberately polite note in my voice, but it was too late to call back the words now. I wanted to say something—anything —to erase that familiar distant expression stealing over his face now; I wanted to—what did I want? To rush into his arms, to feel comforted and secure against the hidden dangers that surrounded me, to beg him to stay with me—this I wanted, and more. And then I cursed myself for being a fool; how could I deliberately ignore the evidence before me? How could I possibly feel secure in the arms of a man whom I suspected of trying to kill me?

I raised my head, forcing myself to look steadily into his eyes, fighting back the tears of frustration and helplessness. We stared at each other for a long moment, and then Julian bowed politely and turned to go. I held myself stiffly, willing him to pass through the door and be gone, but he hesitated, turning back to look at me again, and I saw the uncertainty in his eyes. It was that look that was almost my undoing; I knew that if he spoke one more word to me I would not be able to control my headlong flight into his arms. I looked away from him quickly, reminding myself with a fierce effort of will what had happened last night, and without another word, Julian was gone.

The tears I had been trying to hold back flooded down my cheeks as the door closed, and with a shuddering sob I put my face in my hands. It had to be Julian, I told myself hopelessly; but if it was, why had he looked at me that way, as if he wanted to protect me?

I had to remind myself that Julian was an accomplished actor; I had seen him pretend time and time again when he didn't want anyone to know his true feelings; I had seen that distant expression steal over his face to mask his thoughts too many times for me to be fooled now by an attempt at concern on his part. So why did I feel that I had misjudged him? Why did I want to rush after him and beg him to stay with me?

Tears were useless at this point, I told myself; what I should do was force myself to take stock of the situation and try to discover why Julian would try to frighten me with the rocking horse. And it had to be Julian, I reminded myself grimly. It was senseless to ignore the evidence before my eyes; no matter how much I tried, I could not forget the breeze that came in through the balcony door that I had closed before going to bed. And the balcony connected Julian's and my rooms. How simple it was for him to bring the rocking horse, whisper his threat, and then, when I screamed, go back to his room by way of the balcony and come rushing into my room again through the connecting door. The only flaw in his scheme was that I had sensed the breeze from the ocean, had felt it drift across my face, had seen the curtains billow out into the room as the salty air came rushing in.

But why would Julian do such a thing? He had too much at stake to try such a trick, I thought. He had to depend upon the continuing good will of my grandparents to make certain I would eventually come into the inheritance they would be sure to provide. It seemed obvious that he would not risk my grandparents' displeasure; he could reasonably assume that if I thought he was responsible, I would go to them and tell them the whole story.

But if it wasn't Julian, who could it be? Norman had counted on my influence with Julian to allow him to marry Rose Streitten. Had Norman been so angry at my failure that he had tried to frighten me into trying again? It didn't seem possible that Norman, spoiled young man that he was, would try such a senseless trick. No; if it was Norman, he would have had another reason.

And then again, I was caught up in Saramary's death, for I knew that whoever had threatened me last night had also killed Saramary. Just as he—or she—had killed Tom because Tom knew something about her death and might tell me about it. But Tom had died for nothing, and I was about to die for nothing, too, unless I could discover the murderer before it was too late.

CHAPTER ELEVEN

I spent the rest of the day shut in my room. I didn't care what the servants might think; with the sound of that terrifying threat still ringing in my ears, I couldn't force myself to follow my usual routine. I wandered aimlessly about my room, and the new furnishings seemed to mock me. It was useless to pretend that everything would come right in the end; that Julian and I would achieve, if not love, then some kind of friendly rapport; that his family and I would learn to live peacefully with one another. The elaborate fairy-tale ending I had so carefully constructed in my mind during these long weeks now crumbled into the dust of what it was —a fabrication based upon my desire to ignore the numerous warnings and near-fatal disasters that had haunted me since my arrival.

How could I have been so willfully blind, I wondered, and then knew the answer: I was not brave, not the sort of heroine who willingly confronts all adversaries and then beats them at their own game. No, I thought bitterly; I preferred to go about with my hands over my eyes, ignoring the obvious because to confront it would take more courage than I possessed. But now, when the would-be murderer had openly declared his intention to kill me, there was nothing to do but strip away all my pretenses, all my inner reassurances that nothing was really wrong, and somehow dredge up enough courage to face the situation.

I thought briefly of going to my grandparents for help, and then rejected the thought immediately. Whatever danger haunted me, I did not want them to suffer the consequences of any foolish action of mine. I was alone as I had never been, even after my mother's death. And somehow, alone, I would have to bring the murderer out into the open and confront him. For my own peace of mind, for my own confidence in myself, I must.

But how?

My eyes strayed again and again to the connecting door between Julian's and my rooms, and suddenly I found myself standing on the threshold, the doorknob held tightly in my shaking hand. Taking a deep breath, I wrenched open the door and stepped into Julian's room. My heart pounded uncomfortably in my ears as I stood there, afraid to move farther; it was no use telling myself that Julian had gone out—what would I do if he came back and found me here? I would have no excuse to offer except the real reason: that I was searching for some evidence that would prove once and for all that Julian was trying to kill me, just as he had killed Saramary and then Tom.

Resolutely, I pushed the thought of Julian's finding

me here out of my mind, and concentrated on what I must do. A massive roll-top desk stood in one corner, piled with ledgers and files, and stacks of papers arranged neatly in order. I went to the desk first, thinking that if there was evidence to be found, I would find it here, although it hardly seemed likely that Julian would casually keep incriminating evidence here where anyone could see it.

Ten minutes later, my senses acutely alert to any noise from the hall, I admitted that my search was fruitless. The ledgers were simply an accounting of household matters, as were the papers on the desk. I had been foolish to expect anything else, and I was just about to turn away when I saw something pushed back into the recesses of the numerous compartments hidden under the roll-top part of the desk. Beyond any feeling of guilt for prying into Julian's private papers, I pulled out the letter and read it quickly. It was from Jeremy Bluntridge and said:

> Dear Julian,
> I'm on my way to Italy. Have located the palazzo where Dorothea St. John stayed during the time in question. Must tell you that the investigation has turned up some questionable evidence, and hope to have some news for you when I return. But I must warn you, my friend, that it might not be pleasant—Edward's assertions are possibly correct. Do you want me to continue the investigation?
>
> Jerry

Blankly, I looked up from the letter and stared at the wall, thinking furiously. If what Jeremy said was correct, there was a strong possibility that the rumor about Julian's illegitimacy was more than rumor, it could be true. And if it was, then Edward's claim that Peregrine House should be his might be upheld in a court of law, and Julian would lose everything. But what did that have to do with Saramary, or Tom—or me?

Suddenly, I heard a footstep in the hall. Was Julian returning to his room? Panicked, I folded the letter and pushed it back where I had found it, but in the process, the lid of the desk slid down. It hit with a force that sounded deafening to me, and I held my breath wondering what on earth I would say to Julian when he found me in his room. But there was no time to think about that; my hands were trying to push the roll top back to where I had found it, and it wouldn't move. Frantically, I raised the lid and shoved it back as hard as I could, trying not to think of Julian standing outside, about to come in and discover me. I pushed as hard as I could, and then realized that something was preventing the lid from coming up. Tears of frustration slid down my cheeks as I desperately slid my hand under the top and tried to feel what was blocking the way. It was a book of some kind, and I grabbed it and pulled it out, shoving the lid up at the same time, praying that whoever was in the hall wouldn't come in before I could race back to my own room. I took a last frantic glance at the desk to make certain everything was as I had found it, and then I was through the connecting door and into the safety of my own apartment. I closed the door and leaned against it, gasping. My heart thudded furiously in my throat, and for a moment I thought I would faint with the relief of not being discovered in Julian's room.

Staggering over to a chair, I fell into it, and willed my pulse to stop that suffocating pounding in my ears. I was safe; there was nothing to worry about. If Julian came in, he would find nothing amiss; there was nothing to prove that I had gone through his desk, I told myself again and again. And at last my fright subsided and I was able to breathe again.

I took a deep breath, and noticed with surprise that I still had the book in my hands. I didn't even remember bringing it with me, so great was my fear of discovery. But now, as I looked at it, I realized with another thrill that, unbelievably, it was the same book I had found in the nursery and had believed lost! And then, close on the heels of my delight at finding the book, came another thought, one that sent a stab of despair knifing through me: there was only one way in which Julian could have this book in his possession again, and that was because he was responsible for the accident with the trap. The book had been in my trunk when I left for my visit with the Ashtons; only Julian, close enough to see the accident, could have found it in the wreckage on the road.

I closed my eyes in pain. That meant that Julian was responsible for Ellie's death, too. I didn't think I could bear it, so great was my disillusionment and loss.

The book felt like a dead weight in my lifeless hands, and suddenly I didn't want to read it. I was just about to put it away when it occurred to me that if Julian thought it was important enough to take it and hide it, then perhaps there was something in it I should know.

Numbly, I turned to the first page, forcing myself to read it. The name on the flyleaf was indeed Julian's—but it was written in a childish hand, and the date of its beginning indicated that Julian started it when he was only about seven years old. I leafed through it, stopping to read only a few of the entries out of all the closely written pages.

The first entry read: "Edward and Aunt Arminta have arrived. I wish Aunt wouldn't bring Edward with her when she comes to visit. I don't care for him."

I skipped a few pages and read another: "Edward and Aunt Arminta have gone. I hope they never come again. I wish Mother and Dorcas would come back. Father spends so much time in his room that I feel quite alone. Even Dorcas would be company at least."

Another entry read, simply: "They're back." And I knew Julian was referring to the arrival of Arminta and Edward. I wondered at all this traveling back and forth, but then I remembered Arminta's telling me once that she felt it was her duty to watch over Julian while Mrs. St. John was away. Apparently Arminta believed in doing her duty to the fullest.

The next entry was written hurriedly, the careful precise hand that had marked the previous ones disappearing in a flood of emotion. "I despise Edward. He said that Mother was a bad woman. I fought him, and the head groom had to separate us. Father was furious. Edward lied and said the fight was my fault. Father told us that gentlemen do not fight with their fists and we had to apologize to each other. But I will fight him again if he ever says such things about my mother."

The careful writing had returned in the following entry, but it was the stilted writing of someone who is desperately trying to control emotion. In spite of myself, my heart went out to the small Julian who had written: "Today Edward killed my dog. He denies it, but I know he did. I found him at the bottom of the steps at the beach. I know Ruff wouldn't have fallen by himself. Edward pushed him. Ruff was my only friend, and now he's gone. . . ."

It was a few minutes before I could read on. But the next several pages were blank. I turned the pages sadly, thinking that even the short lines I had read gave too bleak an insight into the lonely thoughts of a little boy.

A long page of wavering lines written in the middle of the book seemed to leap out at me after all the empty pages I had leafed through. The words were poignant and angry at the same time; it was not difficult to understand why. Julian had written: "Father is dead. He hanged himself in his room and now I'll never know the truth about him and Mother. The funeral is to be tomorrow. I don't want to go. How could Father leave me without telling me? Mother can't come home. She is very ill, the doctor told me. Is she going to die too?"

My eyes were blurred with tears so that I could scarcely see the page before me. I remembered Arminta's saying that Julian had been only seven years old when his father died. I read the last line again, experiencing the grief I had felt when my own father died.

I had been young then, not as young as Julian, but still a child. What would I have done without my mother to comfort me, to explain away the horror of death in terms my young mind could try to understand? But Julian had had no one to comfort him, to stave off the nameless fear of being left alone in the world. Oh yes, I remembered, Arminta and Edward were here, but that wasn't the same as having one's own mother to comfort and explain. Arminta and Edward . . .

I let the book fall into my lap, a feeling of vague unease overshadowing me as I thought about what I had read. There was something wrong, some undercurrent I couldn't quite grasp. I reread the entries again, hoping to stumble upon some clue that would explain my unease, but only the loneliness of a small boy thrust abruptly into an adult world came through to me. Why, then, did I feel as though I had missed something important, something that would help me in my own situation?

The book slipped from my lap as I sat thinking and fell to the floor with a thud. I bent to retrieve it and could only stare in surprise. The jolt as it fell had separated the pages from the binding and there on the floor, looking incongruous among the white pages of the book, were two sheets of lavender-tinged writing paper. I picked them up and smoothed away the creases where they had been folded and tucked into the leather flaps that made the covers of the journal. Both were covered with tiny, spidery writing that filled each page. With a gathering sense of excitement, I looked closely at the fine writing and knew instantly that a feminine hand had written them. My pulse began to race; could it be that these closely written pages belonged to Saramary Synclair? It seemed too good to be true, I thought, as I carried them over to the window so I could read them more easily in the waning afternoon light.

With the sound of the murmuring sea outside the window, I deciphered the first line, then read on with stunned disbelief.

I found Julian's diary today when I was measuring the nursery for new furnishings. How clever of him to have a secret hiding place for his little treasures—and how cunning of me to have found it! What a lark it will be to write my own secret thoughts and tuck them away in his little book. A delicious irony, I think. Julian is not the only one who can have secrets, and it will be exciting and frightening at the same time to know that I have written my own secret down and have it hidden in this little cupboard in the nursery where it is possible that someday someone will find it. But how can I help it? I have always loved adventures, and knowing that my secret is here to find will make life deliciously exciting! But even now my hands begin to tremble when I think of writing it down. Suppose the worst happens and someone finds this little book and reads what I have written? The results could be catastrophic! But, of course, by then it will be too late. Julian is far too proud to admit that he has been a fool—for the sake of propriety (that dread word!) we will go on as before, with none the wiser. I'm sure that in the event my little addition to his journal is found, Julian will find a way to keep my secret safe. How could he do otherwise?

Poor Julian! It is comical to see his pride in the coming child—if only he knew! So many times I have had to bury my face behind my fan so he won't see me laughing when he makes a reference to the new heir of Peregrine House. How I long to tell him the truth and see that smug complacency wiped away! But I know it would be disastrous and not worth the momentary pleasure of hurting him. Sometimes I believe I am truly wicked—but then I think that anyone who has ever been so rapturously in love as I would understand that it is not wickedness but a desire over which I have no control. It is unfortunate that Julian cannot understand the desires that consume me—but it is his own fault really. He makes no effort to give me the attention I need. He understands only the business of his estate that keeps him occupied all day. Is it any wonder that I have turned to someone else? For there is only one man who understands me. When I am in his arms, only then do I feel alive. I am not sorry that I am bearing his child—only sorry that it will never be known. For how could I face the disgrace and scandal if the truth were known? All of Julian's and my friends would shun me, there would be no more invitations to parties and balls, the house would be shut to guests. My life would be over. I could not bear to be locked away in this house forever! But if I keep my secret, it will not be forever. My lover has a plan, and when the time comes, we will be free. So I will continue the deception, and all the while I will long to say the name of my lover aloud, for all to hear. Oh, Edward! Edward! How can I bear the thought of living with Julian when I know you are near!

The finely written pages fluttered to the floor, falling heedlessly from fingers grown suddenly numb. I moved in a daze to the nearest chair and sank into it, staring blankly before me. In all my speculations about Saramary, I had never for a moment considered this! I shuddered in revulsion at the thought of Saramary and Edward laughing at Julian while they lay entwined in one another's arms. What a cruel deception they had planned, and with what delight they had carried it out! I felt a tremendous anger toward the woman I had never known. What a shallow, thoughtless, uncaring person she must have been, keeping the secret of her child's parentage from Julian in order to retain the admiration of the people around her. Not a thought for the hurt Julian would suffer should he ever discover the truth; not a thought for the child itself, passed off as another man's son to protect Saramary's selfish interests. It was despicable, monstrous!

Then a thought flashed unbidden into my mind, and I knew it had been forming even as I sat here and thought about Saramary. I pushed it from my mind, but it intruded again: a thought so awful in its implications that I gasped aloud and shut my eyes tightly because it was too hideous to believe.

What if Julian had discovered the truth? Had somehow discovered that the child he was so proud of was not his at all—but the child of a man he had despised since childhood? It would be agonizing enough to find out that his own wife had been unfaithful; to discover that her lover was none other than Edward, at whose hands he had suffered so much in his early years, might have been unbearable. Had his anger been great enough to kill the woman who was responsible for deceiving him?

I knew now for a certainty that her death was not suicide. She herself had written that she intended to carry through the deception, had planned to have the child and give it Julian's name. The closely written lines I had read carried with them no remorse, no guilt at what she had done. In fact, I thought bitterly, she had seemed proud of her actions; only a hidden grain of common sense or, more likely, simple selfishness had caused her to keep silent about her affair with Edward. No; the woman who had written these lines was not suicidal.

So, someone in this house had murdered her. Reluctantly, I came to the conclusion that had been in everyone else's mind when they had talked to me about the day Saramary was killed: Julian was the only person in the house who had sufficient reason for murdering the unfaithful Saramary.

Yet no matter which way I twisted it, in the end it came back to the fact that I could not make myself believe that Julian was capable of murder—under any provocation. No matter that all evidence seemed to point to him; no matter that he had sufficient motive and opportunity. There must be some other explanation. There had to be!

But if Julian had not murdered her, who had? And how was *I* going to find out if even Julian had failed? It seemed an impossible task.

Suddenly, I heard a voice whispering my name. A chill ran down my spine as I recognized the same hoarse whisper that had called to me the other night in this very room.

"Who is it?" I called, fear cracking my voice.

The only answer was a long-drawn-out "Lar . . . issssa."

"What do you want?" I cried, straining desperately to discover the source of that sibilant whisper. My eyes searched the darkened shadows of my room fearfully; it was as though I expected some grotesque monster to take shape before my eyes.

"Lar . . . issa."

The whisper came again—from the hall outside my door, I thought. I was beginning to get angry at such tricks. I sprang out of the chair, where moments before I had sat transfixed, and wrenched upon the door.

"Stop this at once!" I demanded, my fear and anger warring with each other.

But the hall was empty, wrapped in murky darkness because the servants had not yet been up to light the lamps at either end. No one lurked about in the dim twilight of shadowed doors. But was that a ghost of whispered laughter I heard?

I stood on the threshold, my hand gripping the door handle for comfort, and listened intently. Was that a slight sound, a muffled footstep, at the end of the hall? The sound came again, moving ever so slightly away from me.

"Who's there?" I called again.

The sound of a swinging door brushing back and forth against the doorjamb broke the eerie silence. Whoever it was had gone up to the third floor. Was it intended that I follow—or was the whisperer merely seeking escape from detection?

Grimly, I acknowledged to myself that unless I followed immediately, the person responsible for that threatening whisper would vanish once more. I moved silently along the length of the hall, my slippered feet making no sound. When I reached the short flight of stairs that led up to the nursery floor, I paused. My heart hammered against my ribs as I stood there, trying to decide what to do. More than anything else, I wanted to run back down the length of the hall and shut myself safely in my room. But how could I? Was any place in this house safe for me? An overwhelming desire to confront the whisperer and be done with the fear I had lived with for so long made me reckless. Summoning up the tattered rags of my courage, I mounted the steps and pushed open the door quickly before I could change my mind.

CHAPTER TWELVE

The nursery door stood partly open. I could see its outline in the murky shadows that surrounded me. The silence hammered at my ears, yet I was afraid to breathe, to make any noise that would betray me. Step by step I approached the door, willing my legs to carry me forward. I paused before the half-open door and the house held its breath with me.

The high windows in the nursery let in the last fading rays of sunset, then abruptly even that light was gone. I peered into the gloom, my eyes straining against their sockets. But nothing moved; there was no sound.

Suddenly there it was again. That horrible spine-chilling whisper. "Lar . . . issa. . . ."

The sound came from the nursery; I was certain of it. I couldn't go in. But my hand reached out, gave the heavy door an ineffectual push to open it wider. The door did not move. I would have to go in. I could bear the suspense no longer. With my heart pounding in my throat, I stepped into the room.

The silence was absolute. I heard my voice, shrill with fear. "Who's there? What do you want?" But the room did not answer.

A movement caught my eye. I whirled around, my hands half raised, and stumbled against something. I choked back a scream; my fingers traced the outline of the low table I had backed into. I gripped a small chair for support. Panting, my breath rasping against the stillness, I looked around, terrified of what I would see.

Some trick of light and shadow pinpointed the horrible gleaming pale eyes of the rocking horse as it nodded up and down. I stood impaled by the nodding . . . nodding . . . of the painted head. Unbelievably, it was moving toward me.

Sheer terror broke my trance. On legs that had turned to rubber, I struggled toward the door, straining across a floor suddenly turned into a sea of mud that hampered me, held me, dragged at my skirts. My feet refused to obey the frantic signals of my brain; I could hardly move. I was certain that the rocking horse had somehow come to life and would reach me before I could get out.

But the final horror was yet to come. Peal after peal of high-pitched laughter—insane laughter—filled the room. I stood, rooted, frozen, inches away from the door, and safety. The laughter went on and on, filling the room, bouncing from the walls, pounding at me. I clapped my hands over my ears, trying to drown out the hideous sound that surged around me. I was going mad. . . .

The laughter ceased abruptly. The door slammed shut. And I was left alone with the impossibly alive toy rocking horse, and the echoes of that insane laughter.

My fear became hysteria. Get out! my brain screamed—get out! I threw myself against the door, crying for help, forgetting that no one could hear me. My hands beat against the solid wood, jerked at the handle. But the door would not yield to my frantic attempts to wrench it open. At last, my arms hanging limp at my sides, exhausted, sobbing, I slid down the length of the unyielding door until I was in a huddle on the floor. I was beyond feeling, beyond caring what happened now. Even the rocking horse held no more terror for me. I waited numbly.

As if through a fog, I heard heavy footsteps running up the stairs. Someone was coming. But it's too late, I thought dully; no one can save me now.

The footsteps hesitated on the other side of the door. What if the whisperer had come back? If he had, maybe it was not too late. As long as I had breath to fight, I would try to save myself. Fear and anger banished the hopelessness I had felt moments before; I vowed that whoever was on the other side of that door would not find me an easy target. I held on to that thought and did not dare consider the odds against me.

The sudden noise of pounding on the door made me start violently. I tried to get up, stumbled on my skirts, and caught my heel in the hem. I fell heavily to the floor on my hands and knees. I heard a rip as I wrenched my foot free, but was already staggering over to the table. I leaned against it for support and brushed away damp strands of hair that clung to my face. I listened to the pounding at the door and waited, forcing back the hysteria that I could feel building again. There was no escape; I had to face whoever was on the other side of that door.

There was a splintering sound as the door was forced open. I could see a dark shape silhouetted on the threshold. The light glimmered behind it, and I could see that it was a man, his face indistinguishable. The silent way he stood there, after the noise of the pounding, made him seem all the more ominous. He hesitated, and in that instant I seized my chance. I grabbed one of the small chairs that circled the table and threw it with all my might straight at him. It hit with a crash, and I heard a muffled curse as the man staggered back under the impact. The doorway was clear only for an instant, but it was long enough. I rushed through it, pelted down the stairs, and ran for my life. Dimly, I heard a voice call my name, but such was my fear that it only made me run the faster.

I took the stairs two at a time, bunching my skirts in one hand so that they would not hinder me. I flew down the hall, past the merciless doors whose faces were closed to me, my breath already beginning to hurt my throat. The sound of pursuit following close on my heels lent speed to my feet. I made the turn onto the balcony in one leap and tore down the stairs to the first floor, stumbling once as my heel caught. Frantically, I grabbed the banister for balance and used it as a lever to propel me the last few feet to the ground floor. Dimly, I noted that only a few lamps burned in the gallery, but there was no time to wonder where everyone was. Heavy boots clattered on the stairs behind me, and I knew that if I looked around, I was lost.

I dashed across the gallery, trying to ignore the sudden pain in my side, and reached the front door. I grabbed the handle and jerked it open. The door flew out of my hands and crashed back against the wall. The noise boomed out across the gallery, but already I was outside, flinging myself down the steps and across the short expanse of lawn. If only I could get down to the beach, I thought; the rocks would hide me until I decided what to do.

I heard my name called urgently, but I did not stop to identify the voice. The call came again, but was blown away on the wind as I struggled with the gate. My hands found the latch at last, and I was through the gate and running down the steps to the haven of the beach.

The steps were slippery with mist and salt spray; I had to grasp the rail tightly so I wouldn't fall. Splinters from the aged wood bit into my hands, but I scarcely noticed the pain, aware only of the shadow that loomed suddenly by the gate I had left open in my haste. One quick look above me, and I was tearing down the rest of the steps, praying I wouldn't break an ankle.

Then suddenly, mercifully, I was running across the sand toward a large group of rocks that loomed out of the darkness. The sand dragged at me, slowing my pace, until I felt I was hardly moving at all. I struggled forward, weeping with exhaustion. My legs felt like lead weights, my heavy skirts a prison that would allow my pursuer to catch up to me. But I heard a voice call, "Larissa . . . wait!" and that was enough to provide me with a last burst of energy.

I reached the dark shadows of the rocks and sank down into the sand, taking great drafts of air into my burning lungs. My gasps for breath seemed to rasp against the sudden stillness, and I was certain that my pursuer would be able to hear me clearly. I put my hands over my mouth and buried my head in the folds of my skirts, trying vainly to silence my ragged breathing, hoping desperately that he would not discover my position.

When I was able to breathe without that tearing urgency, I raised my head cautiously and looked around. Wisps of fog were moving in from the sea, and in the peculiar gray light they brought I could make out the waves as they broke and raced in to shore, their white froth gleaming ethereally in the dim light. A sliver of moon appeared briefly through the gathering mist, giving me enough light to see that I was alone on the beach. But wait. Was that the shadow of a man moving carefully and slowly among the rocks? I strained to see. Yes. There he was, not far from me. My heart gave a painful lurch as I realized that it was only a matter of time before he found my hiding place.

Desperately, I considered my position. I knew that it was hopeless to expect that I could reach the steps to the house without his catching me; he was too near. I could not hope to run from him a second time; my strength was almost gone. I could not make that wild dash again, in the hope that I would meet someone at the top who would protect me. There was no one to rely on but myself; the thought was chilling.

Then I thought of the caves. I had explored the beach thoroughly in the time I had been here, and I knew where the caves were located. If I could reach them I might be able to hide successfully until he gave up his search. Then I could make my escape to my grandparents' house. What I would do then, I did not stop to think. My grandparents were the only people I could trust in this nightmare. I did not want them to be involved, but I had nowhere else to turn. I tried not to think how alone I was, but concentrated instead on the problem of how I was going to get to the caves without being seen.

I looked for him again, and saw him a short distance away, prowling around the rocks, looking in the opposite direction. Cautiously, I raised myself to my feet, and when I was sure he was looking away from me, moved quickly toward the next group of rocks. In this fashion, a macabre game of hide and seek, I worked my way down the beach to the caves. The last step was the most difficult; I had to cross an area about forty yards wide that was without cover. I looked fearfully over my shoulder, and saw that he had moved closer to me than the last time I had seen him. That decided me; I waited until I thought it was safe and, gathering my heavy, damp skirts in both hands, dashed toward the darkness of the mouth of a small cave. Bending low, I ran inside and turned quickly toward the entrance to make sure he hadn't seen me. No; there he was, still moving to my left. I breathed a sigh of relief, and then almost choked. Another, smaller shadow detached itself from some rocks and came running toward me. Such was my state of tension and fear that I didn't recognize Berus until he came into the cave and pushed his nose into my hand. I sank to my knees and buried my face in the thick fur of his neck thankfully. At least now, whatever happened, I was not alone.

The dog's body was warm and comforting as he

turned his head to give me a quick swipe with his tongue in greeting. I wound my fingers through his fur and whispered the command to be quiet. He seemed to sense my fear, for he gave a low whine before settling himself as close to me as possible. Together we looked out and waited.

We did not have long to wait. The shadow of the man was coming closer all the time, and suddenly I realized with horror that my footprints were easily visible in the wet sand. The trail led straight to the cave and it was obvious that the man had seen it and was following.

In the fitful moonlight, I could see that he was almost at the empty stretch of sand before the cave. I leaned against Berus and wept uselessly, my tears dripping down to mingle with the salt spray that dampened Berus' coat. I was at the end of my strength; I could only wait for him to come with a hopelessness of exhaustion and failure.

Suddenly, Berus stood. To my amazement, I could feel his plume of a tail brush back and forth against me, welcoming the shadow bearing down on us. He made a low sound deep in his throat, which I instantly recognized as his sound of greeting.

There was only one person, beside myself, that Berus would approach like this. I had known it all along, and refused to let myself believe. I had recognized his voice calling to me at the house, and again on the steps leading down to the beach, but had refused to let my mind acknowledge it. I had struggled for so long to deny the evidence before my eyes, the clues that everybody dropped, that to admit it now was the final blow. But there was no choice; even as the last barriers came crashing down in my mind, he was stepping into the cave.

"Larissa?" he called questioningly.

I said nothing, but Berus left my side and went eagerly to his master, his plumed tail signaling his happiness and foretelling my defeat at the same time.

Julian reached down and ruffled the fur of his dog. "Good boy, Berus. You found her for me. Good boy."

CHAPTER THIRTEEN

Julian struck a match, and in the sudden tiny blaze of light his face seemed to float disembodied before me, a satyr's face that was all hard planes and deep shadows. I backed away from him, unconsciously seeking escape although I knew there was none. This time there would be no running from him; I was caught in my own trap. Sharp projections of stone bit into my spine as I flattened myself against one side of the cave and waited for him to speak.

Berus paced back and forth between us, whining anxiously, not understanding the tension that vibrated between us. Finally, the dog went to the mouth of the cave and sat there, gazing watchfully into the darkness. Julian and I stared at each other. The match burned down toward the end, and I watched it, mesmerized, my whole attention absorbed by the flame as it licked its way toward Julian's fingers until, with a muttered exclamation, he shook it out. Another flared immediately as though he were afraid I would somehow manage to disappear in the brief interval of darkness.

I wanted to ask for, to demand, an explanation from Julian; I wanted him to tell me that he was innocent of all that had happened to me. But the horror of my experiences came crowding over me; the whispered threat to kill me seemed to hang in the air between us, and the looming shadow of the man on the threshold to the nursery mocked me. I stood silent, realizing with a sense of fatalistic wonder that all my doubts and fears, my near-fatal accidents and panic-stricken flight from the horror of the nursery, might end in this small cave by the sea, facing a man whom I knew I would always love, no matter what happened now.

"Larissa . . . I . . ." Julian began unsteadily. "Larissa, please don't be afraid of me—"

I couldn't help it; reaction to all the horror I had experienced swept over me. I laughed—a high-pitched sound of hysteria that echoed the laughter I had heard in the nursery. It frightened me because I could not recognize it as my own. I put a hand over my mouth to choke back that horrible sound, but still it came forth, forcing its way through my fingers, ringing out around us until Julian took a step forward and grabbed my shoulders. His fingers tightened unmercifully as he shook me back and forth.

"Larissa! Stop it!" he shouted. "Stop it!"

The sound penetrated my hysteria; with a last gulp, I stopped and looked up at him.

"Larissa, why did you run from me?"

The extremes of emotion into which I had been plunged took their toll on me at last. Because I had been so frightened, I now reacted with anger. "I was afraid of you! Have you ever given me reason to be otherwise? You and your family united to treat me as an outsider, determined to keep your secret safe from me. How you must have laughed at me! Innocent, naïve Larissa, who didn't even know about her husband's first wife! Stupid Larissa, who tried to believe that the accidents that kept happening to her were merely that—accidents—because the alternative was to believe that her own husband was trying to kill her!"

"Larissa—"

"No, let me finish," I interrupted hotly, the words I had kept inside me for so long now pouring out. "I tried, Julian, I really tried. But it was hopeless from the start. You turned me aside again and again until finally even I realized that from the beginning the only thing you wanted from me was money. Money," I repeated bitterly. "I wonder now why you bothered with me at all when you had everything you wanted right on your doorstep. Why didn't you marry her, Julian?

It would have been so much easier on everybody if you had!" I stopped, almost choking with anger and humiliation now that the words were spoken.

"What are you talking about?" Julian asked quietly.

"What? You mean whom, don't you, Julian?" I cried. "The beautiful, rich Rose Streitten, of course!"

"Rose? What has she to do with this?"

"How dare you deny it! I saw the way you looked at her. . . ." I could not go on, remembering the night of the ball and the first time I had seen the two of them together.

Julian laughed bitterly. "Is that what you thought? Even though Rose is six years younger than I, we grew up together—I could no more think of marrying her than I could think of marrying Dorcas! There is nothing between us but friendship, whatever you may have heard to the contrary."

"Then why . . . I mean, the night of the ball . . ."

"Ah, yes. The night of the ball. You know Rose's father was responsible for slandering my father after his death. Well, Rose has done everything she can to stop his lies, even at the expense of her relationship with him. I will always be grateful to her for that. I did not want her to come to the ball because it was rumored that I had killed Saramary in order to have Rose. It would be laughable if it weren't so serious. But I knew if she came she would be subjected to the same sly looks and stares I would have to endure, so I tried to convince her to stay away. But she came anyway, to show her support." His voice hardened. "And that is why I looked at her as I did. She is the only one who has never believed that I killed my first wife."

I could not doubt the sincerity in his voice about Rose Streitten, but there were so many other things I had to know about. I started to speak, but Julian continued, in that same hard voice:

"I forbade anyone to speak of Saramary to you because I did not want to frighten you. I can see now that was a mistake; it was too much to hope that you wouldn't find out eventually, but I thought to spare you the morbid details until I could prove who was responsible for her death."

"Then you know who—"

"Yes," he answered grimly. "I know who. That's why I wanted Jerry to open the case again—because he is convinced, as I am, that Saramary's death was not a suicide."

I was confused by Jeremy's role in all this. I asked, "Who is Jeremy Bluntridge?"

"Jerry is an old friend of mine from school. He is also an inspector for Scotland Yard. He is helping me to investigate Saramary's death, and when Edward began to take a sudden interest in you, he helped me there, also. Edward never does anything without good reason, and I wondered why he was asking so many questions about you. I told Jerry to find out what he could; it was he who suspected the relationship between you and Lord and Lady Ashton. That's why I was so anxious for you to visit them. I knew by that time it was possible you were their granddaughter, and I thought you would be safe with them."

"Then you knew—"

A note of pain crept into his voice. He said, "Yes. I knew you were in danger—God! Do you have any idea how helpless I felt, knowing you were at the center of things, and having no way to stop him! I could kill him with my bare hands!"

I was shaken by the violence in his voice. I asked, desperately trying to keep my own voice even, "But what about Tom? Why did you want me to pretend his death was an accident, when we both knew it wasn't?"

"Because I thought you would be safer that way. I knew that if you insisted that Tom was murdered, you would be in even greater danger than before."

"But I thought—"

"Yes, I know what you thought. You believed I was trying to protect myself. Old Tom was a well-meaning fool. He knew something about Saramary's death, but for some reason he refused to say anything about it to me. And then, that day, when I saw him talking to you,

I realized that he was trying to protect you, too. I had no way of knowing what he told you, but I knew that whatever it was, the knowledge could be dangerous. When he was murdered, I knew I had to get you away. That's why I wanted you to go to the Ashtons. I thought you would be safer with them than with me."

I laughed bitterly. "And all the time I thought—"

"Yes," he said, his voice suddenly savage. "You thought I was pleased about your relationship with the Ashtons because of money. Well, that was to the purpose, I suppose. You despised me for it and that made it easier for me."

"Easier . . ." I was beginning to understand, but before I could say more, Julian continued.

"I did know that you were not an heiress at the time I married you. Mother's assertions to the contrary, I did take time to learn about that. I didn't care about the money, but I did care about the fact that your aunt insisted you knew about the scheme to deceive me. In fact, when I asked her at the reception, she told me you were responsible for concocting the whole story. I wouldn't believe it—I damn near called her a liar to her face. She laughed and said it didn't matter what I believed. When I learned that she had forced you to marry me—"

"That's not exactly true," I interrupted. But Julian continued as if he hadn't heard.

"And then, the first morning after we arrived, you said that you had been deceived also, and were content to have a marriage in name only, to act the part with nothing else expected, I thought that was what you wanted, so I tried to act accordingly."

"But you had turned away from me even on our wedding day!" I cried. "You would have nothing to do with me from the moment you received that note before we went to the reception!"

His flare of anger matched mine as he said, "That was when I first learned that you were compelled to marry me. I felt like a fool! Damn it—I couldn't force myself on an unwilling bride!"

I groaned inwardly. All those precious moments lost because we had both misunderstood. I said, "But Julian, you never asked me . . ." But even as I spoke, my voice trailed away because I realized that the fault had been as much mine as his. I had never asked him to explain, either. Both of us had been caught in a trap of our own making, and it was galling to have to admit that only our pride had kept us silent, when a word from either of us would have set us free.

We spoke at the same time:

"I wasn't forced to marry you, Julian—"

"I didn't marry you because of money, but because I—"

"Oh, Julian!" I stumbled forward, and then with a blessed sense of relief felt his arms encircling me, holding me tightly against him. I leaned against him, sobbing uncontrollably. Julian held me closely, murmuring above my head, stroking my hair, both of us too caught up in emotion to say anything coherent.

At last, when I was able to control myself, I looked up at him. His face was a white blur in the darkness of the cave, and I could not see his expression. But I had no need; I knew what it contained.

"Oh, Julian, I've been such a fool," I said at last.

"No more than I," he answered tenderly. "Let's go home."

"Oh, I think not," said another voice. "Touching as this scene is, I fear I must interrupt."

Edward stepped confidently into the cave. The only one to move was Berus, who backed away from his position at the cave's entrance, his lips drawn back in a silent snarl as he came to stand by me, a self-appointed guard. I could only gape at Edward; I was frozen with shock.

Julian stiffened by my side, and we watched silently as Edward lit a small lamp and placed it on a shelf of rock. The yellow light from the lamp washed over the cave, illuminating Edward and the gun he held in one hand.

I gasped when I saw the gun, and Julian drew me

protectively to his side. I cowered there, unable to take my eyes away from the deadly weapon that was trained so steadily on us. Julian faced his cousin and said coldly, "What do you think you're doing Edward?"

"Don't be obtuse, Julian. You know very well what I'm doing. You have forced my hand, cousin, and much as I regret it, I will have to kill you both now."

"But why?" I whispered. I stared stupidly as Edward sneered at me.

"You don't think that after all my carefully laid plans have succeeded I will let you get away, darling Larissa? Oh, no, my dear. I have worked too long and too hard for that."

"Plans?" I echoed.

"Larissa . . ." Julian said warningly.

"I think I should tell her, don't you, Julian? After all, you and your inspector friend have suspected me for some time now, I know. I think it's only fair that Larissa should know why I'm going to kill her."

He turned to me, but the muzzle of the gun remained steadily on Julian. Edward bowed politely, a travesty of manners that seemed all the more deadly in view of the gun he was holding with such calmness. "You still don't understand, do you, Larissa?"

I shook my head, understanding all too well, but unwilling to do anything that might provoke him into using that gun.

"Ah, I thought not," Edward said condescendingly. "Not even with all your amateurish probing into Saramary's death and your own subsequent . . . accidents. You were foolish, my dear, as I'm sure you realize now. But of course, now it's too late. You should have left well enough alone."

In the light of the lamp, Edward's face took on such a malignant aspect that I wondered why it had taken me so long to understand. But then, Edward was so much more clever than I. He had taken such pains to paint Julian as an unscrupulous and unprincipled man; had seen that in my loneliness and confusion I was an easy target, ready to acknowledge my suspicions of Julian. Edward's game had been deadly, and I had been a helpless pawn in his schemes. Suddenly, I felt faint with the realization of what my stupidity had cost us.

I turned to Julian and saw that his expression as he looked at Edward was like granite, even as his arm drew me tenderly against him. How could I ever for a moment have suspected Julian, my mind cried bitterly, when all the evidence was there for me to use, had I been intelligent enough to see it? I pressed against Julian in a wordless apology, and he glanced briefly down at me, reassuring me with a swift smile.

"Then you did kill Saramary." Julian's voice was flat, his tone a statement rather than a question.

"Ah, yes. A regrettable incident, that. But of course I couldn't take the blame, could I? I thought it a most convenient way to remove you, Julian, after I had time to think about it. Unfortunately, it didn't work."

"But why did you kill her?" I asked, feeling repulsed by the calmness with which Edward admitted his crime.

"It really was an accident. But then, she was becoming burdensome. She thought that since she was going to have my child she could use that as a lever to make me come to heel. I was bored with the whole thing, really."

He paused and glanced keenly at Julian. "Ah. So you knew about Saramary and me, Julian?"

"Yes," Julian answered coldly. "You have always had the unfortunate tendency to underestimate everyone but yourself, Edward. I told Saramary that final day that if she wanted you, she would have to go with you. I wanted nothing more to do with either of you. That was what our quarrel was about—and of course, I couldn't tell the police. I had no intention of creating any more scandal for Peregrine House than I could possibly help."

"So that was why she was frantic that day," Edward mused. "She insisted that we go away together. She became quite hysterical. . . ."

"But if it was an accident, as you say, Edward, why didn't you just explain to the police?" I asked quickly, as I saw Edward's hand tighten around the handle of the gun.

"Because, my simple darling, I saw a way to turn her death to my advantage. If Julian was proved guilty of murdering his own wife, he would be taken away and I would be free to claim the heritage that is truly mine."

"What are you talking about?" Julian grated.

"Oh, come, Julian. You know I have always wanted Peregrine House. It is mine by right, you know. You are the usurper. Don't tell me you didn't know that your precious mother had an affair while she was married to your father—an affair of which you are the result. Consequently, as the son of Adrian Synclair—your supposed father's brother—I am the rightful heir. Julian Synclair had no sons. You have no claim."

"You're lying!" Julian's voice rasped out in the darkness, and I put a restraining hand on his arm to stop him from leaping at Edward. I was terrified that Edward would kill him if he attacked, and frantically sought a way to keep Edward talking, but it was not necessary; Edward continued smugly, enjoying his role of torturer.

"On the contrary, dear cousin. Or should I call you my cousin, after all? You have only to ask your mother —or at least, you won't be able to ask her now, so you'll have to take my word for it. Arminta and Dorothea conveniently took a trip to the Continent some years ago. Supposedly the strain of travel brought on a premature birth. A convenient excuse, I should say, since Dorothea's husband was away from Peregrine House for those first two vital months when she conceived the child of her lover. Poor man—he wasn't supposed to know about the deception. But he knew, believe me. I made sure of that the day he died. He couldn't stand the evidence of your mother's duplicity. He hanged himself, as we all know."

With a great effort, Julian controlled himself. His

voice hard, he asked, "What does all this—assuming for the moment that it is true—have to do with Larissa?"

"There are several reasons, Julian," Edward said condescendingly, as though explaining a very simple problem to two witless children. "The first is obvious, I should think. If you and Larissa had a son, the claim to Peregrine House, which is rightfully mine, as I have said, would be more difficult to make. After all, the secret of your questionable birth has never been common knowledge. Secondly, and much more to the point, if I had succeeded in killing Larissa, all the old scandal about Saramary would rear its ugly head; the police would put two and two together, and it would be obvious what would happen to you. You would be out of the way, Larissa would be out of the way, and the field would be clear for me. But I had to kill her before Lord and Lady Ashton recognized her as their granddaughter. I couldn't quite see convincing the police that you would kill a suddenly wealthy wife. It would make much more sense from their point of view that you would rid yourself of a penniless one. It is well known, thanks to me, that your finances are somewhat ... ah ... in arrears."

I found my voice at last. Ignoring all of Edward's other statements, I focused on the one concerning my grandparents. "But how did you know that I was the granddaughter of Lord and Lady Ashton before they did?"

Edward laughed cunningly, and the sound drifted through the cave, a subtle echo of that mad laughter that had resounded through the nursery before he locked me in. "The first night I met you, I knew. I told you that I had been to the Ashtons' often, didn't I, my dear? I saw the portrait of your mother. I saw the pin you were wearing. I recognized it as the same pin worn by the woman who sat for that portrait. I knew that if I could recognize the resemblance, even the doddering old Ashtons could. So I stole the pin from your room before the party; even if Lord and Lady

Ashton said something about your resemblance to their dear, lost daughter, the final proof would be lost to you."

"So when you learned that I was going to visit them, you came to my room and tried to push me over the balcony."

"Yes. I saw their reaction at the party, although I tried my best to keep you away from them; I thought that if I could prevent you from seeing them, everything would work out perfectly for me."

"But you didn't succeed. . . ."

"No." There was a regretful tone in his voice that was chilling. I moved even closer to Julian when Edward continued, "No. I didn't. More's the pity. I was forced to play out a more dangerous—to me—plan. As I was rigging the trap that day, Julian almost discovered me. But I succeeded in weakening the bridle rein before you came rushing down to the stables, Julian. I knew that mare was skittish; one or two shots in front of her nose and she would be off, and no means to stop her. Unfortunately, Larissa was only injured. Not killed, as I had hoped."

"And what about Tom, Edward?" Julian interrupted. "Why did you kill him?"

"It's obvious, I should think. Tom knew about Saramary and me. Saramary, for all her beauty, had very little intelligence—as you know, Julian. She wasn't as discreet as I wished her to be. At any rate, Tom heard us talking one day—quarreling, actually, about whether you should be informed of our little affair. I knew any testimony from him after her death might put me in an unfavorable light, so . . . I threatened him. Suffice it to say he did not go to the police with his little story. But I heard him talking to Larissa one day—ominous mutterings from a guilty conscience—and arranged for him to have . . . an accident. I couldn't afford to have Larissa become suspicious of me, especially since I had done such advance planning to convince her that you were the guilty one."

There was a sudden ugly silence. Edward caressed

the barrel of the gun casually as he regarded us. He continued, in a soft, insinuating tone, "You know, Larissa, when I first met you, I thought killing you would be easy. You were so shy and afraid of everyone. I misjudged you. I apologize." Again that mocking little bow. "I had no idea you would summon the strength to fight me. I was getting desperate. Already two attempts had failed. I didn't think I should risk a third. But then I had the brilliant idea of trying to drive you out of your mind. If I succeeded, you would no longer be a danger to me. That was when I got the idea of using the rocking horse. It was a fortunate choice, was it not? Mrs. Harmon, who has been known to succumb to pretty little compliments, innocently told me about the visit to the nursery. She let slip that you seemed to have an aversion to that rocking horse, and when you went the second time, I followed you to determine your reaction. That was when you found the book, remember?"

I nodded. "Julian's diary," I said, noticing Julian's startled movement by my side.

"Ah," Edward said to Julian. "You didn't know about that diary, did you? There was quite a mess on the road that day Larissa had her . . . accident. The trunk had fallen off the trap and everything was scattered on the road. I saw the book lying there, and since it had Julian's name on the cover, I took it. I thought it would come in handy, and it did."

"So you hid it in Julian's room," I said evenly.

"Yes. I knew that you were suspicious of Julian, and I thought that you might have the courage to search his room for evidence. Which you did, I take it?"

I nodded again, feeling sick at the thought of his treachery. I had walked blindly into his trap, and I cursed myself for being a fool. "How did you know that I would find it?" I asked hopelessly.

"I didn't," Edward said complacently. "But it really didn't matter, did it? You already knew—or thought you knew—that Julian was a murderer. If you found the diary, it would be only one more piece of evidence; if you hadn't found it, well . . ." He shrugged.

"You were talking about the rocking horse," Julian said coldly.

"Oh yes. I had no idea the first time I used it that it would strike such terror into Larissa. I must be congratulated. Of course, it was a bit tricky going through your room"—he nodded toward Julian—"but I knew that Larissa would see that the balcony door was open and draw her own conclusions about who the guilty one was. After she screamed, I knew you would come rushing to her aid, so I waited on the balcony, and then went through your room and presented myself at her door, as puzzled as all the rest over what had happened. You never suspected, did you, Larissa?"

Hopelessly, I shook my head, and Edward smiled. "I had hoped that you would follow me to the nursery after I had played that little trick on you in your room, but of course, I was only guessing at the extent of your courage. You must admit you were frightened, weren't you? A few more incidents like that, and you would lose your mind. In a way, that would almost be better than killing you outright. Either way, I could have contrived to have Julian take the blame."

"So your plan is to kill us now?" Julian interrupted again. His contempt was not lost on Edward. Suddenly, Edward's face became twisted with ugliness, and his rage was so great that the gun wavered in his hand. I knew that he was beyond reason; a few seconds more and he would pull the trigger. Julian knew it too; he tensed beside me.

Everything happened so quickly then that only a confused recollection remains in my mind. I remember Julian pushing me away from him so suddenly that I stumbled and fell to the floor of the cave. Sharp stones bit into my hands as I fell, but the pain was nothing compared to the confusion that whirled above my head. I looked up in time to see Julian leaping past me toward Edward. Edward, startled by the sudden attack, aimed a shot at Julian. I screamed as the bullet roared from the gun; my screams mingled with the shrieking sound it made as it glanced off a rock, a shot gone wild. Julian and Edward came together with a crash that seemed to shake the stone walls of the cave. Both men fell heavily to the ground, Julian on top for only an instant before Edward, with a furious lunge, twisted away from him and tried to grab for the gun he had dropped. Julian was after him instantly, and both men wrestled for possession of the firearm. In the lamplight, their faces were contorted. I could hear grunts and muffled curses as they swung at each other.

Berus whined as I held him fiercely, afraid to let him go. The shadows of the struggling men flashed back and forth on the cave walls, looming hugely over me as I cowered on the floor. The gun was only a few feet away from me when Julian panted, "Larissa . . . the gun . . ." I only stared at it as if I had never seen it before. With a last jerk, Berus twisted away from me. He bounded over to Julian's side and hesitated, waiting for an opening.

I saw Edward reach behind him, one hand blindly seeking, while the other tried to push Julian away. I screamed a warning, but it was too late. Edward's fingers closed on a heavy piece of rock and brought it around to crush Julian's head. Stone and flesh met with a sickening crunch. Julian crumpled to one side, unconscious. In that same instant, Berus leaped. The dog hit Edward just as he was beginning to roll away from the weight of Julian's body. He fell back heavily as Berus stood astride him, jaws open, poised for the attack.

At last I was free to move. I leaped up and grabbed the gun, pointing it unsteadily in Edward's direction. The gun was heavy; it took both hands to hold it. The muzzle wavered back and forth as if with a life all its own. I was terrified that I would somehow set it off.

Edward stared into the wide-open jaws above him, his eyes dilated with horror. He screamed, "Larissa! Get him off me! He'll kill me!"

Fleetingly I remembered Edward's belief that Berus

was a witching dog; that he could mesmerize with that one blue eye before slashing his victim's throat. In that moment it seemed true; in the light of the lamp—which mercifully had not been knocked over during the struggle—I could see that Berus stood unmoving, his whole body concentrated in the effort to hold Edward on the ground. His strange eyes seemed to bore directly into Edward, and Edward stared up at him, his eyes bulging with superstitious, and very real, fear. His once handsome face was contorted with terror. He screamed again at me to call off the dog.

I could not believe it was my voice that answered, "No. I'll not call him off. Perhaps this was the way Saramary felt, and Tom, before you killed them. It would be what you deserve for Berus to do the same to you."

"Larissa . . . please!" He pleaded, but I had no pity for him. Instead I was trembling with rage. How dare he plead with me to save his life; Edward, a murderer twice over! I looked at Berus, whose jaws were beginning to drip with saliva, and am ashamed now to recall the triumph I felt to see Edward reduced to the terror he must have inspired in his victims.

My triumph was short-lived. With one eye on Edward, I knelt beside Julian and put my hand to his temple. To my horror, my fingers came away red with blood. In the lamplight I could see the crimson stain that soaked his hair and dripped slowly down the side of his face. Grimly, I faced the possibility of trying to get back to the house with an unconscious Julian. I dare not trust Edward to help, even with the gun in my possession.

I would have to do *something*—but what? I stood again, trying to point the gun steadily in Edward's direction, hoping he would not notice how afraid I was. I called to Berus, my voice a cracked whisper that held no authority. The dog glanced briefly at me, then back again to Edward. I called again, louder this time, and, reluctantly, the dog came to me.

"Get up, Edward—and slowly," I said, trying to

control my voice. "I wouldn't want the gun to go off accidentally...."

Edward threw me a look of such hatred that I wanted to shrink back from him. But it wouldn't do to weaken now. I forced myself to hold my ground as Edward slowly got to his feet and took a step toward me.

His face was contorted with rage, but he said softly, "You don't think I will let you get away with this, do you, Larissa?" He took another step toward me.

"Stay where you are or I'll be forced to fire this gun," I answered, hoping desperately that I sounded convincing.

"No, I don't think you would do that." He held out his hand for the gun.

"I mean it, Edward." My thoughts were racing. What if he did try to take it away from me? What would I do? I looked down at Berus, trembling by my feet, his lips drawn back in a snarl as he looked at Edward. "If Berus attacks again, I don't think I can call him off," I said, praying that his fear of the dog would force him to reconsider.

"It would be foolish of you to try such a thing, Larissa," he said softly. "Don't you see that I'll have to kill you now? You know too much about me. Give up, Larissa, and I promise it will be quickly done."

His words were confident, but I saw his eyes glance toward Berus uneasily, a trace of fear showing briefly in them before he looked directly back to me. Dare I take the chance? He was coming closer, and I knew that I could never fire the gun. The weapon seemed to drag me down, and I had the absurd desire to burst into tears and surrender so this nightmare would be over at last. But then Julian moved slightly and groaned, and I knew I couldn't give up now. Edward would kill us both. He was one step away now, so close that even in the lamplight I could see the color of his eyes with their impossibly long lashes staring directly into mine with such a look of hatred that I knew I would remember it for the rest of my life. It was that sneering look that strangely enough gave me courage to face him again.

The gun trembled in my hand. I was desperate, but so was Edward. He reached out and grabbed my wrist so suddenly, so fiercely, that a stab of pain shot up my arm and I could feel my fingers weakening their hold. Desperately, I held on to the weapon, for I knew that if Edward succeeded in taking it away from me we were lost. We struggled, Edward gasping in pain as Berus sank his teeth into his leg, but he did not release his grip on my wrist. I couldn't hold out much longer; as Edward brought my arm up to take the gun away, I struck him in the face with my other hand. Edward staggered back, thrown off balance by my sudden attack, and in that instant I seized the opportunity to dart by him toward the mouth of the cave. Edward lunged after me. The gun went off in my hand, and I was thrown backward with the force of the charge. Edward screamed and clutched his arm, where already a red stain was blossoming through the fabric of his coat. He bent double with pain and shrieked a curse at me before he crumpled to the ground. I watched him in horror.

"Well, it looks as though I'm too late. You seem to have things well in hand, Larissa," a voice drawled behind me.

I turned blankly to stare into Jeremy Bluntridge's grimly amused face. He looked reassuringly at me and gently took the gun from my stiff fingers. I sagged against him, not even wondering in that moment why he should be here instead of London, where I had thought him to be. His presence was the most comforting I had ever felt as he stood with one arm about me, the other holding the gun on Edward.

The release from terror brought forth shuddering sobs from me, even as I darted to where Julian lay. I dropped to my knees in the sand, holding Julian's head in my lap, using a tattered remnant of my skirt to press against the wound in his temple. Berus came to stand by us, and when suddenly the cave seemed to be filled with men in uniform, I could only stare at the miracle that had saved us.

A stretcher was brought for Julian, and two men picked Edward up and carried him away between them. I went with Julian, holding his hand, watching the blood seep through a makeshift bandage that one of the men had fashioned until the doctor could attend the wound. We were the last to leave, and as I looked back at the cave, the sea was already claiming it for the night. I shuddered at the thought that Julian and I could have been trapped in there, waiting helplessly, while the tide rushed in and covered us, and Edward, safe outside, laughed triumphantly at his success.

CHAPTER FOURTEEN

The trial is over now. Edward has been removed to an institution for the insane, where he is well taken care of by a man under Julian's employ. The man is necessary, Julian tells me, to cope with Edward's sudden violences before he lapses again into that empty staring into which even the doctor cannot reach. I can find it in my heart to pity poor Edward now; the shock of discovering the truth was too much for his already unbalanced mind. Julian says he will never leave the institution. Arminta Rossmore and Dorothea St. John visit each other regularly, their friendship strengthened by the need to comfort each other, and perhaps because the strain of keeping their secret is no longer between them they will come to learn eventually that Julian bears them no resentment. Mathew and Dorcas, free at last of the legal entanglement regarding Mathew's estate, have built a home of their own, which I suspect will soon be filled with children, if Dorcas' radiance is any guide. Norman, who visited us just the other day, has changed immeasurably—perhaps due to his new responsibilities in developing a stable of racing horses under the guidance of Colonel Huxley, he has acquired a new image of himself, as well as calloused hands and a sun-browned face that no longer appears petulant and spoiled. He and Rose Streitten are to be married in the fall with Julian's smiling permission; Julian feels that at last Norman will make a good husband for Rose, although he says jokingly that Norman will have his hands full with her. And Julian . . .

Sometimes in the quiet of my sitting room, I find my eyes wandering beyond the pages of my household accounts, remembering the last of that long, terrible night. In a way, I suppose, we can be grateful to Edward for precipitating the events that were to bring the truth to light at last, but even now I shudder to remember the awfulness of the scene in the drawing room, when Arminta Rossmore had finally come forward with the truth.

Jeremy Bluntridge commanded the scene. It was he who sent one man for the doctor to examine Julian and Edward, another to summon Dorothea St. John from Dower House, and a third to gather the rest of the family. I scarcely recognized Jeremy that night as the same person I had come to know; his blue eyes were flinty as his gaze raked each of us assembled before him. He stood in the center of the room, exuding such authority that even Dorothea St. John was silent in the face of that fierce stare.

I sat by Julian, who had been stitched and bandaged, and found my hand stealing into his for support. Edward's arm had been attended to—a surface wound, the doctor assured me—and he sat in the corner guarded by two burly policemen, who were alert to his slightest move.

Dorcas and Mathew had taken their places on the sofa, while a white-faced Norman stood stiffly beside Mrs. St. John, who had seated herself in her high-backed chair. I could not look at her; she seemed to have aged immeasurably in the few minutes it took for

Jeremy to describe Edward's confession of double murder, and of his plans to kill Julian and myself.

Arminta had been the last to arrive; she and Dorothea St. John held a whispered conversation together before she turned to the rest of us. She stood now by the crackling fire, telling her story in a flat voice that belied her high state of emotion. Once or twice her glance rested briefly on Julian, and I had to turn away from the pain in her eyes as her voice moved on, condemning Dorothea and herself.

"Edward was correct when he suspected the reason for Dorothea's and my long-ago visit to the Continent —but his conclusion was in error. I was the one with child—and that child was Julian."

Arminta paused at Julian's violent start. She held up her hand in silencing gesture, as though she must say what she had to before she lost courage. "It pains me to reveal a secret so long and so carefully kept, but now is the time for truth. Don't you agree, Dorothea?" She turned to Mrs. St. John, who leaned against the back of her chair and closed her eyes as if the truth were too much to bear. Dorothea gave the barest of nods, her hands tightening on the arms of the chair. Arminta looked at her for a moment, then she spoke again.

"Dorothea and Julian had a marriage of convenience, as the saying goes. They were not close; neither were Adrian and myself. Adrian was away much of the time—and . . . I became Julian's mistress. We even managed a brief holiday together before we realized that to continue was madness. When I discovered that I was with child, Dorothea and I formed a plan. We would go away together, and when I had the child, Dorothea would take it as her own. Julian—the father —need not know. He was anxious for an heir; Dorothea would avoid the scandal that was already threatening; I would extricate myself from a somewhat compromising situation."

Arminta paused again and stared into the fire. The room was silent, but I could sense unasked questions vibrating in the air. When she continued, it was in a voice totally lacking in self-pity; it was almost as though she were relieved to be telling the truth at last. She said, "I know it was a foolish plan. You may well ask why I did not have the child and pretend it was Adrian's. I cannot answer, except to say that we were young—all of us—and I dared not consider the consequences if Adrian discovered the truth. It seemed best at the time. Dorothea and I came home directly after the baby was born. And Edward"—Arminta cast a mute look of appeal at Edward before continuing resolutely—"Edward is the son of my maid who accompanied us; she was a good girl, of whom I was very fond, but she died in childbirth and I kept Edward to compensate for the loss of my own son. Adrian was lenient with me in this one respect at least—he gave Edward his name and allowed me to raise him. He kept silent about Edward's true parents, but he never regarded him as his own son."

I was filled with reluctant admiration for Arminta Rossmore—not for what she had done, but for her courage in making it known at last. How she must have suffered during Julian's early years when Dorothea had neglected him. I realized now that it was less a sense of duty that had prompted so many extended visits to Peregrine House than it was love for her own son. I was sorry that Julian had been made to suffer because these two women had not had the courage to make the truth known; but who was I to judge? Who can ever be certain that they would not react the same way, given the same circumstances? But it was indeed sad that Dorothea St. John had never been able to overcome her aversion to the son of her husband and his mistress, even though she herself had consented to the deception.

But Arminta was not finished. "It is said that Julian, senior, was mad. Dorothea and I did nothing to dispel this notion because we were afraid the truth would come out and we would be discovered. We could not face that. We could not face so many things. . . ."

She turned directly to Julian, looking directly into his eyes. "It is through our weakness and selfishness that you were made to suffer, Julian, and I think it is for that I am most ashamed. Your father was not mad —only driven to despair because he suspected how Dorothea and I had deceived him. There were others, including Gerald Streitten, who were misguided by us, but who suspected the truth also, and your father's pride would not allow him to be made such a fool. He was a kind, honorable man—and together Dorothea and I destroyed him."

Her glance flickered to Edward who sat withdrawn into his own world, unmoving after that violent start when Arminta had made known his parentage. She said, "It is a just punishment that I will now suffer what you have had to endure all these years."

For the first time, tears shone in her eyes, but her indomitable will held them back. She turned to Jeremy, who stood silently regarding her with a measure of both pity and admiration. "I believe that is all you require of me, Inspector?" She glanced once more at Julian, and then, her head held high, left the room.

We all sat in stunned silence, until Dorcas broke the spell. With an indignant exclamation, she said, "What are we to do now? The scandal will simply ruin us!"

"Dorcas . . ." Mathew put a restraining hand on her arm as she tried to stand.

"Don't you understand? We'll be disgraced!" she cried, trying vainly to free her arm from Mathew's grasp.

I was shocked at this callous disregard for the feelings of others, but even more shocked when Mathew leaped to his feet and almost shouted, "Dorcas! That will be enough!"

We all stared at Mathew, who had never before asserted himself. Dorcas could only gape at him, mouth open in surprise, as he stretched himself to his full height and glared down at her. "You will apologize for that outburst immediately!" the transformed Mathew demanded of his wife.

"But—"

"At once!"

Dorcas turned crimson, but after one look at Mathew's livid face, stammered an apology.

Mathew nodded to Jeremy. "If you need us for any further questions, we will be upstairs. I apologize again for my wife's rudeness. She is overwrought." Then Mathew turned to me and said, "I'm afraid we must make an apology to you also, Larissa. If you remember the first night after you arrived and Julian's dog was on the balcony outside your room? I found out later that Dorcas and Norman had somehow coerced the dog up there to frighten you; they knew how vicious he was, and thought you might be frightened enough to leave. A foolish, dangerous plan, but one worthy of their selfish interests, I'm afraid. Dorcas has something to say to you now. . . . Dorcas?"

"I . . . I'm sorry, Larissa," Dorcas said in a small voice. "I did not know until later, when Julian told us he had married you knowing your situation, that I had misjudged you. It . . . it was awful of us, and I'm sorry. It's just that we could see all the old scandal about Saramary rearing its ugly head, and I didn't think I could go through it all again. You see . . . each one of us felt responsible in some way for Saramary's death—we were all touched in some way by her personality and . . . and . . ." She burst into tears.

I touched her hand, saying softly that I understood, and when Norman came up and stammered an apology, I nodded at him also. The three of them, Norman, Mathew, and Dorcas, left the room, Dorcas sobbing quietly into Mathew's shoulder.

When they had gone, leaving a stunned silence behind, Dorothea St. John was the first to move. Painfully, she roused herself from her chair and came over to Julian. She walked like an old woman; gone was the authoritative, commanding figure that could inspire such fear and dislike. I looked away from her, knowing that her confrontation with the man she called her son, and who was not her son, would be too painful to watch. I glanced around the room and was not surprised to find the others looking away, as though they, too, realized what an intensely personal scene was about to take place. I thought fleetingly that Julian's family had come full circle—with one exception. Arminta and Dorothea had succeeded in their deception, while Saramary had not. I wondered if Julian was thinking of Saramary as he stood and faced Dorothea St. John.

Suddenly, I could not bear to witness what these two had to say to one another. Quietly I slipped from the room and let myself out the front door. I don't think anyone noticed me go, and for that I was glad. I needed to be alone for a while, to sort out my tumultuous thoughts.

I let myself through the gate that led to the sea, shuddering in remembrance of my headlong flight down these same steps only hours before. There was an emptiness inside me; it was as though the shock of finding out the truth about so many things at once had numbed me.

The waves rolled gently in to shore, and a light breeze caressed my face as I walked down to the beach. The faintest of gray and lavender tinted the sky in the east; it was that time of morning when everything seems hushed, waiting peacefully for the new day. I felt out of place, a disturbing element in an otherwise serene atmosphere.

I stopped at the edge of the sand, with the foam-flecked waves washing gently on the beach before me, and looked out over the water. A single gull floated above me, catching the breeze and soaring effortlessly. I tried to think of all that had happened during that long, terrible night, but events had crowded themselves one on the other so rapidly that I knew it would take time to sort it all out.

I wondered what Mrs. St. John would say to Julian, and what Julian would reply. I wondered if he could ever forgive her for what she had done to his father, and then I knew he would forgive. Julian, like his father, was a good man—a kind and considerate man when the truth was not withheld from him.

I sank down onto the sand, oblivious of the damp spreading through my skirts, and faced the fact that I had been at fault as much as any of his family. Endlessly, I had jumped to conclusions, never stopping to ask Julian for explanations; I had condemned him always, before he had a chance to speak. I wanted to go to him and tell him that I had been wrong so many times, but I was too ashamed. I knew I did not deserve a second chance at love. I had squandered something precious between Julian and myself before it had even had an opportunity to develop. And I had no one to blame but myself.

Berus came loping down the beach, appearing out of nowhere as was his habit, and I called to him. It seemed that whenever I felt most alone, he would appear and come to me, offering silent companionship. The dog bounded up to me, and then raced down to the water, intent on some private search of his own. I watched him sadly.

The sun rose in a cloudless sky. I watched the gray transform itself into pale pinks and the lightest of blues, wondering if I would have an opportunity to welcome a new day as Julian would, now that all the mysteries surrounding Peregrine House were solved. My misery overwhelmed me as I realized I had no place in Julian's new life, and I rocked back and forth, my arms about me, suddenly cold.

Berus stood by the water, his plume of a tail waving back and forth as he looked beyond my shoulder. I turned and saw Julian coming toward me.

"I see Berus found you for me again," he said as he came up to me. "I always send him to guard you whenever you go walking on the beach."

I could not look at him; could not bear his half-teasing manner when I had so much to say and no words to say it. I stared miserably at my hands, clutched tightly in my lap.

Julian reached down and drew me to my feet. He put one hand under my chin and brought my head up. As I looked into his eyes, his teasing expression had changed to one of complete seriousness. "Do you know why I sent Berus to protect you?" he asked softly. And when I didn't answer, couldn't answer, he said, "Because I was too proud to come myself. Too proud to tell you that I loved you when I thought you could not love me."

He bent his head and looked directly into my brimming eyes. "And I do love you, Larissa. . . ."

"Oh, Julian," I sobbed. "I'm so ashamed . . . I was so afraid that you didn't love me that I . . ."

"It's over now," he said, pulling me fiercely against him. "We'll start again. . . ."

He kissed me, gently at first, then with an urgency that made words and explanations and apologies unnecessary. And I answered that kiss with all the pent-up longing I had suffered these long, long, empty months without him.

Above us, the gull circled and wheeled; the dog below danced joyfully around us. The sun struck golden sparks on the dazzling white of the gull's wings, and glinted off the strangely colored eyes of the dog who came to sit contentedly before us. And Julian and I . . .

It was going to be a perfect day.